guilty pleasures

Maria Isabel Pita

First Magic Carpet Books, Inc. edition September 2005

Published in 2005

Manufactured in the United States of America
Published by Magic Carpet Books, Inc.

Magic Carpet Books, Inc.
PO Box 473
New Milford, CT 06776

Library of Congress Cataloging in Publication Date

Guilty Pleasures by Maria Isabel Pita
$16.95

ISBN# 0-9775531-5-0
Book Design: P. Ruggieri

For my dear friend, and over-all
wonderful person, Richard Kasak

Table of Contents

Author's Note   7

Out of Control   11
Toronto, Canada 2015

Thorsday Afternoon   21
Coral Gables, Florida 2005

Milagro   31
Copan, Honduras 1983

The Integral   49
London, England 1966

Covenant Transport   59
Dorchester, Massachusetts 1933

Relative Relationship   77
Vienna, Austria 1909

Laila   91
Zanzibar 1863-1880

Bride of Christ   107
Lisbon, Portugal 1735-1755

Song of the Blood   129
Transylvania 1636

Secret Societies   155
Florence, Italy 1500

Lady of the Lake   179
England, Dark Ages 12th Century

Sea Lion Soles   191
The Aleutian Islands, the present & 1,000 years ago

Shiva and Parvati   205
Mahabalipuram, India 7th Century

Theron and Rhodopis   227
Athens, Greece 5th Century B.C.

Prince Maj-Ra   253
Egypt, New Kingdom, ca. 1,000 B.C.

The Double Axe   263
Crete, Knossos, ca. 3,000 B.C.

Star Crossed   269
Another Solar System – Date Unknown

Light After Breath   287
A Parallel Universe – Date Unknown

author's note

Ever since I was a little girl I've devoured history books. I grew up reading about ancient Egypt and Greece, Medieval and Renaissance Europe, ancient Ireland and the England of the Romantic Poets... the list goes on. I was researching details of daily life in different times and places for the novels I was going to write when I grew up. I filled binder after binder with typed facts, and with illustrations I copied from the books myself. *Guilty Pleasures* is the realization of a lifelong dream; of an ever deepening fascination with the different ways human beings – men and women – have expressed love and desire throughout the ages.

You can read *Guilty Pleasures* three different ways – from beginning to end (from the near future to the distant past) from the past to the present, or by traveling back and forth through time as the mood strikes you. I placed *Star Crossed* and *Light After Breath* at the end of the Table of Contents because they occur outside earth's current timeline in another solar system, and in a parallel universe.

Women know there is nothing more important in life than what we feel and who we feel it with. Intense fantasies aren't just a delicious way to pass the time; they also help keep us in touch with our deepest selves. Personally, there is nothing I enjoy writing about more than the power of sexual love and the imaginative desires it never ceases to inspire in us.

Maria Isabel Pita
Baton Rouge 2005

"This strange obscurity I could not understand; and I tried to remove it with my will, and with my wit, and with my heart and mind... How do they live, these people? How can they laugh, and sing, and praise the stars, thinking each day the sun that rises brings them yet nearer to a timeless dark?... We know that beauty is permanent, and that, being permanent, it is beyond the confine of the five senses of the body and can be apprehended only by the spirit...In the future...you will remember how to remember."

Joan Grant, Winged Pharaoh

Out of Control

Toronto, Canada 2015

"...The Aichi Museum in Japan unveiled a 12-foot-high, 15-foot-long LCD video wall that features Opticality's technology and forms the world's largest 3-D display."

Dan Dubno, Discover Magazine, May 2005

'm thinking the coffeepot resembles an old Apollo rocket just as a fragment of a 3-D music video steps around the corner from the living room and begins playing in the kitchen doorway. I deliberately ignore it and resume my catatonic contemplation of the tall white percolator. It seems to be taking longer than an antique launcher did to reach the moon to deliver the stimulating black space of my coffee.

The singer's runaway hologram disconnected from the sound system, Michael Bon has once again escaped the laser bars containing his passionate outpouring of emotion. His image stands with the round wooden dining table vaguely visible through his lean hips, a hanging plant flowing down the length of his back as though twining around his invisible spine. I know it's because he's singing that he seems to have something urgent to tell me. I also know he's glancing back at the other band members still imprisoned in the display frame and not towards the bedroom to make sure my husband is still in there; however, knowing all this doesn't change the way his intense focus makes me feel. Of the numerous electronic problems I have experienced in our state-of-the-art home, this one is by far the most disturbing...

Rick finds it amusing; he laughs as he walks through the musician's ghost into the kitchen.

I finally cradle that first blessed cup of coffee in my hands. 'What's the good of keeping the heat turned down to save energy,' I grumble, 'if *he's* using up God knows how much running around the living room all day?' I feel compelled to pretend I'm annoyed by the problem because the truth is it excites me on some perverse, or on some profound, level, I'm not sure which, but I am sure Rick would make fun of me either way.

'He's in love with you, Moira.' My husband of five years slips four slices of bread into the toaster. 'Your beauty has his crystal cells spinning out of control. While you were watching his video one day he saw you lying on the couch like Goya's *Maja* and desire gave him the power to rise out of the machine.'

'Stop joking about it,' I snap, breaking my New Year's resolution to be more patient with my sarcastic partner.

'Sorry, honey, I should know better than to try and have some fun with you so soon after you've risen from the dead. Butter?'

'Very little.'

Michael abruptly sinks to one knee and lowers his golden-brown head as though he is infinitely tired, then he just remains there genuflecting on the threshold and glowing like a candle flame in his white suit. Rick walks casually through him again biting into his toast and Michael looks beseechingly up at me, but I tell myself it is *not* his expression that shoves me down into a chair. Apparently, the auto-rewind is now also on the fritz; the deviant tune should have kept replaying itself and Michael should have delivered his urgent message to me over and over again. The 3D player has been broken for over a week, but both Rick and I have been so busy with the holidays and all the shopping and partying involved that a musician's occasional appearance in doorways isn't enough of an incentive to spend badly needed money on repairs. So the machine keeps turning itself on and playing just this one particular video over and over again.

Despite his semi-transparent luminosity, Michael looks much too real kneeling there watching me eat breakfast; I have to keep remind-ing myself he's only a lifeless hologram. Yet it really does seem that his laser-fashioned face is perspiring as he exerts himself beyond what is possible to communicate with me...

Forcing myself up out of the chair, I reward my overactive imagi-nation with another cup of coffee, conscious that my silk robe falls open to reveal one of my breasts as I sit down again.

'Hey, what are you and that rock star doing in there?' Rick demands from the living room.

I don't bother to reply as Michael continues staring up at me as intently as an Olympic runner about to take off, his fingers bridging the dining room's forest-green carpet and the white glacier-like tile of the kitchen floor. Instead, I smile silently at this handsome man whose veins are made of ultra-fine colored lasers and whose cells are tiny, multi-faceted crystals, and whose heart...

'Get out here and watch the news with me, Moira. Don't you care what's happening in the world?'

'*You're* what's happening, Michael,' I whisper.

Holographic video players can only project three-dimensional, life-size musicians where you place the display frame, or so I thought until the system malfunctioned, because apparently the projection is limited only to the room the display frame is in. Three days ago I was home alone resting on the couch after an exhausting shopping spree on *The Way* when Michael suddenly appeared right beside me. I cried out and sat up before I remembered he wasn't real, but my heart was still beating furiously in my chest when I fell back across the black leather cushions again. He took a step back, clutching the shirt over his chest as if in sympathy with my racing pulse, and the passionate grace of his gestures as he silently poured his soul out to me through his eyes made me succumb to an irresistible impulse... I hooked my thumbs into the elastic of my black cashmere tights and shoved them over my hips and halfway down my thighs along with my red cotton panties, exposing my warm pussy to the cool air of the living room... and to the musician mouthing words I couldn't hear but which affected me as if his lips were moving intimately against my labia. I sensed that our feelings were in mysterious harmony, our thoughts and desires perfectly in tune even though my reason argued that when he was filming the video he wasn't imagining a woman he didn't know taking her clothes off for him. Yet naturally that didn't stop me; I pulled my gray sweater up around my neck, revealing my soft white breasts, and he genuflected beside the couch as if desperate to take one of my pink nipples between his lips. The band stopped playing behind him as the song came to an end, and for a breathtaking moment I was alone in my living room with four sexy men all fervently watching as I touched myself, gently fingering my clit with two fingertips and arching my back as if offering them my breasts. Then for a disappointing instant I was alone, until the song started up again. I knew just how much time I had to bring myself to orgasm, and at the critical moment when Michael sank to one knee before me I climaxed to the throes of an excruciatingly exquisite illusion that he was proposing an eternity of boundless pleasure, not just to me but to everyone who could hear what he was really saying through his music...

'You can't have me,' I taunt him now, pushing my chair back.

When he smiles it seems so natural I'm half way to the sink with my empty cup before it registers... that smile is *not* part of the video I'm very familiar with by now. Yet when I look again his expression is once more intensely sober; his smile was only a trick of the sunlight shining through the kitchen window.

I put my cup in the sink, wipe the counter Rick has left strewn with breadcrumbs, and then stroll towards the doorway tightening the sash of my robe.

Michael surges to his feet.

Despite my rational resolve to ignore him, I pause uncertainly before him. Now that I'm closer to him I can see his image flickering ever so slightly. I hold my breath, close my eyes, and step into him...

His lips are surprisingly cool and they expand slowly beneath mine as my reason collapses on itself caught by his tongue's spiraling galaxy full of life's wet heat...

I suddenly find myself bent breathlessly over the dining room table.

'Moira?' Rick helps me up gently and turns me to face him. 'Are you all right?'

'Um, yeah... I just felt a little dizzy for a minute... I'm fine...'

He holds me tightly against him for a moment and I feel the fervent hope in his arms. 'Do you think maybe you're... you know?'

'No,' I say firmly, noticing that Michael is no longer projected in the kitchen doorway. 'I just drank too much last night.'

'We both did.' Rick lets go of me and disappears into the bedroom to hide his disappointment.

I follow him in, afraid to let him out of my sight. 'I can't believe they're making you go into work today,' I say inanely.

'Only for a few hours.' He enters the bathroom to shave and the buzzing of the electric razor makes it even harder for me to think straight. Like a humming bird's wings my heart is beating so fast I appear perfectly calm, yet my entire being is concentrated on the glimmering, pollen-like stars into which my blood transformed when I entered the musician's hologram. My brain insists I simply blacked out for a few seconds, and that in those few seconds I experienced a dream as vivid as it was brief...

Rick emerges from the bathroom caressing the silky snake of his gray-and-white tie. 'You look like hell, baby. Go back to bed.'

* * *

The virtues of a hot, candle-lit bath should never be underestimated.

I'm not surprised when Michael eventually appears in the doorway, until I remember that the bathroom opens up off the bedroom, not the living room where the display frame is. My brain quickly explains to itself that the 3-D system has an even greater range than I believed, yet my pulse helplessly reacts to the way he stares down at my naked body, visible beneath the water's pale blue surface. My curves fluctuate ever so slightly, an effect disturbingly similar to the subtle pulsing of his luminous form, and my wet arm when I lift it out of the water to reach for my tea cup gleams just like his holographic skin.

'What do you want?' I ask him wishing the phone would ring and break the spell of his unwavering regard. 'Okay, don't say anything,' I continue lightly, but my hand trembles slightly as I set the cup down, 'just hand me my towel, please.'

As if intending to comply with my request, he crosses the threshold.

I bend my knees and curl up in a corner of the tub, hugging myself protectively as I suddenly dare to realize it's my name his lips are shaping. It was always my name he was saying over and over again followed by something else... 'Don't be afraid...'

With an urgent expression, as if to help me out of the water and save me from drowning, Michael reaches for me, but the bathtub is the safe confines of the reality I know and I cringe, clutching myself even more tightly, refusing to be born into an impossible new world... into another dimension of sensuality such as I had never conceived possible...

'Surprise!' Rick calls from the living room.

Michael glances over his luminous shoulder in the direction of my husband's voice, and an electrifying blend of anger and despair flashing in his eyes as they meet mine, he vanishes.

'There you are.' Rick smiles. 'Did I scare you? Sorry.' He begins washing his hands.

I relax out of my fetal position, but my grasp on reality is even more tenuous than my footing on the tub's slippery surface as I rise slowly, staring fixedly at the empty doorway.

'You want to hear something strange?' Rick is drying his hands with his usual thoroughness. 'It seems our resident hologram was killed in an accident on Christmas Eve.'

'What?' I gasp.

'Michael Bon is dead.'

Thorsday Afternoon

Coral Gables, Florida 2005

Across the earth there are over one-hundred lightning strokes every second. Cloud to ground lightning is the most spectacular of all, forming a bright and usually forked bolt of light, and more lightning strikes in Florida than anywhere else in the U.S.

Sheryl is working at her desk. The computer screen is a deep blue with white figures flowing across it like schools of tiny glowing fish as she stares through her own personal porthole into a sea of information.

Her cat Merlin finds the screen both intriguing and frustrating. His large black bulk sits beside her keyboard, his golden eyes fixed on the monitor's frustrating fish tank.

'They're only numbers, silly,' she tells him for the hundredth time, banging her forehead gently against his before deftly catching some papers the pleased swish of his tail sends flying off the desk. His loud purr drowns out the computer's quiet hum.

Sheryl and her husband of five years own a small but lucrative Web Design company. Being self-employed is decidedly a luxury, but it's also a two-edged sword in that it demands a great deal of self-enforced discipline. She leans back in her chair and caresses Merlin's supple spine as it rises beneath her hand like a warm black wave, helping relax her own tense back.

He leaps off the desk when the phone beside him emits a shrill purr.

'Hello?' Sheryl answers, as always hoping it's her husband.

Her hopeful greeting meets with dead air.

'Hello?' she repeats, annoyed, then hangs up and returns to her assessment of their quarterly profits.

After another hour of mind-numbing accounting, stimulatingly real hunger pangs demand she take a break.

Hearing her get up, Merlin unfurls himself from a ball on the couch like the black seed of the universe sprouting the legs of time and space as the golden suns of his eyes are born. He follows her sleepily into the kitchen, where she is tempted to have a beer with her sandwich, but she resists the urge. After eating she gets right back to work, but not after brushing her teeth.

She is so deep in the luminous pool of their finances that a rumble of thunder makes her jump. She covers her swimming vision with her hands for a moment. 'That's enough for today,' she informs Merlin, but he is nowhere to be seen. 'Coward.' She smiles as lightning abruptly photographs the room.

Sheryl quickly saves her work, turns off the computer, and stretches her back standing in front of a window. She is enjoying the feel of the coming storm. The darkening afternoon pulsing with a spectral light turns her on. Beyond the trees swift, jagged cracks appear in the sky and send a pleasurable chill down her spine. She loves lightning; it feels like a haunting X-ray during which she truly senses the eternal energy only temporarily contained in her flesh.

She falls back across the couch to enjoy the show and to rest for a while before attacking the problem of dinner with her usual culinary skill. It hasn't begun to rain yet; when the electric bass of the thunder dies away for a moment the body of the house is profoundly silent around her. She props a cushion up behind her for a better view of the sky ribbed with dangerous looking black clouds. It seems almost natural, like something she has been expecting, even wanting, when the black clouds suddenly fall into the room in the form of a black-gloved hand firmly covering her mouth.

'Don't even think of screaming,' a man's voice whispers in her ear. 'If you do exactly as I say, I won't hurt you.'

A silent flash of lightning seems to split the sky and her feelings in half. She is pleased and excited that Mark finished his presentations early and is in the mood to play, but a small, anxious part of her wonders why she can't see his car parked in the driveway, and especially why she didn't hear his key turning in the lock, a sound she never fails to register just as Merlin always appears when she uses the electric can opener.

'Do you understand me?' His voice remains a toneless whisper.

She nods once.

He lifts his hand, but before she can turn around to face him the room goes completely black as a cool cloth falls over her eyes. He quickly ties it behind her head, then forces her wrists together in her lap and secures them with another cloth.

She doesn't want to spoil the mood, but she can't stop herself from asking, 'Mark, is that you?'

'Get up.'

She obeys him even though she is suddenly desperate to prove to herself this man is her husband so she can enjoy the game, but bound and blindfolded, with the rumble of thunder blending unnervingly with the blood pounding through her heart, she can't quite get a grip on her thoughts. His gloved hand painfully gripping her arm, she senses him leading her in the direction of the windows and a decorative wooden table.

'Mark, please tell me it's you,' she begs softly, and then cries out in shock when a crashing sound is the only response she gets from him. She can't believe he would deliberately break an expensive vase just to arouse her fear and it makes her wonder how well she really knows her husband.

'I told you not to scream.' A more muted clatter is followed by a delicate splintering sound that tells her the lamp is down. 'Do you want me to hurt you?' He presses her against the edge of the table and shoves her back across it, prying her legs open around his hard body.

The patter of rain on the window behind her foolishly makes her picture a crowd of little feet running away from the serious trouble she is in. Starved for reassurance, she reaches up in an effort to feel his face, but the way he tied her hands together with her palms facing away from each other makes it impossible.

He forces her hands over her head and then roughly caresses her short little housedress over her breasts, bunching it up around her throat before quickly tearing off her panty, but there is no ripping sound and the gesture is much too smooth... the blade's cold tongue licks the flesh of her inner thighs slowly, one after the other, as if savoring their tenderness. Tears fill her closed eyes, her awareness flickering beneath a rush of terror; her consciousness a vulnerable flame kept alive by the mysterious wick of her spine.

'Don't be afraid...' he urges in that same anonymous breathy voice, and surprises her by pressing the hilt of the knife into one of her hands. 'Take it.'

She clutches the weapon, but then realizes it's useless to her since she can't possibly be sure those really aren't Mark's hands in leather gloves hungrily kneading her breasts.

'I want you to feel this.' He snatches the knife back and rests a cool plastic sphere against her palm for an instant.

Mark would never willingly use a condom with her, he absolutely hates them, and she moans, stunned by this evidence that the dark force between her legs belongs to a stranger.

He grips her behind the knees, and it's impossible to recognize Mark's loving touch through the impersonal leather gloves. He feels tall like her lover, and strong, like so many men, and his costly violence is frighteningly out of character. He lifts her legs up around him and the cool, dry air of the room makes her even more intensely aware of her warm, moist sex lips. She can see absolutely nothing while he is able to see and enjoy absolutely all of her. She gasps beneath the electrifying sensation of a rigid penis lodging its head at the entrance to her pussy. Fear and guilt tell her to dread being penetrated by a complete stranger, yet her flesh languidly betrays her soul by desiring the experience... she is horrified by the possibility she is actually being raped, but the truth is she is even more afraid his erection will disappoint her, that it won't be big and hard and devastating enough to somehow redeem her.

'Do you want it?' he whispers. 'Do you want my big dick inside you?'

'No, please... Mark?'

She cries out as his cock rends her open. She tells herself it's her husband's hard-on stabbing her even though it's impossible for her to be sure she recognizes the feel of his length and girth as the rubber impersonally separates her most intimate flesh from his. The pleasure she experiences is shocking, unforgivable and undeniable. He puts her legs together and leans some of his weight against them to open her up even more. Mark has never fucked her so hard, not with such a strangely pure violence, the pulsing energy of his hips completely unrestrained by concern for her comfort or consideration for her clit's more subtle needs. She doesn't even know his name yet her pussy can't resist clinging to him, tightening and relaxing around his thrusts as one second she knows he's her husband and the next she's breathtakingly certain she has no idea who the man banging her is.

'Do you like this?' he hisses.

'No!'

'Oh, yes you do, I can feel how much you like it!'

'Oh, God…' If he's her lover he'll know he's pleasing her. If he's a stranger she can say anything she wants to; she can confess her darkest, most politically incorrect longings as though his invisible force belongs not to a flesh-and-blood person but to a sinisterly potent man conjured up by all her most secret fantasies. 'Oh, yes…' she breathes, surrendering to his overwhelming force. 'Fuck me… fuck me!'

'You are so bad!' He stabs the word into her. 'Bad, bad girl!' He has stopped whispering. 'You didn't even fight me!'

'No, Mark, I knew it was-'

'Don't lie to me! You weren't sure it was me.' She feels the sharp edge of the knife against her throat suddenly. 'Come on, Sheryl, admit it, you weren't sure.'

'I was sure, Mark!' she gasps. 'I was sure it wasn't you!'

'God…' he groans. 'You whore…'

When he's finished with her he removes the blindfold and slips off the rubber, grimacing in distaste as he helps her gently up against him so he can untie the cloth around her wrists.

'The condom really made me worry it wasn't you,' she confesses, clinging to him.

'But it also obviously took away your fear of catching something and helped you relax.'

'Don't try to make me feel guilty, Mark, please. There was nothing I could do to stop you, and you know it.'

'And you loved that.'

'Yes… but only because I love you…'

'Meow!'

'Did you hear that?' Mark asks. 'How do you explain that little paradox, Merlin? A complete stranger breaks into our house, ties her up and threatens to hurt her, and she begs him to fuck her because she loves me.'

'Mreow?'

'Oh, I'm sorry, I forgot, you're neutered.'

Milagro

Copan, Honduras 1983

When traveling in a third world country, your American passport is worth all the gold of the pharaohs or the Mayans or whatever ancient culture has drawn you there, or so Margaret Jones feels as she steps off the plane into a hot and humid afternoon in Honduras. She unzips her purse and reassures herself that the thin blue book is safely tucked away next to her return ticket – two paper wings giving her the power to fly out of the hardship and poverty she glimpsed from the plane and which now surround her. Yet even if she loses her purse (God forbid) her father works for the U.S. government, which puts her in a better position than a king's daughter in the Dark Ages. She trusts he's waiting in the small, one-story building that is the country's second largest airport.

Margaret is nineteen-years-old and, by her impatient reckoning, a mature woman ready for just about anything. The adventure of her life stretches before her, yet it is also reassuringly defined. She enjoys the stability of the Western Roman road through the landscape of her emotions. Having read voraciously since childhood, she is acquainted with all the artists and philosophers who have explored and mapped out her soul, offering comforting signposts as she prepares to follow her own mysterious direction. She is in her second semester at college, where she is majoring in History with a minor in Literature.

* * *

Milagro Ortez stands in the shadow of an open doorway watching people walk by on the stone-cobbled street.

Copan is full of foreigners. Located high in the mountains and accessible only by a narrow, twisting road (made dangerous by sudden mudslides) it is a small treasure chest overflowing with cultures. The reason for this is the splendid Mayan ruins. Milagro has grown up with the constant presence of archaeologists, and recently their numbers nearly doubled when an entire underground city was discovered. Through the web-like grid of locked gates, she and her friends have glimpsed serious, moon-pale faces buried in the dark earth. It doesn't matter that she herself is a descendant of the Mayans. She is told to stay away from all the places where the Gringos spend the whole day digging, rising straight up from holes in the ground with faces as white as the ghosts they do not hesitate to disturb. And they haunt Milagro, the Gringos not the ghosts of her ancestors. She goes to sleep at night wondering about them. It fascinates her the way the women share in the same tasks as the men and later join them in the restaurant-bar that has become *their* place. These white women don't stay at home with the children and the laundry and the flour to be kneaded and the beans to be soaked.

Milagro cannot imagine what these foreigners do all day deep in the earth. Her brother tells her they use tiny brushes to clean the dirt off long dead faces. He was hired to work on the growing dig, but he sweats and laughs in the sun using shovels and picks while the tall, cool archaeologists speak quietly with each other, and then vanish into the underworld, rising and setting like moons.

Milagro is sixteen-years-old. She helps her mother with the chores and with their small produce shop at the front of the house. The little schooling she received – the rudiments of reading and writing – is a distant memory. She is unusually tall for her race, and her excellent bone structure makes her slenderness appear a matter of aesthetic choice rather than of inadequate nutrition. Her black hair shines like the star-filled sky at night and falls straight down to her waist.

* * *

Margaret tosses her short brown hair away from her face and sighs plaintively. She and her father and his third wife, Elaine, are making their slow, torturous way up the mountain to Copan. Every mile or so they encounter a group of children wielding sticks and shovels who pretend to fill the potholes in the road, which is in dangerous disrepair, and then eagerly thrust twig-like arms through the open windows of the car for a reward. With a magnanimous air, her father and stepmother sparingly dole out the light Honduran coins, and the bright smiles disappear as dark heads bow to count them.

At least the scenery is enjoyable. To their left lush forests and tobacco fields stretch for as far as the eye can see below and above them, while only a few feet on their right the mountain's muddy brown crags loom menacingly. Her father casually tells her they often dissolve into fatal avalanches during the rainy season, and Margaret tries not to think about how easy it would be for their car to plummet off the edge of the road into a green abyss. She will be very glad when they reach their destination. The twisting mountain roads have made her carsick on and off for two days ever since they left Tegucigalpa.

When they finally pull into Copan it is like driving back in time. A woman is washing her hair in the bend of a wide creek as they cross the bridge onto a surprisingly clean street paved with stones and lined by quaint, whitewashed buildings with colorful trims. It is by far the prettiest town they have encountered so far, and the facade of the hotel they pull up in front of looks promising. Heat, nausea, the absence of roadside facilities, and being forced to drink soda or beer instead of the local water, have led to major disagreements between Margaret's imagination and her body, which she has discovered doesn't give a damn about anything except its own comfort no matter where she is.

It is with intense relief that she sets her heavy bags down in a room that is Spartan but clean. The air conditioner is an old dinosaur, but it roars to powerful life and blessedly begins transporting her back to the Ice Age. She is so grateful that she can almost forgive the lack of hot water, or of any water pressure whatsoever. The shower is a cold trickle beneath which it takes her forever to rinse the shampoo out of her hair as she dreams of the powerful hot shower she will take back home in the real world.

* * *

Milagro's mother tells her to stay away from the white men. 'Falling in love with one of them would be as foolish as trying to walk on a moonbeam.' Milagro loves the silver path of light on the water which seems to lead to an enchanted land, yet she understands that trying to follow it would only get her drowned. Many of the tall Northern men have eyes the color of water shimmering in sunlight, and she wonders what the currents of their thoughts would feel like if their attention was directed at her for more than just a shallow second. The need for them to notice her is becoming so strong it is almost painful, like suffering from an illness her own people cannot cure. The blue-gray eyes of these foreign archaeologists have seen as much of the world as the sky above her, and more and more Milagro feels she is not truly alive because they never see *her*.

At last the red dress she ordered from a catalogue arrives. Her mother protests against its color, and crosses herself when she sees how little there is of it, but Milagro is thrilled that it fits her like no homemade dress ever has. It is as if she paid not for what she got but for the material that was cut away to reveal her true self.

That night all the local boys pay more attention to her. Her girlfriends, however, are not interested in going near the bar where the Gringos hang out drinking to that loud, throbbing music that doesn't have any real rhythm to it, and their idea of dancing is just clinging to each other and talking. They are always talking, the men and the women together. Milagro's friends have also been warned to stay away from the white men, but it's easy for them because they don't share her obsession with these infinitely careful and tireless diggers who spend their whole day in the dirt, and then stay up half the night just talking.

* * *

Later in the evening, Milagro slips off by herself. A group of young men trail after her, tossing compliments and insults at her like stones mingled with flowers – they like the way she looks tonight, but they cannot respect her for it. When she turns onto the street which 'belongs' to the Gringos, they fall back, and soon there is only silence behind her.

Awkward as a new-born calf learning to walk on its long legs, she makes her way up the steep hill in the red high-heels she ordered along with the dress. Alone and in the dark, it makes her nervous that she has chosen the devil's color, and her arched soles start burning as if she has both feet in hell already, because every step brings her closer and closer to the sin of disobeying her mother.

Ashamed of herself, protectively clutching her bare arms in the cool March night, Milagro pauses outside the Gringos' bar. She forgets her fear as the deep throb of their music embraces her, filling her with a strange sense of power, so that instead of blending into the shadows as a part of her longs to do, she stands in the middle of the street staring into the bar's smoky glow with hungry eyes.

Lewis steps out of the bar onto the street as his friend, John, turns back to answer a question someone calls after them. Lewis pauses to wait for him, gazing at the red-and-gold sign for the *Llama Del Bosque* (Flame of the Forest) restaurant hanging on the dark horizon at the top of the hill like a perpetually setting sun covered with black graffiti.

Music surges through the open doorway and lifts Milagro's heart deliciously up into the sky pulsing with stars when the man's eyes fall on her.

Emerging from the bar, John immediately notices the girl standing in the street. She looks young enough to be dangerous and good enough to eat, nothing like the usual local fare. 'What a waste,' he mutters, and with a knowing glance at Lewis starts down the hill alone.

Milagro holds her breath. It is too dark to see the color of his eyes but she *knows* they are blue and that what her mother said about white men and moonlight is true because she feels herself drowning in them. She does not know how to use her arms and legs to swim or to walk away from this man. His direct contemplation is an element she has never experienced, and he is so tall the sun's rays have become confused with his hair.

'*Hola.*' His quiet voice bridges the space between them as he approaches her.

'*Hola,*' she breathes, paralyzed by a whole new sense of herself beneath his regard, which makes her feel precious as a Mayan statue and equally unable to move.

He caresses one of her high cheekbones lightly with his fingertips. 'What's your name, sweetheart?'

'Milagro,' she answers breathlessly.

'Milagro...' he whispers. 'Will you be *my* miracle?'

She nods, not caring at all that she doesn't understand him.

* * *

It should seem like a dream come true actually being alone with this handsome man from another world much richer than hers, instead everything feels more sharply real than ever. Her daydreams never got past the part where his eyes acknowledged her presence in the world, never venturing beyond the moment when he reflected her beauty back at her in a way none of the local men ever could. What happened after that was always a glowing cloud of amorphous feelings in her mind; she had never pictured the uncomfortable reality of his jeep. When he straps her in, her awareness of everything flickers strangely as for a heart-stopping moment he leans intimately close to her. She thinks she hears him whisper her name again, 'Milagro...' but so softly the syllables of her identity become tangled and lost in her hair as if she only imagined his voice. When he slams the door closed to walk around to the driver's seat she feels the impact deep in her body and the sensation is so hot and sweet it further compromises her ability to think. She gazes at him, her eyes wide with indefinable emotions as he takes his place behind the wheel, because he barely touched her yet he wounded her somehow.

'Milagro... What a beautiful name.' He smiles at her as he shifts gears with a confidence she experiences deep in her pelvis again. 'And you *are* miraculously lovely, all things considered.'

The tone of his voice helps relax her against the hard seat; she once heard her uncle speak to a stray cat in such a way before he took her in. She clutches the dashboard as the jeep accelerates down the dark and bumpy road.

'You don't speak a word of English, do you, baby?'

'A very little,' she replies, wanting him to be proud of her.

'That's okay,' he smiles, concentrating on the headlights slashing through the jungle, 'we don't need to talk.'

She wonders where they are going, but only vaguely; it really doesn't matter. There is a focused intensity about him that assuages her soul in a mysterious way, as if every time he glances at her an invisible, divine hand caresses her from the inside out. She refuses to think about the devil and his purported powers; they have no place in her positive nature. It is enough for her that he knows where they are headed. Now that she's getting what she has wanted for so long it's easy to feel this night is special, that it might never end, which makes worrying about their destination almost irreverent in the face of how blessed she is to be in this very special man's company. She can't really see him; it's too dark in his rocking vehicle, but the way his hair shines reassures her. Such a tall man can stride towards unseen enemies with confidence, armed only with the invisible machete of his willpower. Her brother's head would barely reach this Gringo's broad shoulders, which in her eyes look as if they can indeed support the weight of the whole world.

When they pull up in front of the ticket kiosk at the head of the path leading into the temple, Milagro isn't surprised; she knows he spends his days there and that he loves it. But when he reaches over and caresses her knee the hot stab she experiences just above the unexplored passage between her thighs is sharpened by anxiety. Her respect for her ancestors has always been tainted by a touch of dread, and the silence when he turns off the engine is so absolute she holds her breath, afraid how fervently alive she feels tonight will make whatever spirits haunt the ruins jealous of her living, beating heart.

'Are you up for a moonlight stroll, Milagro?'

She gazes at him mutely, wishing she could see his eyes.

'Come on.' He slips out of the jeep and she unconsciously continues holding her breath as he walks around to her door. He opens it and she closes her eyes as he leans towards her, but this time he doesn't whisper her name as he frees her from the strap pressing against the hard tips of her breasts. Then he grabs her around the waist and she has to open her eyes to cling to his godlike shoulders as he lifts her down onto the ground. How close she is to him is so impossible she stumbles in the high-heels when he lets go of her and turns away to close the door. 'Easy there, sweetheart.' He steadies her, and she cannot believe her eyes when he genuflects before her, making her feel precious as the statue of a saint in church. And the devilish nature of her shoes is confirmed when he blessedly slips her feet free of them one after the other.

'I'll carry these for you,' he says, looming over her again. 'I hope you don't mind walking barefoot.'

She doesn't understand a word he says, but the silent statement of
his fingers slipping between hers is eloquent enough that she willingly allows him lead her down the tree-lined path into the temple of
Copan.

The moon is out and three quarters full just above the trees.
Milagro is accustomed to walking barefoot; it isn't the uneven ground
beneath her soles that bothers her, and certainly she has no problem
with this dream man's possessive grip on her hand, but the closer they
draw to the ruins the more anxious she becomes. Her powerful ancestors were also inconceivably cruel, completely unacquainted with
Christ's love and mercy, and leaves rustling in a restless breeze easily
begin sounding like warning whispers urging her to turn back and run
home to her mami who is always right about everything and who will
forgive her for disobeying her because she loves her and will always
love her no matter what... then the path curves and all at once the
temple grounds stretch out before them. Across the neatly trimmed
grass of the ancient playing field stone steps ascend towards the moon,
but he turns away from them and heads towards the sacrificial altar.
Like every local child, Milagro was once morbidly fascinated by the
circular stone upon which the winner of the sacred games was sacrificed every year. She thought it horrible that the victor was rewarded
with death; her Christian soul recoiled at the thought of gods who cruelly thirsted for the blood of the strongest and most accomplished of
their subjects. She had struggled to understand what it would be like
to play a game striving to be the best and to outshine your competi-
tors all the time knowing you would die if you won.

'No,' she says out loud, still haunted by the paradox.

'It's all right,' her companion squeezes her hand, 'you don't have to be afraid, there's nothing out here that can hurt you, trust me.'

The sacrificial altar is clearly visible in the moonlight shaped like a big egg surrounded by a narrow hollow ring of curving stone designed to catch the blood of the victim's heart. Short wooden stakes are planted in the grass around it with a thin metal wire strung between them to keep tourists away from the gradually eroding artifact. She clearly remembers her first sight of the channel down which the blood flowed after they slit the unlucky athlete's throat, and how the porous rock still looks faintly stained with the life of its victims. The slender, muscular body of the victor was arched back across the curved surface, his arms and legs spread wide open in the most vulnerable of poses… she prefers not to think about what happened then.

'No!' she gasps even more anxiously when her foreign friend steps casually over the wire into the forbidden space around the altar, clearly expecting her to follow.

'Don't be afraid,' he repeats, but his tone is slightly different now, not so patient as he tugs on her hand and forces her to scale the symbolic fence.

Everything that happens after that is so shockingly cold and hard and painfully hot all at once that her thoughts seem to drown in the experience like swimmers in a tempest of sensations. First her dress is whipped up over her head, and then her worn white cotton panties are effortlessly torn from her body.

'*Ay, Dios mio!*' she gasps, forced to cling to him to recover her balance. She barely has time to comprehend that she is standing naked in the heart of a pagan temple before he pushes her back across the altar. The surface is rough against her skin even as her spine molds submissively to the curved stone, the tips of her toes just barely touching the earth. She spreads her arms out, desperately clutching the unyielding surface beneath her as he lifts her slender legs in his hands and spreads them open. All she can see are stars above her, and suddenly it's as if they fall to earth and start burning at the entrance to her flesh directly between her legs. The pain is so intense it seems to fill the pulsing universe, yet beyond her body's misery her soul is mysteriously triumphant. She did everything she could to win the tall, powerful man sacrificing her virginity to himself, and now her proud blood is flowing, feeding the hunger of gods she doesn't believe in but who obviously still believe in her, and need her... she can feel their eternally selfish power surging up into her body and possessing her, violently using her flesh for their own terrible pleasure as the archeologist's fingers dig into her tender thighs, remorselessly holding them open.

'*Ay, Dios mio! Dios mio!*' she breathes as if praying because she feels as if he's killing her... yet her heart beats faster and faster beneath her quivering little breasts as he thrusts himself deeper and deeper between her legs.

* * *

I don't believe this, dad,' Margaret is close to tears. 'I was so thrilled when I saw that bottle of *Bombay Sapphire*. I asked for a gin and *tonic*. I explained it to her very clearly. "*Tonic* water," I said at least three times. I made it *perfectly* clear. But no, what does she give me? A fucking Gin and Perrier.' She stares down at her glass in outrage, mourning the barbaric murder of a great spirit.

'Watch your mouth.' Her father sucks on his pipe, amused and worried in equally mild measures. 'Who taught you to drink *Bombay Sapphire* anyway? Is that what you're learning in college?'

'It's the best Gin there is.' Margaret glances resentfully at the small woman behind the bar.

'Then drink it.'

'I'm *not* having Gin and Perrier.' She pushes her glass away. 'It's bad enough they don't have any decent wine in this country.'

'You're getting a degree in alcoholism, I see.' He empties his pipe into an ashtray and promptly begins refilling the lion's head bowl, a gift from his daughter. She also brought him a large container of his favorite tobacco, unavailable in Honduras.

Margaret tries to forget the sparkling disaster in her glass by looking around her. They are sitting in the *Llama Del Bosque* restaurant theoretically enjoying cocktails before dinner without Elaine, who is lying back at the hotel with one of her migraines. They ate here last night as well and she was amazed by how delicious the food was. Her father explained fresh ingredients from neighboring farms are what make everything taste so good, but she is still dying for a real drink.

'Shall I order you some *Botran*?' He finally takes pity on her. 'I told you, Rum is all you can get around here besides beer, and even then it has to be the right brand.'

Margaret enjoys a small revenge a few minutes later when they are served two Rum-and-Cokes and after taking a sip her father angrily informs the waitress the rum in his glass is *not* the Botran he ordered.

'Yes it is, sir,' she insists unhappily.

'Then bring me the bottle. I want to see it.'

The bottle never materializes even though they linger over dessert. The restaurant resembles a large screened-in porch dropped in the middle of the jungle and Margaret is thankful for the cool nocturnal breeze. However, her body has had more urgent concerns ever since two handsome young archaeologists (they are clearly not tourists) entered the restaurant just as she was finishing her three-cheese pasta. After that, every bite became a tasteless struggle as she dreaded they would look her way just when she was sucking up a wormy strand of spaghetti. But she has already ordered dessert and the blonde one (the one she has her eye on) is still engrossed in conversation with his friend over straight shots of rum. Then as large plates of the local fare – rice, beans, plantains and chicken – are set before them he finally looks around him, obviously so at home there he has only just remembered he's in a public place.

Margaret doesn't know how she is surviving his intense scrutiny. He makes no bones about his interest in her, and her body temperature rises thinking that his profession must have something to do with his lack of manners, archaeology being such a strange marriage of hardworking realism and imaginative romanticism. When she musters the courage to meet his vivid blue stare for more than a second it has the same warmly intoxicating effect on her as straight shots of *Bombay Sapphire* and her thoughts begin walking the straight line of an obsession – she has to get away from her father so this man can approach her.

She gets up to use the bathroom, which is just outside the restaurant at the edge of the jungle.

She lingers inside the filthy little stall for longer than necessary, and somewhat dizzy from holding her breath, she stumbles against a chair as she emerges.

A rough hand grips her bare arm to steady her.

Looking up she feels as though he is pulling her up to the luminous surface of his eyes and saving her from the deep despair not having him in her life will condemn her to.

A few minutes later Lewis and John are having coffee with Margaret and her father while she smiles in disbelief at the treasure she has found for herself in the middle of nowhere. Her father is impressed by the archeologists' manners and pleased they share his daughter's love of history since they appear to be doing well financially. Lewis especially makes it clear he appreciates and respects Margaret's intelligence. His smile is so encouraging that she dares to try and express her more profound thoughts on human culture, and the way he looks at her makes everything she believes feel beautifully real.

Margaret leaves the *Flame of the Forrest* intoxicated with desire and hope. She and Lewis start slowly down the street together, but the hill is so steep they find themselves giving into its gravity, laughing as they fall into an elated run away from her father, who follows at a more sedate pace with John, deep in some conversation.

No one notices the slender figure standing in the shadows watching them go.

The Integral

London, England 1966

Rain lances around the hooded figures of streetlights, falling gently in the darkness beyond them. Golden snakes slither along the curb glimmering water's shape-shifting power. They vanish at a sudden hiss of tires, but the luminous atoms immediately coalesce again without effort and flow into the night.

Beyond the stiff clerical collar of the sidewalk, inside an old three-story building, a naked bulb offers a dim view of the forest-green carpet's faded design of flowering branches. Down the narrow hallway six black doors look like portals into the universe, their rusted doorknobs hanging in them like burned out suns.

In the first floor apartment at the front of the building, a woman sitting at a vanity in her bedroom flips open a black compact. The mirror rises over the powder's fine sand like a crystal-clear wave reflecting the curving island of her mouth, but then dimensions collapse when she snaps the compact closed again. She drops it into a wooden drawer filled with the plastic shells of lipsticks and liners, blushes and eye shadows. They make it impossible to say how many years have broken against her flesh; her muscles keep a passionate grip on her handsome bones.

Light crests on the wall beside her as headlights novae on her windowpane, turning the raindrops into twinkling galaxies before fading away again. Naked, she is in full view of the street for a moment as she rises. Her closet is coffin-sized and the single lamp is behind her, making it impossible for her to see the different textures of the garments rippling beneath her fingertips like a live current. The rain sounds like a vast black cat purring around the building, intensifying her sensual restlessness. Yet if she goes out again tonight she knows she will only come back drunk and with the wrong men. At least this nameless longing makes her feel deep and mysteriously hopeful.

The temple silhouette of her four-poster bed begins moving along the wall as out on the street a vehicle approaches. She gazes at the wall, seeing one of the shadow-plays branded into her memory... between the bars of the four-poster bed are three silhouettes, one of them hers. She is on her hands and knees like the desperately hungry, masterless pussy she is, two dark erections remorselessly penetrating her vulnerably slender shadow. She is never more at peace than when she is impaled on two cocks at once. The silhouettes of the men are always the same in her memory, looming large and relentless, the synchronized stabbing motion of their hips picking up brutal speed with the black holes of her mouth and her pussy absorbing them as if she is boneless and bottomless. In reality she has to struggle to breathe around the hard-on packed into her mouth reaching for her throat, and yet she wants it there, she invited to there; she essentially created it with her talented tongue while another erection plunged into the sensation-rich depths of her cunt. Whenever she brings two men home at once she knows she will be used for all she is worth. She was taught that isn't much for a woman like her, yet her flesh is blessedly free of abstract beliefs. She never feels more fulfilled than when she has a womb full of cum deliciously warming her, while another ejaculation burns deep in her rectum and she can still taste a third man's flood of pleasure on her tongue. The occasional pain, the physical strain sometimes tainted with discomfort, is more than worth the sense of truly being herself and fulfilling her nature for a few hours in the darkness before daylight and normality and her boring job return to haunt her...

A second car driving by outside raises another erotic specter of memory on the bedroom wall, this one showing the erect nipples of her breasts feeding a hovering specter while another one crouches between her legs feasting on the rich warm juices of her sex...

She stands daringly in the window as a third car begins driving by on the street outside.

Slanting headlights give the elegant black vehicle a powerful feral look. Billions of organisms died and were fossilized over millenniums just to satisfy its hunger for one day. Suddenly, as if its molten nose picks up the trail of a scent, the car swerves over to the curb just below her apartment.

Her pulse speeds up wondering if the driver sees her standing naked in the window. Her natural impulse is to lower the blinds, but instead she pulls up the window to let in the night air, exciting herself with its frigid caress.

The luminous swords of the headlights are sheathed and the driver's door opens. A man emerges. She sees him clearly even though he is wearing black. He is tall and blonde. His black boots reflect the wet street as they stride across the sidewalk, and then up the steps into her building.

Wanting to get a better look at him through the keyhole she hurries into her dark living room, but then stops dead when she hears the lock on her door resist for an instant before surrendering to an expert touch.

'Oh, my God!' she gasps, and runs back to the open window in her bedroom, but the screen is rusted closed. Hyperventilating wordless prayers, she struggles wildly with the metal net trapping her.

The lamp clicks off behind her.

Fear short circuits the synapses in her brain as the darkness takes form, becoming a hard arm around her chest and a cold leather glove pressed against her mouth.

'Don't be afraid,' a man's voice whispers. 'Isn't this what you wanted?' He lifts his hand an inch from her lips. 'Don't make a sound,' he commands, and turns her roughly to face him. 'Just do as I tell you.' He slips an arm around her waist and cradles her against his side. 'Say "Yes, master".' His other hand cradles her face. '*Say* it,' he commands quietly but firmly.

'Yes, master!' she breathes.

'Very good.' His embrace at once threatening and protective, he stares down into her eyes.

Her bones feel dangerously light robbed of the weight of her willpower. She is so frightened she barely feels it – an emotional hypothermia her reason tells her she has to fight. Yet the terrified rush of blood trough her heart is ebbing like a tide beneath his steady gaze. In the dark room his irises are the faint blue of intensely hot suns thousands of light years away, and she feels herself falling against gravity into the mysterious lunar landscape of his features… the ideal geography of his face can't just be her desperate imagination…

'We're going for a ride,' he says quietly. 'Look.' He turns her head like a doll's towards the window. 'That's the coin you need to pay the toll.'

Outside the full moon has broken through the clouds.

He's crazy, she thinks in total despair. 'Where are we going... master?'

He answers in an undertone, 'That all depends.'

'On what?' she whispers.

'On how good you are.' His gloved fingers spread like black rays over one of her pale breasts without touching it as his thumb lightly orbits her aureole. It puckers in on itself like a flower retiring for the night, yet at the same time her nipple juts out long and firm and hungry in a way that is mysteriously immune to the terror darkening her mind.

Her eyes close. 'What do you mean?'

Abruptly gripping the back of her head he presses her face against his chest and makes her gasp for air in the starless space. He holds her firmly, until the beating of his heart against her lips mysteriously flat-lines her resistance.

When she stops struggling he strokes her hair and lifts her face to his again. 'I *mean*,' his voice is dangerously soft, 'you're going to do as I say.'

She answers breathlessly, 'Yes, master...'

He turns her in his arms, pressing her back against his chest. His left hand wraps around her throat as his right hand slips between her legs. He grips her neck just below the chin, cutting off her breath, and her clitoris instantly comes alive beneath his cool leather fingertips, the legend of the mermaid becoming a vivid reality in her blood as it rushes into the rocky harbor of her pelvis in response to his swift strokes. The more his fingers tighten around her throat the more her clitoris feels like a haunting gill inhaling ecstasy like oxygen as the tide

55

of her vaginal juices rises between her thighs so swiftly she suffers a breathtaking climax almost instantly. He makes sure she can't breathe at all as her body stiffens in his arms, yet she scarcely notices as pleasure sustains her deepest being like the purest element.

Her silk robe is lying across the bed. He releases her abruptly and picks it up. 'Put this on,' he commands.

Her legs weak from the powerful orgasm still charging her blood, she manipulates her limbs into the slippery red silk as he watches in silence.

The sash of the robe is lying coiled on the floor. He kicks it up into his hand with one black boot, wraps it around her waist, and uses it as a leash to pull her out of the apartment.

She nurtures the faint hope of running into someone in the hallway, but she normally never does and tonight is no exception.

Outside the moon is gone and it is raining hard. Her robe clings darkly to her curves as a shudder of oddly intoxicated disbelief causes her to stumble off the sidewalk, which feels roughly unfamiliar.

Opening the passenger door, he shoves her into the front seat.

She falls trembling against the skin-soft leather as he tosses the robe's sash into her lap like a bloody umbilical cord. The second he closes the door, she tries to open it again, fumbling desperately for the lock.

He quickly slips in beside her. 'Come here.' He pulls her over to the edge of her seat and thrusts a hand into her robe. 'Stay close.'

His fingers leave warm trails across her thigh as they squeeze it painfully and she begins to cry silently. Her stomach turns over with the engine, and the satisfied hiss of tires accelerating up the street robs her of breath for an incredulous instant because this simply can't be happening. He turns the heat on, and runs a red light at the corner that feels like her heart powerless to stop him from doing whatever he desires. She prays for flashing blue lights to come to her rescue, but only the windshield wipers sympathize with her pulse.

'What are…?' She clears enough fear out of her throat to speak. 'What are you planning to do, master?'

His voice is an inexorable undertone, 'Everything you want me to.'

'Then… then you won't hurt me?'

'I didn't say that.'

Her silk robe starts drying stiffly against her. *Like blood*, she thinks. The sinister sensation overwhelms her, and then leaves her feeling unnaturally calm. He is racing down a dark street she doesn't recognize, and suddenly he takes a sharp left onto a concrete ramp that almost glows beneath the headlights. She grips the edge of the seat as they spiral upwards at reckless speed, and when he shifts gears she feels it in the base of her spine. Gravity pushes her towards him. He raises his arm to hold her, and suddenly she sees the steering wheel as a snake swallowing its tail. *I'm dreaming! This is just a nightmare*! Profoundly relieved, she closes her eyes and relaxes against him.

'Falling asleep?' he asks.

'No because I'm already asleep and this is just a dream.'

'Then why don't you wake yourself up?'

She tries, but she can't manage to turn his hard chest into her soft bed or his heavy arm into her comforter's safe warmth. Reluctantly, she opens her eyes again.

His gloved hand is gripping the rubberized plastic of a steering wheel, not a serpent eating itself. Apprehension is working in her blood like a drug and making her hallucinate.

He allows her to pull away from him and sit up straight in her own seat. Far below the bridge the red-and-gold glimmer of a busy street makes her think of a grade-school film of blood flowing through an artery... cells swerving urgently around each other, flowing in congesting clumps, slowing down and speeding up again...

'What's your name?' he finally asks her.

'Does it matter?'

'Yes, it does.'

'What's *your* name?' she demands weakly.

'I told you to call me "master".'

'Please tell me where we're going, master,' she begs softly, submissively.

'Please tell me what you're going to do with me...'

He pulls over onto the side of the road and stops the car. 'I'm going to put my tongue in your mouth, like this...' The gearshift thrusts painfully into her womb as he pulls her to him and kisses her violently. 'I'm going to let my tongue wander around slowly,' he continues in a whisper, his lips moving against hers, 'licking the tombstones of your teeth and forcing you to remember every body buried inside you. Then I'm going to unzip your spine and caress your soul until you beg me to finish stripping you down to the bone; until you beg me to take you. Then, when you're conscious again, I'll get you a new dress and let you enjoy how beautiful you are. After that I'll come for you again, and you'll be waiting for me, you'll be waiting even more desperately than you were tonight, and I'll be even harder on you, because you'll want me to be. Nothing else will ever really satisfy you. Only I can do that.' He pauses and looks directly into her eyes. 'Do you understand now?'

'Yes,' she takes a wonderfully deep breath, 'My *Lord!*'

Covenant Transport

Dorchester, Massachusetts 1933

Six days a week at four o'clock in the morning, Elizabeth Reed drops her brother off at the bakery and then heads home again for a few more hours sleep. Rising before the sun depresses her; it mysteriously robs her of her sense of direction and she knows where she is going only in the most literal sense.

During the relatively short drive, traffic signals flash yellow suns over the empty black space of the roads. One morning it rains gently on her way home and a rising fog imbues the streetlamps with a ghostly aura. Hers is the only car in sight except for a truck pulling up to the curb on the opposite side of the street. Its multiple headlights are shaped like a cross around which the mist flows in restless sheets. Two words are written in white letters across the truck's dark body: COVENANT TRANSPORT.

* * *

Three mornings later, Elizabeth passes the truck again. An abundance of stars are visible above the empty office buildings as she catches sight of the driver jumping lightly down from behind the wheel. He is strikingly tall and his silhouette in a long black coat flows like a solid shadow in front of the headlights' luminous cross.

* * *

The struggling ad company where she works as an invoice typist finally goes under, forcing her to look for another job like so many others, and Sunday she begins the dreary search through the meager classifieds.

On Monday she answers an obscure little ad for a receptionist that feels in keeping with her brief resume. She suffers a strangely pleasant shock when she drives to the address, 1048 Elder Street, the numbers visible now without the truck parked in front of them. Elizabeth is somehow certain the job is meant for her. She considers 'coincidence' a dirty word; she has always imagined she senses invisible forces working around her, perhaps because it's inconceivable to her that her unique beauty is only a random combination of chemicals.

Stepping out of the old Ford Model-T her brother manages to keep running, she glances down at her faint reflection in the driver's window. She has recently sacrificed most of her long hair to the indifferent altar of a salon floor. Like cupped hands, two neat black curves now offer her face to the world, the trim bangs combined with her full mouth giving her a seductive look. It's the latest fashion and in keeping with the independent spirit she exhibited since birth, to her late mother's chagrin.

There is no sign beneath the black metal numbers on the heavy wooden door, and the large front room she steps into is empty. No paintings hang on the stark white walls, no furniture breaks up the polished gleam of the wooden floor, and the ceiling is an unfinished web of black beams rising much higher above her than she would have thought possible from the building's facade. The space is dimly lit by sunlight filtering in through the opaque glass of two windows flanking the door, and by a brass lamp sitting on a small desk she suddenly notices tucked into a corner.

'Good afternoon,' she says to the blonde woman seated behind it. 'My name is Elizabeth Reed. I've come to apply for the position advertised in the paper.'

'Good afternoon, Elizabeth.' The woman rises from behind the desk. 'Come this way, please.'

A natural blonde judging by her complexion, the current receptionist is as tall and beautiful as Ginger Rogers. She leads Elizabeth into a narrow corridor faintly lit by a naked light bulb where she opens a door and smiles her into the room beyond. Then the door clicks shut behind her, leaving her alone with a monstrously large desk and the figure draped in black seated behind it.

'Good afternoon, dear,' the nun says, her smile weary. 'Please, have a seat.'

Elizabeth perches on the wooden chair facing the paper-strewn surface.

'You are the ninth girl I have seen today, Elizabeth,' the nameless sister states sadly, her watery green eyes framed by a delta of wrinkles. 'Not one of them was right for the position.'

'Oh...' Elizabeth has no idea what else to say as she produces her painstakingly typed resume.

The old woman accepts it and studies it for a moment, her thin lips pursed. 'Mm... very good, and now you are here.'

Elizabeth takes advantage of the opening. 'Where is *here* exactly, Sister?'

'Forgive me, my dear, I thought you knew where you were. This is an annex of St. John's Church. Primarily it serves as a storage facility, but a kitchen in the back is where volunteers bake the Host on Saturdays. We store all charitable donations of food and clothing here. You met Candy. She answers phone calls and accepts gifts during the day, but we also need someone to be here at night, because God's servants never rest, you know.'

'Oh, I know, I've been driving my brother to a bakery every morning at four a.m. and I've seen one of your trucks.'

'Oh, excellent.' A childish grin smoothes away her wrinkles before vanishing like a mirage in a cracked desert. 'Candy will give you the appropriate forms to fill out. I trust ten dollars a week is acceptable?'

'Oh, yes, thank you, Sister!'

'We need you to begin tonight, Elizabeth. I will give you the key. Your hours are midnight to nine, Monday through Friday. The women who do the baking only come in on Saturdays, so you will not have to deal with them. The young man who handles our deliveries will introduce himself. We're expecting new cushions for the pews tonight at around four a.m.'

The tall, dark figure in the long black coat... the thought of him more than the generous pay makes this graveyard shift feel potentially intriguing instead of mind-numbingly dull.

* * *

Elizabeth is back in the echoing front room seated behind the desk with the brass lamp and its green glass shade. She is wearing a long-sleeved black dress with a lace-trimmed collar that buttons down the front, and the pearl-drop earrings her grandmother left her, her most treasured possession.

She let herself into the office at six minutes to midnight according to the black-and-white clock hanging over her head now. The absolute darkness and silence intimidated her, and she still cannot quite shake off a subtle feeling of anxiety.

Except for a trip to a closet-sized bathroom, she has been sitting in the surprisingly comfortable desk chair for two hours reading. The first thing she did was explore the slightly warped drawers, but she found nothing of interest, only the usual pens and pencils, paper clips, loose staples and writing pads.

She tries to keep her attention buried in the plot of her book, but boredom is sucking the energy out of her drop by drop, second by second, and she doesn't know how she can possibly stay awake all night.

Standing up to get blood flowing through her stiff muscles, she walks over to one of the windows beside the door and flips open the dusty blinds. If she can wait another two hours for the driver to show up she can just as easily survive two centuries. Her only companion in this silent vigil is the streetlight on the corner. The way the top of the lamp post curves over the black asphalt evokes a person with his head lowered in grief, yet even through the walls of the building she senses the subliminal hum of the power flowing through it.

Headlights abruptly cut through her thoughts as a truck pulls up outside and the words COVENANT TRANSPORT fill her vision.

She opens the door and steps out into the cold darkness just in time to see the driver walk out of the headlights' luminous stream. He is concentrating on the clipboard in his hand, but he looks up instantly in response to the sound of her high-heels on the sidewalk.

For once reality outdoes her imagination; he is so intensely handsome her voice seems to slip on his features and all she can manage is a breathless, 'Good evening!' Hugging herself, she hurries back inside, and retreats all the way behind the desk.

He follows her. 'Good morning,' he corrects her, setting his clipboard down in front of her. 'My name is John.' His voice is deep and quiet.

'Pleased to meet you, John, I'm Elizabeth.'

'You are beautiful, Elizabeth.'

The direct compliment literally takes her breath away. 'Thank you...'

'How many men have had the pleasure of using your lovely body, Elizabeth?'

'What?' she gasps. 'It is none-'

'Do not tell me it is none of my business, Elizabeth, because you would be lying.'

'I may have bobbed my hair, sir, but I'm a respectable woman and a very particular one.' Naturally she has allowed a handful of men to make love to her, but they all disappointed her in the end for one reason or another; however, that doesn't make her a tramp. 'I still subscribe to the old-fashioned belief that there's someone special out there I'm meant to be with, and until such time as-'

'Do you really believe that, Elizabeth?'

'Yes,' she replies fervently, transfixed by the ideal symmetry of his features. Despite the freezing temperatures outside there is not the slightest hint of color in his cheeks.

He turns away abruptly with a cape-like flourish of his coat and leaves the front door open behind him, letting in the cold.

Even though he just raped her sensibilities by asking her such an intimate question, his perfect bone structure and proud carriage make it impossible for her to resent him. She remains rooted to the desk chair thoughtlessly awaiting his return, shivering.

A minute later she watches him wheel in what looks very much like a narrow wooden coffin.

'I assume those are new cushions for the pews,' she remarks. Daring to venture out from behind the desk again, she follows him down the long corridor to a door at the end. 'Let me,' she offers to open it for him and the knob turns so easily she nearly stumbles into the pitch-black space. Moving lithely out of his way, she searches the wall for a light switch as the darkness swallows him and his burden. At last she finds the switch and flicks it up, but nothing happens.

'Don't bother.' He reappears dragging the empty two-wheeler behind him. 'It's dead.'

She does not want to act like a puppy trotting at his heels, so she sits back down at the desk as he returns to the truck.

His next trip to the storage room is made in a silence punctuated by a long, penetrating look as he passes her desk. 'Well, Elizabeth,' he says on his way back out again, 'do you think you will like your new position?'

'That all depends, John. How long have you been doing this?'

'Doing what, flirting with beautiful women or driving a truck?'

'And I'm sure you could easily fill that truck with all your conquests,' she retorts.

'Naturally,' he pauses beside her, 'but that does not mean I am easy to please. A girl like you should not be alone all night, Elizabeth. Or do you enjoy being awake while most everyone is asleep?' He glances around them. 'Can you feel all their dreams flying through the air like spirits? It is so much easier to come up with interesting ideas at night, ideas too subtle to be born when everyone's mind is awake and tuned into rational fears and concerns.' He holds her eyes. 'If you know what I mean, Elizabeth.'

'Oh, yes, I do. I've been driving my brother to a bakery every morning at four o'clock and the atmosphere is different at that hour, and not just because it's dark… I've seen your truck parked out in the mist…'

He perches on the edge of the desk, looming over her in his black coat. 'Do you believe in an afterlife, Elizabeth?' he asks quietly, gazing steadily into her eyes.

'Yes, but I don't believe it's something that just happens to us,' she answers thoughtfully, intrigued by the unusual conversation. 'I believe there are as many different afterlives as there are people. I mean, unless you develop your spiritual senses in this life you'll probably have a pretty scary experience. Death isn't just one big black empty space we all vanish into, and I don't believe it's a perfect ready-made heaven, either. To believe that is like being a baby in the womb imagining life after birth as either a featureless void or a carefree paradise.' Sharing these profound thoughts with him excites her so much she forgets to feel shy. 'I think dying must be like another birth, except that everything gets turned inside out and your inner world manifests around you.'

'I have some free time,' he says quietly. 'Will you share a cup of tea with me in the back, Elizabeth?'

* * *

The cavernous kitchen is dominated by a long wooden table worn shiny smooth from years of pounding and kneading the body of Christ. It is flanked by rows of ovens, and the fact that half the overhead lights are dead makes the room feel strangely morgue-like. It is dark in the corner where a decrepit little gas stove adjoins a large porcelain sink. She seats herself at the small wooden table in front of the stove while John starts some water boiling in the kettle, his back to her. Except for the occasional white flash of his hands he is three different degrees of darkness from his black hair to his coat down to his leather boots.

'I like your ideas, Elizabeth.' He sets a chipped tea cup in front of her and seats himself opposite her.

'Thank you, John.'

He crosses his arms over his chest and his intensely serious expression makes him almost too handsome to look at. 'Are you pleased to find out everything you believe is true, Elizabeth?' His choice of tenses confuses her but she ignores it. 'I would have to be dead first, so I think I can wait to find out.'

'You do not have a choice, Elizabeth. Do you really believe in this strange position in the middle of the night doing nothing?'

She smiles to conceal a climax of emotions inside her as she suddenly realizes what he is up to. 'You mean I'm… I'm dead?' She crosses her legs to hide how much it arouses her to think of him as a dark angel.

He continues gazing silently into her eyes.

'I don't know it yet, but I've… I've died,' she goes on, imagining that he's waiting for her to develop the macabre plot, 'and this place is just a metaphor my soul is fashioning around me. And that beautiful receptionist, and the old nun who hired me, are the two aspects of my nature, sensual and spiritual. Also, it's after hours, so everything is dark and silent as the grave.'

'You are very bright, Elizabeth.' His smile is sinister. 'But what does that make me?'

'Either an angel or a devil… yet I hope you can somehow be both.'

'Then they will have to come together inside you, Elizabeth.' Rising abruptly, he walks around the table to her.

Her eyes close from the weakening blow of desire she experiences as he grips her arm and pulls her to her feet. She doesn't resist as he leads her over to the table. He grasps her around the waist and lifts her on to it, and still she doesn't protest as he pushes her dress up far enough to spread her legs and stand between them. His mouth opens over hers, luring her into a warm, fluid realm alive with the rising, rhythmic excitement of flight. His deep kiss is a substantial yet unrestrained dimension in which his controlled force overwhelms her and makes it impossible to think clearly about what is happening. Only vaguely does she wonder if her wantonness will lose her the badly needed ten dollars a week promised to her by a nun who would promptly fire her if she could see her now. He keeps a firm grip on her upper arms even though there's no chance of her getting away, and she's glad his hands don't wander elsewhere as he explores her only through a lingering kiss. Still, she is increasingly afraid... or excited... she can't quite tell the difference. His haunting insinuations opened her up to his advances, but they are not responsible for the languid way her head falls back as he tongues her more deeply than any man ever has. He almost seems to want to suck the breath out of her lungs and her chest heaves from the strain when he at last pulls away.

Gazing into her eyes, he gently grasps her left wrist and draws it up to his lips. He caresses her sleeve up out of his way and kisses the faint blue delta of veins visible through her delicate skin. She watches him with her mouth parted in growing wonder, her eyes shining with a longing she can't put into words. At first the sight of his strong white teeth and well-defined canines is just another aesthetic revelation, just another visible reason to surrender to her attraction to him, but when their surprisingly sharp ends begin sinking into her skin she instinctively struggles to pull her arm free.

'Stop!' she gasps, but he keeps her slender wrist fiercely planted between his lips. Pain rises inside her in a deafening symphony, its fiery director forcing all her senses and perceptions into one climactic sensation as he bites into her flesh growling deep in his throat.

'Oh, my God!' she cries. 'What are you doing? Stop! Please, John, stop! Stop!'

He raises his head.

She can't believe his lips are stained a deep, beautiful red cosmetics can never hope to duplicate. 'You just... you just sucked my blood!' Yet her exclamation isn't completely one of horror; she sounds more like a child whose playmate has exceeded the boundaries of an exciting game by doing something utterly unexpected and shocking, so that her pain is tempered by a thrilled admiration shining in her eyes beneath a resentful veil of tears.

He whispers, 'Have you heard of vampires, Elizabeth?'

'Of course I've heard of vampires, but they don't... they don't really exist...'

'How do you know the undead are only a myth, Elizabeth? How can you be so sure we are not real?'

She stares at her wrist struggling to understand the puncture wounds in her flesh that might have been made by a very large cat as myriads of fears flock into her mind like bats. The vivid red holes are dangerously deep, and looking back up into his silver-gray eyes – into the bottomless black holes of his pupils – she realizes her soul was lost to him from the moment she saw his silhouette take shape against the luminous cross of headlights. The only question is what will happen to her body...

'You are so beautiful, Elizabeth. Your soul is uniquely intoxicating to me, like no other I have ever tasted. I must have you...'

She wants to say, 'This isn't funny anymore, John!' but it never was funny, it was arousing, and it still is somehow even though the stimu-lating edge of her fear is painfully sharp now.

He lets go of her wrist and steps back. Now is the moment when she should make an effort to get away from him, but she doesn't move. She is transfixed by the way his eyes close as he licks his lips to savor the flavor her of her blood as if earth's most delicious ingre-dients are concentrated within it. His eyelids are so smooth and white they look carved from marble as he gazes blindly up towards heaven. He isn't looking at her, she could theoretically slip off the table and run from the kitchen, but she still doesn't move, and her passivity is a mystery she is so desperately trying to comprehend she can't think straight; she can't think at all. And then it's too late because his eyes are open again.

'Stand up and take your dress off for me, Elizabeth.'

The indignant exclamation, 'What kind of a girl do you think I am?' flashes through her mind like distant lightning; there is no real thunder, no true outrage in it. Her pride and her virtue are still mys-teriously intact as she slips down off the edge of the table and begins unbuttoning her dress, an intoxicating blend of fear and desire caus-ing her fingers to tremble forcing her to concentrate on the task. She gazes demurely at the bone-colored buttons of his coat as she slips the dress off her shoulders, hesitating only for a heartbeat before exposing her naked breasts, too young and pert to require the sup-port of a bra.

'Look into my eyes, Elizabeth. I want you to see how beautiful you are.'

She obeys him, and caresses the dress down carefully over her garters, exposing the soft bush concealing her sex followed by the firm pale flesh of her thighs. A moment later all she is wearing in the middle of a church kitchen are a black garter belt, black stockings and black high-heels.

He is upon her so swiftly she doesn't have time to take a breath to cry out. The cold depths of his coat enfold her slender body as he bends her backwards and clutches her left thigh, roughly lifting her leg up against him. A shrill scream echoes through the cavernous kitchen and drowns out her shocked gasp as his teeth easily penetrate the fine skin of her neck. He shifts her weight in his arms in order to get the best possible grip on her, and she clings to his shoulders to keep her awareness from being swept away on a blinding current of pain hopelessly confused with an irresistible erotic undertow... the harder she struggles against the powerful sensation the more relentlessly she feels herself carried away on it... she doesn't have the strength to fight it... then suddenly she doesn't understand why she's resisting something so intensely pleasurable... she closes her eyes, vaguely aware that only his arms are holding her up as her racing heart begins slowing down, willingly obeying the sensual rhythm of his throat swallowing her blood in increasingly generous, powerfully warm mouthfuls...

When the kettle stops screaming she can hear herself think again. 'Stop!' she cries. 'Oh, my God, please stop!'

His teeth feel like two long and impossibly hard erections slipping slowly out of her body. He releases her, and she sinks to her knees as if her black stockings are only ashes or shadows without substance. She rests her cheek against one of his cold black boots, and its unyielding reality reassures her. When he grabs her by her bobbed hair and forces her back up to her feet again, she welcomes his rough handling like the most profound tenderness, and some part of her can't resist offering the other, virginal side of her neck up as a willing sacrifice to his vicious kiss.

'You are mine now, Elizabeth.' He takes her hand and leads her back down the narrow corridor into the empty front room. 'Sign here,' he commands, handing her his clipboard, 'and release your soul to me.'

She finds a red pen in the desk, and with an unsteady hand signs her full name on the blank white page.

'Look at the clock, Elizabeth.'

She glances up at the black-and-white face. The arms are still at 2:09, the moment she got up to look out the window and saw his truck pull up.

He heads for the door.

'Wait, John!' The last thing she wants in the universe is to be left naked and alone.

'I will be back as soon as you have accepted the truth, Elizabeth,' he promises without looking back, and the door closes silently behind him.

Standing at the window, she listens to the rumble of the truck's engine starting up and watches the golden stream of his headlights flow away before she walks slowly back to the desk, staring anxiously at the clock's unchanging face. She returns to the kitchen. The sight of her dress lying on the floor should shame her, but she is strangely numb. He hurt her. He did something she had never dreamed a man would do to her. He penetrated her flesh with a part of his body but he didn't make love to her, he sucked her blood. She can hardly believe it, and if it wasn't for the sinister red wounds in her wrist she might be able to convince herself she only imagined the unearthly experience. The punctures aren't bleeding, they don't hurt at all, and this worries her more than anything.

Listlessly slipping her dress back on, she makes an effort to ignore the haunting evidence he left behind on her flesh by sitting down at the desk and opening her book, but she finds it impossible to resurrect any interest in the sweet romantic plot.

Longing for the normal sound of a car rushing by outside, she picks up the phone.

It takes her a full, incredulous minute to accept the fact that there is no dial tone.

She sets the receiver back down and makes sure the line is connected to the jack in the wall, but when she checks again there is still no dial tone.

She sits staring into space.

An eternity passes before she hears the long sigh of the truck's tires outside like blood beginning to flow along the roads of her veins again. She suspects the sound is only an illusion, but it no longer matters. As the door opens and he crosses the threshold she knows their infinite hunger is all the reality she needs.

RELATIVE RELATIONSHIP

Vienna, Austria 1909

I t is early evening and the gray, feathery quilt of the sky is tossing pillows of mist to earth, restlessly changing the shapes of things as if in a dream. The old-age of erosion spoiling their eternal youth, statues decorating a stone bridge arching over the Danube seem to writhe in despair as they envy the mortal woman walking beneath them, her black ankle-length coat and wide-brimmed hat glistening with drops of water reflecting the hidden stars above. The stone figures silently desire her power of motion – her miraculous ability to journey from birth to death – and a pale hand beckons to her through the fog.

She pauses, and after the ticking of her little square heels, the silence is absolute.

The rigid finger is pointing down at something.

She looks, and sees that on the bridge's stone railing are two abandoned wineglasses. One crystal goblet lies on its side, a faint trace of color shimmering on its rim. The other glass stands tall and erect and is still half full of a light-golden wine.

Rachel keeps her hands respectfully sheathed in her muff in the face of this mysterious evidence, tentatively touching the scene of the love with her imagination. The river – gray as steel and unstoppable as time – rushes on below her as she pictures the man who abandoned his wine… He is in his thirties, he must be, his glass is still half full, and the woman is very much in love with him for she finished her drink. His feminine companion is perfectly fulfilled, but he appears to have a taste for something more…

Rachel wonders what he is like and what inspired them to share a private toast on a public bridge. Were they celebrating a special (perhaps illicit) occasion far from the prying eyes of their family and loved ones? Perhaps the man is wealthy enough to casually discard two fine crystal glasses…

A final faint shaft of sunlight glints off the wine he abandoned.

Rachel steps forward, and before she even realizes what she intends to do, her right hand slips out of the muff and she pushes the woman's glass off the edge of the bridge into the river. She glances self-consciously up at the statue that seems to be watching her. With its stone eyes as witness, she picks up the man's glass and boldly drinks what he left for her. Then she hurries away almost feeling as though she committed a crime.

* * *

Rachel is sitting at the desk in her drawing room, but she is only pretending to be writing a letter to her aunt. She is possessed by the irrational certainty that her life is now linked with the man from whose glass she drank yesterday evening on the bridge. Some inexorable impulse prompted her unsanitary gesture. Around her neck she is wearing the golden cross her mother gave her before she died, and glancing down at it she cannot help but admire the way it rests between the swells of her breasts, exposed by the deep cleavage of her dressing gown, her flesh soft and smooth as the desert hills on which Christ was crucified.

She picks up her fountain pen again, and idly sketches the crescent moon on the rough, ivory-colored paper. Gazing down at the shape, she observes the fact that the moon's sickle is also a backwards 'C' of sorts, the first letter in 'Cologne' and 'Clothing'...

She clips the cap back on her pen, sets it down, and glances over at the grandfather clock. Clothing does not make the man; it is only part of his cultural skeleton. She wonders what he is like...

* * *

Later that evening, after she has eaten alone and the sun has long since set, Rachel goes for another walk. Her aunt thought it scandalous that she chose to stay alone in the city after her mother passed away and keeps insisting her niece move out to the country with her, but Rachel is relishing the solitude, and the vibrant anonymity of the city, where she feels free to think (if not actually to do) whatever she pleases.

Her heart is beating faster than her sedate pace calls for when she steps onto the bridge. As she approaches the center where the stones arch high over the black water, she sees a man leaning against the ledge in the very place where three days ago she discovered the wine glasses. A gas lamp a few feet behind him shines on his golden hair but leaves his face in shadow as he glances over at her, the clock-like ticking of her heels the sound of his privacy running out.

'Good evening,' he says quietly.

'Good evening,' she replies just as softly, and forces herself to continue walking past him.

'Are you anxious to be somewhere?' he asks.

Surprise and excitement catch her like hands and turn her back to face him. The lamplight now pools around his handsome features. 'No,' she replies, 'I always go for a long walk in the evening.'

Abruptly he looks down at the water again, leaning heavily against the stone. His shoulders slump defenselessly in a fine dark suit, allowing her curiosity easy entry.

'Is there something troubling you?' she dares to ask, moving a little closer to him.

His hair glimmers as he shakes his head. 'She is dead,' he intones. She cannot see what color his eyes are, but they are vertiginously deep in the shadows when he looks at her again.

'Oh… my condolences,' she whispers, and experiences an odd stab of guilt.

'We came here three days ago,' he goes on quietly, gazing down at the black river again. 'We were just engaged and were on our way to the Opera to celebrate… I returned this afternoon… I walked all the way from… from her wake… my glass was still here but hers had fallen into the water just as she did… you see, she drowned.'

'Oh…' Rachel can scarcely breathe; she feels as though her reason is also drowning in fatally deep currents of possible and impossible.

'She was boating on the pond in her garden when for some reason her little boat capsized… she became tangled in her skirts and petticoats, and she was never taught how to swim…' He straightens up. 'But please forgive me. I should not be burdening you with this sorrowful tale, although it has been very kind of you to listen.

Might I ask your name?'

'Rachel Steiner.'

'Thank you, Miss Steiner, for your patience with a sad stranger. My name is Alexander Harling, and it would be my pleasure to escort you home.'

'Yes, thank you…' She has no right to deny him anything.

* * *

In the dark bedroom the pale gray linens resemble a portion of the sky that has been falling to earth all night in sheets of rain, the bed's loved-in disorder brooding clouds in the window of the vanity mirror.

Alexander lies with one arm bent around his golden head. Emerging quietly from the water-closet, Rachel stands gazing down at her husband. With his eyes closed and his features relaxed in sleep he looks so innocent that all the wicked things he does to her at night seem like a dream. He is not as wealthy as she imagined him to be when she drank from his wine glass on the stone bridge, but he is rich in wit and warmth and in skills it makes her blush to think about, as does the fact that he will not permit her to wear a nightgown to bed. Respectable couples can afford the privacy of separate bedrooms; if her aunt knew her niece slept naked in a man's arms every night she would be shocked speechless.

Alex wakes as she slips into bed beside him again shivering with pleasure as his body heat embraces her chilled flesh. 'Good morning,' she whispers, smiling into his sleepy gaze.

As always he returns her smile, until he remembers, then his mouth sets into the hard horizon her heart races towards desperately without ever being able to cross into his soul and comfort him. His expression is a two-edged sword – it arouses her with the depth of his love for his dead fiancé, and cuts her with despair because she is not enough to make him forget her.

She closes her eyes as he erects the muscular columns of his arms on either side of her to arch his body over hers like a bridge. She feels blissfully at home in this sensual temple, but her heart is heavy as a stone. The passionate depths of his personality are both her joy and her torment. She *must* make him truly love her and forget there ever was another...

'And what is so good about this particular morning?' he asks finally, gently kissing her mouth.

She keeps her lips sealed as tightly as the marble mausoleum she imagines his dead bride is buried in even though he has never taken her there. None of their acquaintances have ever even spoken of his first love, as though they dare not mention her name in his presence.

'Answer me,' he commands, and she cannot resist letting him have her tongue. 'Mm, that is good,' he murmurs, thrusting his knee between her legs.

Their marriage night is still fresh in all her senses... the fire-lit bedroom flickering with shadows that suddenly seemed full of cherubs wildly circling their bed – the almost grotesque crudeness of physical conception silently beating the divine wings of her tumultuous emotions. The feather mattress was transformed into a cloud that rose into the heaven of his eyes and the love shining in them even while sinking into a burning hell as he impaled her on his agonizingly large erection, the profound silence broken only by the crackling of the fire and her gasps of pain. Thank God the vintage of her virginity could be harvested only once for it was almost too much for her; her soul had never tasted such an intoxicating mix of fear and excitement, pain and pleasure, shame and desire. The blood of Christ neatly contained by the gem-encrusted chalice held in the priest's hands at church had not prepared her for the sight of her blood staining the Eucharist-white of her inner thighs, or for the half cross of a man's amazingly hard penis slowly but remorselessly stabbing her. The prolonged sight of her naked body was bad enough. He literally ripped her white nightgown off impatiently, the tender, considerate man she had married suddenly a fierce stranger who took her breath away. She had been taught not to look at her naked body anymore than was necessary, so she could not understand why he wished to torment her with his open contemplation of the most shameful parts of her. She could not blame him for his obsession with her soft, round breasts, for they were more beautiful than any statue's, even though she knew it was sinfully vain of her to think so. But when he commanded her to lie back across the bed and spread her legs for him... that was when the trembling shadows came alive like the cherubic wings of her schooled innocence and latent sensuality beating against each other. Standing at the foot of the bed, he gazed down the length of her body and into her exposed sex, and his expression was so reverent she almost forgot her intense embarrassment. The penetrating look in his eyes actually made her want to curiously touch the slick petals protecting the vulnerable heart of her flesh, but she resisted the wanton impulse by clutching the sheets on either side of her hips. She knew he was a good, respectable man, and in those moments she doubted herself more than she did him, for surely her body was the Devil's creation, his fabled pitchfork responsible for all the tempting holes in her mortal coil.

'You are so beautiful, Rachel,' he told her, and suddenly she was able to appreciate the sight of her unclothed body as she might a fine statue. If it did not shame her to look upon naked men and women made of marble, then why should she be ashamed to look at herself or at her husband as he began undressing before her? The heavy curtains were closed, but she knew that outside the window the crescent moon was harvesting the stars with its silver cycle, and that night she found out what a man was really like beneath his fashionable attire. No words could describe his true nature; she could only experience it and submit to it as his intensity utterly ravaged yet also mysteriously fulfilled her. His concentrated thrusts forced her to accept and to appreciate as she never had before the confines of her limbs, of her arms and legs and especially of the silky glove of her sex clinging to him. He beat himself against her, he stabbed her cruelly and relentlessly, yet all the time he gazed down at her with a wondrous gratitude in his eyes, and towards the end the almost saintly slackening of his features inspired her to relax beneath him, like a willing sacrifice on an altar stained by her blood devoted to the divine force of his lust. On their wedding night he only made use of her sex, but very soon he also claimed her mouth with his penis. And after a few months she even allowed him to venture into the tight passage hidden beneath the soft hills of her buttocks; into the darkest depths of her flesh where it feels as if God has secretly buried all the painfully sweet sins of earth.

* * *

On the night of their first anniversary, when they are finishing a private candlelit dinner at home, Rachel can no longer contain herself. 'If you at least spoke about her, Alex, it would help, would it not? I know nothing about her or about the time you spent together, and I cannot continue fighting a ghost for the full warmth of your affections!'

'But that is how you wanted her, is it not?'

'How can you say that?' she gasps.

'Because if she was alive I would not be here with you,' he answers coldly.

After a long and terrible moment, he pushes his chair back, walks around the table, and genuflects beside her. 'Forgive me, Rachel.' His head falls heavily onto her lap.

She caresses his hair. It is so soft she cannot stop herself from crying.

'I did not mean to take it this far,' he confesses, pulling her up into his arms as he rises. 'It is not your fault,' he whispers. 'I had no idea you would take me seriously.'

'I know why you cannot love me, Alex...'

'Rachel...'

'You cannot love me because *I* am the one who pushed her glass off the bridge and finished the wine that was left in yours. I could not tell you, but I have always felt it was somehow my fault that she drowned. I wished it in my soul... I might as well have pushed her into the pond with my own hands. I wanted her out of your life even though I had never met her. It was my fault...'

'No, Rachel.' He takes her hand and leads her out of the dining room into the cozier confines of the fire-lit drawing room. 'Sit down, please,' he says, and then sinks to one knee before her again. 'I love you, Rachel, I loved you from the moment I saw you on the bridge, and that is why I could not bring myself to tell you the truth. It was only a drama I thought it would be exciting to play with you. I did not mean to let it drag on so long until it assumed a life of its own. But when you reacted so intensely, when I saw you were willing to do anything for me... I could not resist... It was wrong, but after that first night I was ashamed to tell you the truth.'

Rising abruptly, he stares down at her soberly. 'I have never discussed my business with you, but in part it consists of restoring old paintings and statues. I was on the bridge that evening. I watched you from behind a statue as you gazed at the wine glasses. They were left there by a frivolous young couple on their way to the symphony, but I could sense you reading much more into the romantic tableau; it was in your face and in your eyes... you were the most beautiful woman I had ever seen... and when you pushed the young lady's glass into the river and drank what was left in the man's, it excited me... it aroused me so much I could not resist playing along with your fantasy. I almost said something to you then. I did not want you out of my sight ever again, but I stopped myself from speaking and went back every evening after that to wait for you because I knew, I hoped, you would return. I thought you would laugh away my sorrowful act, but because you felt guilty, you did not, and then it was too late, for it had never occurred to me that your passionate reaction would seduce me into believing the tragic tale myself... I actually became angry with you for not telling me what you had done, Rachel, and the longer I nursed this irrational resentment against you, the more impossible it became to tell you the truth.'

She gazes up at him, her eyes wide with wonder, and then she begins to laugh. She cannot stop laughing until he pulls her up into his arms and gently slaps one of her flushed cheeks.

She slips out of his grasp, and tugs on the velvet chord that rings a bell in the kitchen.

Almost immediately their housekeeper appears.

'Alice, dear, please pack a bottle of *Neuburger* and two crystal glasses in a picnic basket. My husband and I have a story to bring to life.'

Laila

Zanzibar 1863-1880

Laila is an old Arab name meaning "dark",
Zahra means "flower" and Amira "princess".

Nowhere in the Qur'an does it state that women are inferior to men. More importantly, nowhere in the Qur'an does it state that men are superior to women, and by their actions men are perpetually proving otherwise. Laila could not understand women who still desired the beings who imprisoned and abused them. Having boundless quantities of time to do so, she thought long and hard on the matter and concluded that women are not seduced by a man's fleshly sheath – which inevitably wears out and is thrown away into a grave – but by the force it contains. These women are enamored of the divine power men believe they embody. As for men, it had long been clear to Laila that they love only the reflection of Allah inside them, and if they cherish a woman it is because she is skilled at worshiping them in every sense. A man can have skin like three-day-old lentils, and shifty black eyes like bugs burrowing into his fat carcass, yet if he possesses power in other men's eyes foolish women can actually believe they desire him. Laila knows better; she was never susceptible to the inexplicable weakness that plagued her grandmother and mother, her sisters and cousins. She did not see strength in her father's violent displays of temper, only the injustice of her mother being forced to pay for the fact that Allah was not as generous with them as He was with other less overtly pious families... except, ironically enough, through Laila herself. Her flawless almond skin, full lips and lush black lashes gave the burning disdain in her vivid green eyes a desirable aura of smoldering sensuality.

She was scarcely twelve years old when her father carted her off to the market frequented by the sultan's eunuchs. She was no more to him than a loaf of bread that was rising and filling out in all the right places. Her teeth were the smooth white of the most precious ivory, a fact potential buyers made note of as her mouth was rudely inspected much like that of a camel preparing for a long journey. And because she was judged worthy as a possession she knew her father bought fresh robes for himself along with a new prayer mat, and she pictured her whole family feasting on the holy days as a reward for her beauty, which was sealed away in the living tomb of the Sultan's harem.

Laila did not grow old enough out in the world to have the light of Allah that shone bright in her heart and mind dimmed by veils and humbly filtered by men's perceptions of her. From the moment she entered the Grand Seraglio she knew Allah had secretly blessed her, for the smooth desert of her life stretching before her as a powerful man's slave was filled with beautiful mirages her growing senses wordlessly promised her could one day become a very real oasis of pleasure and even happiness.

Not including three enviably powerful Sultanas, the man who now owned Laila possessed more concubines than he could name, and once she bled around him she ceased to be of any special interest. The crescent moon had risen over the palace walls to adorn the softly blushing sky when she was brought into his presence for the first time.

After she was bathed and then depilated (a painful ordeal that had her gasping and writhing like a beached fish on a shore of soft white linen) massaged and then hennaed, a handful of women flocked energetically around her for hours, happily preparing her for the loss of her innocence. No treasure was truly worthwhile if it was easily found, and certainly the Sultan had his work cut out for him. She was enveloped in so much brightly dyed and intricately embroidered cloth that, gazing down at herself, she became lost in the pattern over her chest... and then in another design on her arm... and then in the intricate stitching decorating her skirt... she was a maze of passageways all leading to that one mysterious place between her legs. It was the older women who took charge of her as she held herself perfectly still listening to them discuss the provenance of her garments. Their conversation made the world feel vaster than she could imagine while at the same time filling her with the exciting sense that her lovely body formed the borders of everything; that she was magically at the heart of all caravan routes because being able to feel as beautiful as she did that day was the driving force behind all of civilization. Damascus, Gaza and other cities she had never heard of all contributed something uniquely beautiful to her wedding night. The loose-fitting dress was as precious as a lifetime of sunsets... as the splendid hues of desert twilights stirred together and served up in elaborate patterns of circles and squares marching and spinning up and down her body. Her waist was modestly defined by a corded belt worn beneath a jacket with sleeves that billowed out like exotic flowers from the elbows. A *Hand of Fatima* from Anatolia was hung around her neck as a sobering reminder that while she was the beautiful slave girl that night, in the future she would have to share her master's affection with many other women. The necklace also served to remind her that even though as a member of the Sultan's harem she was blessed with abundance and would never have to roast *halvah* for herself, she would still do well to remember the virtues of patience and faithfulness. Her long black hair was gently caught in two loose plates on either side of her face and draped over her still flat chest, and finally a white cotton veil with vividly embroidered edges was placed over her head to flow all the way down to her ankles.

It took most of the afternoon to prepare her for what turned out to be a very brief stay in the Sultan's private chamber. An inevitable feeling of awe kept her eyes downcast as she was brought into his presence. She was glad of the woven splendor concealing her which entertained his eyes, leading his vision along red and gold paths so that (she fervently hoped) he would not notice the dark and contemptuously direct thoughts in her eyes. He was a thundercloud of black robes drifting over to his place on the elevated bed, and after she crawled dutifully towards him from the end the experience was very much like a rare but devastating storm in which pain flashed hotter than lightning. He did not bother to undress her and she felt stiff as a corpse laid out for burial in her finest clothes as the weapon hidden beneath his robes attacked her; brutally aiming for the tender and defenseless wound at the heart of her flesh. Laila's contempt for men reached a terrible climax that night as one of Allah's most revered servant's on earth made her eyes close in distaste as his powerful breath – overly sweet from too many honey cakes –assaulted her face. He was stabbing her, cruelly drawing her blood, yet for some reason he was the one panting and writhing against her as though in his final death throes. Her insides felt dry as sand only briefly moistened by a gush of blood from a slaughtered lamb. It seemed a miracle when she at last found herself back in the harem's soft and comforting embrace.

Laila dreaded that the Sultan would send for her again. She knew she was not supposed to feel this way and was careful to keep her fears to herself beneath the resentful glances of other hopeful young slaves. At least her rigid passivity had not displeased the Sultan enough for him to order her execution; she had been afraid that the rebellious feelings burning in her eyes would condemn them to fish food at the bottom of the river. So it was, in a sense, a relief to still be alive, and Allah eased her burdens even more six days after her royal summons when her cycle began again as usual. And with the onset of her menses pity flowed her way, for she was no longer presently competing for the coveted rank of Kadin. As a beautiful but humble Odalesque, at least for a while, Laila posed no threat to other aspiring concubines and she was now treated with an indifference she much preferred to the active hostility she endured immediately after spending a few violent hours with the Sultan. The assessing regard of the Kislar Aga during the crucial days after the loss of her virginity had also made her feel intensely anxious about her future, but then everyone's calculating attention shifted to the beautiful new slave who had just arrived and Laila was able to relax into insignificance.

Not all the women living in the Seraglio could still hope to rise in the Sultan's favor by way of their beauty or by bearing him a child; they had had their chance and were now considered too old to be singled out again. By unspoken consent these women congregated on one side of the baths, and it was towards their languid groups that Laila gravitated. At first her silent, wide-eyed presence on the fringes of their conversations was viewed with suspicion, for she was still young and lovely enough to fight for special favors from their master. She was pointedly ignored, but Laila was patient; she had nothing better to do than watch and listen as she thrived beneath every casual smiling glance that came her way. She had no musical or dancing skills to speak of, but all who looked upon her seemed to understand why the Kislar Aga allowed her to languish as an Odalesque without pressing her into servitude.

The days were long and unnaturally idle, but Laila found the absence of men as soothing as the massage a less fortunate Odalesque treated her to almost every day. Amira was far from plain, but with hundreds of women to choose from the Sultan could afford to be particular and she had been condemned to serving as the slave of slaves. Laila relished the feel of Amira's hands moving slowly across her body. At first Amira had been afraid of pressing too hard and hurting her, until Laila laughingly assured her that nothing had ever felt as good as Amira's fingers kneading her skin. It was Amira who told her about The Palace of Tears, and Laila at last understood why his concubines passionately hoped the Sultan would live forever – because they wished to continue enjoying all the luxuries of the Grand Seraglio.

For three years Laila savored her secret blessing from Allah in uncertain silence, then one spring night – when the full moon was embroidering vivid black-and-white patterns across the silent bodies of sleeping concubines – Laila discovered a part of her body that felt as luminous and mysteriously powerful as the sun's consort. The Sultan had seemed completely unaware of the fact that a glowing fragment of the moon had been born through her and secreted away in the silky folds of flesh between her legs. It was the middle of the night and she couldn't sleep. She was idly touching herself thinking about the bodies of other women, and of how hers would one day be more like them, when she discovered an intense magic casually hiding between her legs. She didn't know if it had always been there or if like her breasts it was slowly developing, but it didn't matter; she was utterly enthralled by her discovery.

Laila began to see things differently. She wondered why no one talked about the breathtakingly sweet treasure concealed beneath their veils and skirts and the even softer folds of their sex. These ever silent nether lips had much to say to Laila every night where she lay alone on her cushions, far enough away from other Odalesques for the subtle movement of her wrist not to disturb them. She ached to speak to someone about the joy that overwhelmed her whenever she determinedly crushed the seed-like swelling beneath her fingertips. She was glad the Sultan had not discovered it, for if he had made her feel this way she would have longed for him night and day. Even when there was no pattern of moonlight and the Seraglio was black as a demon's mouth, Laila lay awake touching herself. With her free hand she explored her body, cupping one of her delicate breasts and pinching her nipple curiously, as she once had exotic fruit in the marketplace. It intrigued her how hard her nipples could get, and during the day she remained acutely aware of them grazing the inside of her dress. She spent as much time as possible in the baths watching the women around her. The sight of naked breasts floating on the water like Lotus flowers made her wonderfully breathless. It seemed to Laila that breasts were like fruit, and that the smaller, firmer ones were somehow more appetizingly succulent than the larger, softer ones; nevertheless, every shape and size of bosom made her feel strangely hungry deep inside. When she was in the baths the day no longer felt endless as she basked in the vision of women's naked bodies lying all around her undulating like desert dunes, the soft hills of their buttocks leading her eyes down the mysteriously promising horizons of their legs. Massaged and hennaed to a smooth perfection by only slightly less beautiful slaves, their dusky golden skins shone in the lamplight, and whenever one of them rolled lazily onto her back, Laila's breath caught watching her.

'Forgive me, did I hurt you?' Amira inevitably asked as she massaged her more gently.

'Oh, no…' Laila smiled.

She will never forget the day she was fully able to see what lay between a woman's legs. She could only glimpse her own sex from above, a much different experience than looking up from her massage directly into the exotic bloom of a woman's secret lips gaping gently open and revealing a tantalizing glimpse of glistening, rosy depths that made Laila moan beneath her breath in reverent despair. She felt as if some divine, infinitely sharp sword had made this delicate slit she couldn't imagine a baby's head rending open, and yet it also struck her as a marvel that a rock-hard skull could emerge from such sensitive tenderness. She knew the woman who offered her a view of her sex as she rolled languidly onto her back and spread her legs was named Zahra, and when she sat up and smiled at her, Laila savored a sweetness she had never tasted before as she smiled back.

She continued savoring this feeling like a new and unknown ingredient in the lavish platters of food they were served all throughout the long afternoon. She understood its source – the way Zahra smiled at her with the lips on her face when she realized that Laila had been openly staring at the secret lips between her legs – but she could not define what this new feeling was only what it did to her. It made her feel fulfilled and yet lacking something vital… beautiful and yet not

guilty pleasures

beautiful enough... content as she had never been before and yet also profoundly restless...

Zahra was casually sharing a platter and rich, sultry laughter with another young Odalesque, and watching them, Laila felt as though invisible hands were wrapped around her throat making it hard for her to breathe as their pressure slowly increased. She was afraid a demon was seeking to possess her until Zahra looked her way, still smiling from something her companion had said, and then it was as if Fatima herself was gazing at her with a profound understanding that made her want to weep with relief. Yet the compassion in her irises the color of sunlit honey was also somehow demanding, and from that moment forward Laila was blindly devoted to Zahra in that she could think of nothing except pleasing her in any way possible. The moment lasted only as long as it took Zahra to slip a plump purple date between her lips, then she turned all her attention back to her companion, leaving Laila at once bereft and elated.

That night she could not sleep at all. She could not forget the way Zahra had looked at her. The other woman's dark-lashed golden eyes had taken possession of her pulse. With her hand working furiously between her legs, the promising, penetrating regard of those mesmerizing eyes blinded her with joy once, then a second time, and perhaps that was why she was then able to see the shadow moving silently through the darkness. She did not intend to rise and follow it, but this was what she found her body doing. The eunuch was nearly invisible on the moonless night, but Laila had seen him, and for some reason a part of her could not resist following the tall, broad-shouldered silhouette towards the baths, deserted at that late hour. When she suddenly remembered she was risking death with her actions, she hesitated, standing amongst sleeping slaves biting her lip in trepidation...

until her feet quickly led her to the couch were Zahra slept. If she woke her she would not know what to say, therefore the sight of her empty couch should have come as a relief, but instead it felt like a blow struck from so deep inside herself she had no defense against a pain of her own inflicting.

Laila turned and followed the eunuch who was casting a deeply dangerous shadow over her newfound happiness. She nearly lost her nerve when she entered the dripping, echoing baths that frighteningly evoked where she might end up at the bottom of the river in a sack, but then the breathless sounds rising from one of the small steam rooms lured her irresistibly towards them. Her bare feet made no sound on the painted tiles, and the closer she drew to the ghostly moans the more afraid she became. Her eyes were no longer overwhelmed by the darkness, and guided by the subtle sheen of water she peered around a wall into the steam room.

Laila instantly forgot her fears in a flood of anger that a man had arrived first at the place where she longed to be. The eunuch's big black bulk was crouched between Zahra's open legs as if he had just impossibly heard the call to prayer in the dead of night. She did not need to see the woman's face to know who he was worshipping, and even though she was appalled by the sight part of her could not blame him. He seemed to be devouring Zahra, yet the moans rising from her throat above her naked body did not sound like ones of agony. When Zahra reached down and clutched the eunuch's smoothly shaved skull with both hands, Laila unconsciously took a step forward to help her if what she desired was to push him away because he was hurting her. Then she wondered if Zahra had gone mad because she seemed to be trying to force the man's impossibly big head inside her. She arched her back, groaning, and her beautiful up-thrust breasts made Laila gasp out loud beneath a stab of desire.

'Oh, by Allah, we have been discovered!' Zahra whispered.

'No, Zahra, I will say nothing, I promise, if... if...'

'What do you want, girl?' the eunuch demanded.

'What *you* want.'

Zahra's laughter was no louder than the rippling of water in the next room. 'Come!' she breathed, opening her arms, and Laila pounced on her like a starving cat. She had no idea what she was doing only that nothing else mattered. The feel of one of Zahra's nipples hardening between her lips nearly made her swoon, and the soft fullness of her bosom beneath her avid mouth was so exquisite she forgot to be careful; she squeezed the other woman's breasts with a fierce hunger. Zahra moaned even more passionately in response, and all at once Laila understood this wordless language eloquently intensified by the wet lapping sounds made by the man feasting hungrily on Zahra's sex while she wildly licked and sucked her breasts. Yet she discovered that love-making was nothing like eating because the more she stuffed her hands and mouth with as much of Zahra as she could get the more she wanted; the more she savored of Zahra's soft, warm skin, the more urgent the smoldering need deep in her belly became.

'Would you like to know how it feels, Laila?'

'Oh, yes!'

'I wish her to pleasure me now,' Zahra said, and the eunuch rose obediently from between her legs.

Obeying an instinct she had no words for, Laila quickly took his place between Zahra's wide open thighs.

'No, take your dress off first,' Zahra commanded.

'But...'

'Do it!' hissed the eunuch.

Laila

Laila stood up, and shocking though it was she appreciated the big black hands that quickly helped divest her of the heavy garment. Then with the eager innocence of a child offered a special treat on a holy day, she knelt naked between Zahra's legs. She clutched the other woman's tender thighs on either side of her sex, and so intent was she on burying her face in this haunting rift in her flesh that she scarcely noticed the eunuch's fierce grip on her own hips. Of necessity her buttocks were thrust indecently up into the air, and even though she felt the man's hands pulling her cheeks apart, she was too intoxicated by Zahra's perfumed depths to protest. Now it was she who moaned as she tentatively licked the hot, wet heart of Zahra's hole while the eunuch boldly ran the hard length of his tongue up and down her own warm slit. When the tip of his stiff tongue flicked energetically down in search of her body's luminous seed, she gratefully followed his silent instruction and sought out Zahra's shallowly buried treasure. Despite the uncomfortably hard square tiles beneath her knees, her senses all began soaring around each other in a wonderful way that made her think of the designs on her wedding dress. None of the Sultan's cooks could have served up a more delicious feast than that which Laila partook of between the tender thighs of one of his discarded concubines. Her tense fears flowed away on the rich juices as she concentrated the efforts of her lips and tongue on Zahra's hardening little pit at the core of her flesh. No grape, no date, no fig had ever tasted so succulent or been so divinely generous in its flavorful moisture. Laila vaguely wondered if her own sex smelled and tasted as good to the eunuch, the sensations trapped between her thighs evoking hot shafts of sunlight sparkling on the waters of the bath through the circular openings in the wall surrounding the Seraglio. Then she had to suppress a cry beneath a rush of all-consuming splendor no other experience on

guilty pleasures

earth had ever prepared her for. It seemed to her that the three of them would all surely dissolve into one... then Zahra grasped her head and she intensified the agile dancing of her tongue until it was rewarded by a strangled scream from above. The next thing she became aware of was lying on her back across the cool tiles with the eunuch's big black silhouette crouching demon-like between her legs devouring her soul; sucking it ferociously out from the dark hole in her body...

'Oh, by Allah, please stop!' she begged.

'Do not be afraid, little one.' It was Zahra bending over her... faithful, loving Fatima filling her mouth with her nipple so she could suckle it and glean a taste of all the pleasures of paradise promised by Mohammed to virtuous men but not to women because, she realized then, it already existed on earth inside the silky-smooth, lotus-scented skin cushioning her senses, and in the long, soft hair caressing and enveloping her... there was no reason to be afraid and withhold paradise from the slave laboring so devotedly in the hot, magically glowing space where the horizons of her legs met and opened up to another realm... the timeless, blindingly beautiful realm of the Prophets who must surely have known about this secret door but who said nothing in their jealous spite that it could only be found between a woman's thighs.

* * *

For a period of many moons too lovely to count, Laila lived at Zahra's side, or beneath her, or above her, our crouched with religious fervor at the entrance to her favorite temple on earth – the dark sanctuary full of its own mysterious light which no one could see as it suffused their flesh and brightened their lives. Then Laila's world darkened and her will to live set like the sun when the Sultan

Laila

awarded Zahra as a gift to one of his provincial governors. As she watched her closest companion in the world and her only friend being prepared for her new master, Laila could not weep; she could not seem to feel anything except a despair like the heart of the desert where no feelings could ever truly grow again. But Laila was young. The winter after Zahra left her, the Kislar Aga brought in a young slave from a distant land whose sunlit hair, moon-bathed skin and fiercely polished silver eyes suddenly reminded the beautiful concubine that Allah's gifts are endless, and that in another woman's mysterious wound she might once again be able to feel the depth of His compassion.

BRIDE OF CHRIST

Lisbon, Portugal 1736-1755

Until I saw Stepham d'Atayde I was content with my fate. As the youngest of three daughters, I never entertained any illusions of marriage, and indeed, my temperament seemed well-suited to the cloister. When my mother was not within hearing (which was more often than not as I rarely saw the lady) my beloved Nanny assured me the life my sisters were destined for did not deserve my envy. As she was the only adult whose judgment I trusted implicitly, I took her words to heart. I also do not think it is entirely fancy when I say that my mother's unhappiness surrounded me in the womb, so that once I was free of its fleshly confines I was not loath to be spared the dubious honor of service to a mere mortal. Certainly the Lord Jesus Christ was infinitely more worthy of my faithful devotion than the man I called father on the rare occasions he commanded my presence.

I confess there was a great deal of pride in my complacency as out of place as gold thread woven into a nun's sober habit. My lack of a worldly dowry did not trouble me for it was the superior metal of my thoughts and feelings, honed to the divine, I was saving to offer the only man ever born of woman worthy of them. If I chose to clothe my unhappiness as virtue, at least I showed some strength of soul by refusing to cry myself to sleep and succumb to the hopeless fever of jealousy my sisters' rich weddings might have poisoned me with. Having no dowry and hence no worldly treasures I could call my own, I persuaded myself to look forward to the modestly furnished private cell my family's status would entitle me to when it came time for me to enter the convent. Perhaps it was my life-long knowledge of the harshly pure fate awaiting me that caused me to look down in disdain at delicate lace and other rich materials passionately coveted by my sisters. My peace of mind was sealed tight as a tomb… except for Nanny's secret whispers in my ear haunting a part of me I strove to bury so as not to suffer hopes and dreams that would only be sacrificed along with my beautiful long hair when I began my novitiate. Yet because I loved her so much I could not help heeding this serpent in my innocent Eden when she told me my hair was black and lustrous as the sea beneath the stars, and that if a man's fingers were ever to dive into its soft rich depths he would surely lose his heart in my eyes which she said were the soft gold of the sky at dawn. Nanny was present at my birth, and the peasant woman who nursed me was a young cousin of hers, so I trusted her mysterious perceptions of the body I was forced to live with and be cordial to without us ever becoming too improperly familiar. Nanny often told me I was more beautiful than any of my sisters and that a real man would not care whether I possessed a dowry or not.

'Are not all men real?' I asked, and her laughter banished the strange anger in her voice and eyes that sometimes possessed her when she brushed my long hair out for the night.

The only occasion on which I openly defied my parents was the first time they took me to the grand Cathedral on All Soul's Day when I was two-years-old. Nanny accompanied us all the way to the bottom of the stone steps which to my child's eyes looked as if they led straight up to a cavernous black heaven glimmering with candlelight like the souls of the blessed, or of the damned, I was not quite sure which. Until my mother took me by the hand and tried to get me to follow her up the endless stairway while the only human being I loved remained behind. Nanny proudly told the story for years afterwards, but my passionate wails of protest, loud as they were, did not reach the ears of any compassionate angels and I was forced to suffer my first endless Mass with strangers. Whispering furiously, mother assured me Nanny was not gone forever but simply standing in the back of the Church with the other servants, and she crushed my tiny fingers painfully in her hand to stop me from glancing over my shoulders in search of her. Then I saw Christ rising above us and the sight dammed my miserable sniffling as I gazed up at Him in awestruck wonder. He towered over all the men and women and children milling below him, reigning over us on his cross looming above the gallery overlooking the entrance to the Cathedral. How could an innocent girl not feel at once frightened and excited knowing she was destined to become a bride of the only man she had ever seen almost totally naked? And He was not just naked – He was vulnerable and in pain, suffering and yet not angry, not resisting his agony, his submissive forgiveness expressing an infinite strength and compassion. The blood dripping from his thorn-crowned temples and around the nails driven into his sensitive palms and bony feet was a bright, vivid red more beautiful than any I had ever seen. The tones of his skin were deep as a sunset, his dark-brown hair glossy as wet earth furrowed by coach wheels. I never took any comfort from the cold and remote images of the Virgin draped from head-to-toe in immaculate blue-and-white robes on which there was no trace of her son's passionate blood. I remember my sisters whispering reverently as they admired the elaborate large halo around the Madonna's head, but I think it was only how much gold had been used to make it that impressed them. Christ was all-powerful now, the cold and ponderous stone church – filled with hundreds of flickering candles powerless to keep it warm while everywhere casting demon-friendly shadows – was only one of his many rich homes, yet for some reason He remained forever crucified, suspended at the most terrible moment of his life before he rose from the dead. When I asked Nanny about this, she told me not to think so much, that it was not becoming in a lady, and it was one of the few times I ever became cross with her.

'But does it not seem strange that every Sunday rich and splendidly dressed men kneel before a poor and nearly naked one?' I insisted.

'Shame on you, Maria! It is our Savior you are speaking of!'

'But do you not think He must be terribly tired of hanging on the cross? Is it because the master carvers cannot imagine what He looked like after He rose from the dead and ascended to heaven?'

'Oh, child, if I did not know better I would say your mother had lain with the devil when you were conceived you say such things! Christ on His cross is there to remind us that all life is sorrow and that no earthly happiness lasts forever.'

'But no one truly believes that, do they?'

Her only response was to cross herself and murmur, 'Goodnight, little one!' before quickly closing the curtains and leaving me alone in my bed for the night.

* * *

had been married to Christ for three years when I first saw Senhor Stepham D'Atayde. I was walking across one of the convent's inner courtyards towards a well, but not because I was thirsty. I liked gazing at my far away reflection in the dark mirror of water lit up by the sky against which I could make out my formless silhouette in the loose and heavy Habit, followed by the distinct rays of my fingers when I lifted my hand and spread it open as far as possible, the only part of my body besides the white moon of my face exposed to the sun. It seemed to me that my soul was down there in the reflected sky, my physical body leaning over the stone rim mysteriously less important than the invulnerable shape of my shadow. My days flowed by in a routine as old and smooth as the convent's stone archways, never deviating from the harmonic path of my service to a higher ideal than those which occupied the minds of worldly women. I found the stark grandeur of my new home pleasing, and the quiet, often profound conversations I enjoyed with my sisters in Christ was soothing compared to the constant idle chatter of my blood relations, whom I blessedly never saw any more. I would have missed Nanny terribly if she had not been dead for five years and always with me in spirit.

I was walking across the courtyard towards my favorite well when one of the heavy black doors in the open-air corridor surrounding it suddenly opened. A man emerged from inside the room in which our Mother Superior met with visitors from the outside world. I was not aware of pausing to watch him as he closed the door behind him, but I must have done so for I clearly remember the sharp contours of his profile carved into a fiercely dissatisfied expression that touched me somewhere inside like a hard stone wall brushing my soft habit, except that I could not casually ignore this invisible contact. I found myself staring at him as he walked towards me along the corridor, his black leather doublet and boots framed by one open archway, then another and another as I became oddly aware of my heart beating in rhythm. He was tall, his shoulders broad, and the thin, neatly trimmed black beard framing his mouth trapped my vision in a tender courtyard of flesh. He did not see me standing by the well as he passed, I was invisible as a shadow cast by nothing, and for some reason I found this intolerable.

'Senhor,' I said.

He stopped, turning towards my voice.

Our eyes met, and I willed him to see them as my beloved Nanny had described them, as the golden light of dawn on the horizon… I found myself willing him to see my face even though my white wimple and black veil washed out my features and threw my beauty into insignificant shadow. He did not speak, but the intent silence with which he returned my gaze felt much more eloquent; much more meaningful. Then with my next breath, which was strangely difficult to take, I remembered I was not allowed to be alone with a man much less speak to him.

'Forgive me!' I gasped, and fled the courtyard.

That evening at Matins' I thought I understood how Eve felt when the serpent approached her as I found myself remembering the firm yet sinuous line of the man's lips so provocatively framed by the black night of his goatee. When I suddenly realized I was sinning by being alone with him, the instant before I ran away from him, I had seen the corners of his mouth turn up ever so slightly in a smile such as Satan might have worn when Eve took her first bite of the apple.

* * *

I strove to put the man out of my mind, but all this served to do was illustrate the tenacity of temptation. Even though what I was tempted to do with him I could scarcely imagine, I stayed awake late at night thinking and wondering about him. Certainly I had no desire to conceive a child; I had never envied my sisters their noisy, dirty little babies. The self-contained discipline of convent life was much more to my liking than attending to the needs of selfish little creatures mauling my breasts and throwing up all over me. Obviously I did not covet this man as a father for the children I would never have, but as the days (and the even longer nights) passed, there was no doubt I desired *something* from him. I had of course heard of women who lay with men only for pleasure; lost souls who Nanny had whispered to me lusted after a man's body as well as his money. I was forced to consider the unpalatable possibility that what I desired from the tall and handsome nobleman was the mysterious force resting dormant in his leggings. I did not know his name at the time, and I could not ask about him without giving away the intensity of my interest and perhaps revealing the dangerous fact that for a few moments I had been alone with him, and spoken to him. If the Mother Superior suspected one of her young nuns was lusting after a man, she would undoubtedly assign her a penance of numbing prayers and endless mundane chores. Perhaps, however, the punishment would be easier to bear than the terrible desire to sin unquenchable as thirst for which I had no cup of experience from which to sip even the fantasy of relief. And mixed in with my obsessive memory of the man in the courtyard was the dread I would never see him again; that those moments when his eyes held mine were the only time I would ever experience a feeling

Bride of Christ

I had never tasted before or since.

I lay in my hard little bed at night possessed by an indefinable long-ing so acute it seemed a miracle when sleep finally brought me a meas-ure of peace... until one night when my restlessness was so great I flung the sheet off and left my room wearing only the white shift I never took off. My hair had grown long again and, unbraided, it spilled down my back in deep waves that seemed to beg for the naked bodies of a man's strong fingers swimming through it. The cold stone corri-dors were silent and empty. No one saw or even dreamed of my pres-ence outside their cells as I made my way silently on bare feet towards the courtyard and my favorite well. I had been there everyday since I saw the man, rather foolishly hoping he would return. I stared at the black door from behind which he had emerged with an ache like an invisible wound burning in my chest I had tried desperately to clean with pure thoughts, to no avail; I could feel a longing flowing from me like invisible blood; weakening my resolve not to destroy my well-being by surrendering to the terribly sweet pain of this fatal obsession.

The full moon's shining gaze was fixed intently down on the con-vent's empty courtyard, illuminating every little dark crack in the stone tiles as I went and stood where he had seen me, never taking my eyes from the black door that seemed to lead not into the Mother Superior's study but into a dark and irresistibly attractive anti-chamber of the hell I was deliberately choosing over salvation. If the door opened now my soul would surely be lost...

In the dead of night, the moonlight so intense I felt it as a silent scream vibrating against my skin, the only sound in the world was that of centuries-old hinges creaking open, oiled by the quick flick of my tongue against my lips as I caught my breath, watching in mingled longing and dread as the black door opened and a tall, broad-shoul-

116

dered man emerged from the impenetrable darkness beyond it. His goatee was black as the cracks in the flagstones against his pale flesh. I could not see his eyes as he walked quickly along the open corridor, but this time I knew he would see me. He took the steps down into the courtyard with an intent assurance that frightened me into clutching the shift over my heart, yet for some reason I did not run away from him. It was a shock that came as no surprise when he pulled my body roughly against his. I was caught in his embrace and frightened because the strength of his arms around me was not filled with kind affection. I might have resisted then, but it was too late; he clutched a handful of my hair, forcing me to look up at his face, and then his lips fell hard against mine, hurting me until I parted them and surrendered to the warm invasion of his tongue.

No one except Nanny had ever intimately touched my body, and certainly her hands never explored me as his were doing, groping and caressing and squeezing while he pressed me so fiercely against him I could believe woman had sprung from a man's ribs for he seemed desperate to merge my body with his, and suddenly I realized that I was equally desperate to help him succeed. My mouth shamelessly full of his thrusting, probing tongue, I lightly touched the silky trail of his beard with my fingertips, feeling it tremor and move against them as he kissed me almost angrily, much more intensely than I had ever heard anyone speak to me or to anyone about anything. I savored faint traces of what he had enjoyed for dinner, and distracted myself from being afraid about what was happening by trying to define the ingredients... a bird roasted with rosemary washed down by a fine, decade's old Port... yet the flavor of his tongue was all his own, and despite how demanding it was I found it more fulfilling than any food. Then his hands moved down and began kneading my buttocks through my shift in a way that made me feel he was still hungry and planning to have me for dessert, only I knew his lust was an entirely different, much more sinful, appetite. There was no similarity whatsoever between the gentle way Nanny once helped me bathe and the rough fashion this man's fingers dug almost painfully into my flesh. My breath caught only to be sucked down into his chest as he refused to let me pull out of his drowning kiss. Clutching one of my bottom cheeks with his left hand, he thrust his right hand, between my legs. Suddenly my shift felt fine as mist offering me no protection, and as his fingers boldly explored the forbidden space between my thighs, the coarse home-spun cloth became damp and warm, clinging to me like a fog that rose strangely to my head even while making me shamelessly aware of the full, soft contours of my sex...

Slipping my hands down from his face to his shoulders, I managed to break free of his kiss long enough to gasp, 'Oh, Senhor, what are you doing?'

He growled deep in his throat like one of my father's hunting dogs but much more dangerously, for like a wolf he was his own master and no one could command him not to hurt me. I felt my bare feet leave the ground, my toes pointing earthwards as though I had achieved sainthood and was ascending towards the heavenly hosts. For a wild moment I thought perhaps the angels were taking pity on my innocent soul and saving me from the devil's clutches, until I felt the hard edge of the well as he set me down on it. I watched his strong hands grip the shift over my chest and pull me towards him, flinging my head back as he ripped it open down the front. But this did not seem to sat-isfy him; I was only half skinned that way and I knew, without under-standing what it meant, that he fully intended to kill who I was simply for the pleasure of possessing me. I also knew there was nothing I could do to stop him even if I wanted to, and I was not entirely sure I did. He yanked me to my feet, and my shift fainted down my body like a spectral reflection of the languidness possessing me even as I stood trembling before him, because I could not possibly admit to being thrilled by the wicked sensation of his eyes caressing parts of my body only God was allowed to see. His hands loosed their possessive grip on my arms as he took a step back to look at me.

'Please let me go, Senhor, please!' I begged as I covered my sex with one hand and desperately sought to conceal my breasts with the other, a vain gesture indeed, for he simply grasped both my wrists and forced them away from my body, stretching my arms straight out to my sides as though preparing to crucify me, and his violence mysteriously relaxed me even as a sharp, hot feeling drove straight into my belly like a divine nail... if he was going to martyr me on the altar of sin, a submissive, forgiving grace was my only hope of escaping eternal damnation... this sinful thought somehow made sense in the midst of seductively novel sensations clamoring for my attention as, still keeping a firm grip on my wrists to hold my arms open, he bent his head towards my breasts. The tip of one of my tender mounds of flesh hardened beneath the warm touch of his lips, and a moan was wrenched from deep in my belly that seemed to burn my body on the inside all the way up from between my legs to my breasts. He released my wrists to roughly fondle my bosom as he bit and licked my nipples, ravenously torn between them, and yet I kept my arms extended as though invisibly crucified, willingly, compassionately offering him my body, pushing my breasts wantonly into his mouth, how hard he was sucking on them a revelation of pain as the divine face of pleasure... I wanted him to hurt me even more... I longed for him to drive something mercilessly, relentlessly hard into my soft, yielding body as though nailing me down… my growing desire to sacrifice myself to his violent lust was so blindingly intense that I closed my eyes, and woke up.

* * *

I learned the man's name three months later when he came to visit his sister who was preparing to take the veil. I was told to chaperone a young novice in the herb garden where she would be receiving her brother, and thinking nothing of it, I stepped out of the dim corridor into the intense sunshine of mid-afternoon walking a few paces behind her. I blinked helplessly from the dramatic change of light as she ran joyfully into the waiting man's arms. They were just separating from their fond embrace when I saw his face.

'Sister Maria, this is my brother, el Senhor Stepham d'Atayde,' Yelena happily introduced us.

I saw it in his eyes – the profound gray of cathedral stones – that he recognized me. We stared at each other for a long moment, my throat closing tight around any polite words I might have spoken.

'Maria…' His deep, quiet voice seemed to savor my name like a sip of vintage Port. 'Is that your real name, Sister?'

It was a reasonable question; many women took a different name when they married Christ, usually that of the Virgin Mother. 'It is the name I was born to, sir. My father is Senhor Rodrigo de Cunha'

'Sister Maria, you mean he *was*!' Yelena gasped. 'Christ is both your father and husband now!'

Once again Stepham and I stared at each other silently. I felt my dreams were all there in my eyes for him to see, so that when he smiled the way he had when I ran away from him, I suspected my soul was lost and did not care at all.

Yelena tugged on his sleeve eager as a kitten for his attention.

I managed to take my off eyes off his face and walk over to a stone bench nearly overgrown with Rosemary. I was glad of its support when my knees weakened as I breathlessly relived my first sinful dream and the taste of rosemary on his lips and tongue. Vaguely, I heard Yelena asking him eager questions about their family, and I did not blame her for sounding more interested in the dogs and horses she had left behind than in her parents' well-being.

'I will get you out of here, sister,' he spoke again abruptly. 'I promise I will find a way.'

I kept my eyes on my hands clasped in my black lap, clenching them as I resisted an overwhelming desire to look at him.

'Oh, my dear, brother, I am happy here, truly I am. It is not as terrible as you think...

''You are too young to realize what you are missing, Yelena.'

I could no longer bear it, I had to look at him, and he seemed to feel the touch of my longing for he turned his head. This time his eyes held mine as forcibly as hands making it impossible for me to look away, and silently I thanked him for taking the choice away from me.

'Maria knows what she is missing,' he stated quietly. 'Do you not, Maria?'

'I know not what you mean, Senhor,' I heard myself say, a defiant edge to my voice Nanny had warned me was not attractive in a lady, but I was a bride of Christ now so it did not matter.

He considered my reply still staring intently at my face, and when he spoke no trace of a smile softened the hard look in his eyes. 'I do not doubt your virtue, Maria,' he glanced down at my rigidly clasped hands, 'but I feel you would like to know.'

'Have you and Sister Maria met before?' Yelena asked suspiciously. 'No, we have never met,' he answered quickly, protecting me as

Nanny always did when I had done something my mother would punish me for, and I knew then with the certainty of revelation that I loved him.

* * *

He did not call me Sister Maria… He called me by my name, Maria… He saw the woman hidden inside the Habit… He called me Maria…

I was incapable of moving past this thought, perhaps because I knew there was nowhere else to go. For some reason this handsome man was sensitive to my feelings, and I loved him, that was all that mattered to me even though it was beyond my understanding how it could be. I did not pray to God for forgiveness because, stubbornly, I did not to truly believe I was being unfaithful to his Son. Christ had said He was in every man, and so it seemed to me the real sin was never to love at all. I wondered what Nanny would say, and chided her silently for never having told me such a feeling was possible. I suspected she had been trying to protect me from what I could never have, but if she had only hinted at this worldly state of grace I might have done something to convince my father not to bury me alive in a convent. Numbingly familiar scriptures suddenly seemed full of hidden clues I had not perceived before. It was Mary Magdalene who first saw Christ after he rose from the dead; it was to her He appeared, and I cherished the hope He would not mind sharing my heart with a man conceived in sin. I do not know what I expected – nothing considering my circumstances – and yet something had to come of the feeling his eyes had planted so deep inside me I could see nothing but his face when I was awake, and at night I often writhed, perspiring, in the grip of dreams all centering around his lips and hands; dreams that always ended before I willingly surrendered to a martyrdom I had no images for, all I knew was that it could come only from him.

An eternal fortnight passed before Stepham came to visit his sister again, and he saw to it I was once more instructed to chaperone her. The Mother Superior called me into her study to inform me that Senhor Stepham had been kind enough to agree to deliver a message to me from my parents, who were away in the country and so were unable to me visit me themselves. Her small black eyes regarded me keenly as she spoke, for she was well aware that my family had shown little interest in my well-being since I took the veil, abandoning me in God's hands to do with as He willed; however, she could not rudely prohibit Senhor Stepham from fulfilling a duty he had honorably undertaken. Yelena and I were dispatched, not to the herb garden but to a fire lit room, for even though it had dawned a fine morning there was a chill in the air on that first day in November. Stone arches rose high above our heads, and marble walls half covered by white tiles decorated with painted blue scenes depicting Lisbon's tumultuous history made me shiver inside my heavy woolen habit. The fireplace was nearly as large as my cell and half a tree was burning in it, but the profound chill of the chamber could never be completely dispelled.

On this occasion, Yelena did not run joyfully into her waiting brother's arms. Now the time was drawing nearer for her to discard her novice's white veils and don the somber raven attire of Christ's virginal harem, her smiling bravery had dimmed considerably.

Stepham greeted his sister with affectionate concern, gently grasping her chin between his thumb and forefinger, tilting her head from side-to-side as he studied her expression or her complexion or both, I could not be sure of anything except the emotion that scalded me watching them together and waiting for him to look at me. The terrible possibility that he had indeed agreed to deliver a message from my parents and had not invented this excuse to see me again made me more miserable than I had ever been in my life. I stood politely to one side, but I did not avert my eyes as brother and sister kissed affectionately on both cheeks.

'How fare you, Yelena?' he asked gently, and I suffered a distinct, strangely exciting impression that he was deliberately ignoring me, and that by doing so – by not dismissing me with a mere casual greeting – he was telling me something I longed to hear more than anything. All the choirs of Angels above could never be as eloquent as the mysteriously significant silence and inattention he directed my way.

'I am well, brother,' Yelena replied, but anyone who had heard her speak to her sibling a fortnight ago would have thought she was ill judging from the listlessness of her voice.

'No, you are not well, that I can plainly see.' He drew her closer to the fire, turning his back on me, and I knew what all the souls in Purgatory were suffering wondering if I was perhaps only imagining the intense, silent understanding between us... perhaps he was not truly aware of me at all...

He gripped Yelena's upper arms as forcibly as he had mine in the dream, and she gazed up at his stern face with the same helplessness I had felt, not daring to hope, not daring to need, and yet unable to resist the desire to feel. 'There is a way,' he said firmly, and at long last he looked over at me, 'but you must trust me.' He held my eyes as he elaborated very quietly, 'You must both trust me implicitly. Do you truly wish to remain here for the rest of your life, Yelena?' he asked, but it was not his sister he was looking at.

She glanced over at me where I stood with my hands demurely folded in my Habit, reasonably afraid I would report this illicit conversation to the Mother Superior as soon as her brother left the convent.

'Answer him, Yelena,' I urged calmly. 'I promise I will say nothing of your feelings to anyone.'

She looked from me to her brother's face and back again, clearly doubting my sincerity and confused by our complicity.

'Yelena!' He shook her gently, forcing her to meet his eyes. 'Tell me, do you wish to remain here for the rest of your life?'

'But what can be done?' she gasped. 'I have been promised to Christ. It would bring great dishonor to our family if I should-'

He shook her again less gently. 'Do you have faith in me, sister?' he demanded.

'Yes!' I breathed.

They both looked over at me, and the expression in his eyes of surprise and gratitude and admiration... and something else I could not define... warmed me much more effectively than the fire.

'You see, Yelena, Maria will help us.' He caressed his sister's cheek reassuringly while still studying my face, so that I seemed to feel the touch of his fingers against my own skin.

'I do not understand!' she whispered anxiously, her frightened eyes still torn between me and her brother. 'I am afraid...'

'Do not be afraid,' he told her firmly, 'simply do as I say, and as Maria tells you to.'

'But why, brother?' There was a hint of resentment in her voice now. 'What are you planning together?'

He released her arms, stepping away from her, and his obvious displeasure made me shiver even though it was not directed at me. 'No more questions, Yelena, you will do as I say. Do you understand?'

'Yes, brother...'

'Go now. I must speak to Maria alone. Wait outside the door and warn us should someone approach.'

I sensed she was about to protest, but his expression silenced her, and I was almost fond of her when she turned and ran from the room as if the fire had suddenly grown too hot for her comfort.

I found myself walking towards the flames and the man standing before them. What would have happened when I reached him only God knows, for in that instant the Lord chose to punish me, as if the sinful thoughts and feelings of one lonely little nun were the most important things in the world, which suddenly began trembling with His awful wrath. I was both awed and horrified as God at once taunted me and challenged my faithfulness to Him by flinging my body into a man's arms with a thunderous roar. Stepham clung to me with the same fervent strength he had displayed in my dreams, but clad as I was from head-to-toe in black, I felt like Death in his hands and struggled to pull away from him so he might be saved. Yet he would not let go of me. He pulled me forcibly away from the fire and I lost my balance, falling onto my hands and knees. The floor rose up to meet me in a solid wave of stone as I felt him spread himself on top of me, viciously clutching my skirt as if trying to possess me from behind like an animal. He dragged me across the heaving floor, somehow able to distinguish my habit from the demonic shadows cast by the wildly flickering fire. He crawled beneath a marble table sitting in the center of the room, pulling me beneath it with him.

'Be still!' he commanded, burying my face in his chest and pressing me so tightly against him I could scarcely breathe, but I was very glad to close my eyes and think of nothing but him because my sight had been hopelessly confused by a room that trembled as though it was only a reflection in my well... as though we were both only shadows and a single stone plunging towards us would shatter our hold on each other forever... I was aware as I had never been aware of anything in my life of Stepham's hand tilting my face up towards his so he could kiss my lips, and I blessed him for striving to make my dreams real before we died.

In 1755 Portugal was visited by a terrible earthquake. "With regard to the buildings, it was observed that the solidest in general fell the first. Every parish church, convent, nunnery, palace, and public edifice…were either thrown down or so miserably shattered that it was rendered dangerous to pass by them. The whole number of persons that perished, including those who were burnt or afterwards crushed to death whilst digging in the ruins, is supposed, on the lowest calculation, to amount to more than sixty thousand." ***Modern History Sourcebook: Rev. Charles Davy: The Earthquake at Lisbon, 1755***

Song of the Blood

Transylvania 1636

The blacksmith carefully offered Count Lupus the red-hot sword. He grasped it firmly by the hilt in his black-gloved hand, and Erika sucked in her breath where she sat on horseback watching him. The long and deadly blade was the fiery crimson of a clear horizon at sunset. A male slave was brought forward and shoved to his knees in front of the Count. Erika saw her lover shift the hilt of the weapon in his hand, getting a better grip on it, and she shifted sympathetically in her saddle as the wet heat of her sex seemed to rival that of the forge in which the sword had been beaten into its phallic form. Before the terrified man could gain his feet and attempt to run away, Count Lupus thrust the blazing metal deep into his guts with a single assured thrust. An orgasm teased the insides of Erika's pelvis like a vulture's wings spreading, but then settled disappointingly down again without taking flight as her lover slowly pulled the sword out of his victim. The slave clutched the blade as though afraid to let go of it, and indeed, robbed of its cruel support, the hot metal no longer staunching the flow of his blood, he fell face forward in the dirt. The ritual was complete. Cooled by blood, the molten blade steamed in the brisk air. The body was carried away as the Count concluded his business with the blacksmith, patiently waiting a few more minutes before sheathing the beautiful weapon in the scabbard hanging from his black horse's saddle.

Once more Erika shifted restively against her own hard leather seat, firmly grasping the reins in her silk-gloved hands, impatient for them to be on their way again. They could not hope to reach their Castle high in the mountains until late tomorrow evening; they would have to make do with the best room in the Inn at Brasov to quench the lust death invariably kindled in them. The Count was a man of God – he had fought alongside his kinsman Vasile Lupus, king of Moldavia, against the heathens who dared continue demanding tribute from their betters – but in many respects he still honored and practiced the old ways. The impotent little priest to whom they both confessed would never hear of this bloody rite, or of the many other sins the Count and his beautiful bride indulged in. Erika and her husband both believed that all the flames of hell could not be worse than unsatisfied desires. Purgatory was full of souls who never had the courage to feed the feelings that made being alive at least tolerably interesting, and sometimes intensely entertaining. They might both be damned, but if so, Lucifer had reserved a special place for them at his side.

At long last the Count mounted his horse, casting a knowing smile Erika's way, and their entourage proceeded along the road behind them, following at a respectful distance. All it took was a casual wave of his hand to make dozens of men and women obey him without question. Erika had been born into the nobility, yet her husband's casual assurance never failed to speed up her heartbeats. It was not only lands and title that made a man powerful, especially in the bed-chamber when he was stripped of all conventional signs of status and it was only the mysterious metal of his will a woman judged him by; and either scorned his dominance behind his back or gave herself to him body and soul as Erika had.

They were a few hours ride from Brasov. Tomorrow they would reach the Batrana saddle of the Carpathian Mountains and begin the arduous but long-awaited ascent to their Castle. How many more living treasures they would collect along the way remained to be seen. Erika was content with their prizes for the time being. The smallest, most remote villages sometimes yielded delectable unspoiled youths. Peasant girls were more common, readily offered up by parents who greedily traded away their daughters' warm and silky young flesh for small velvet purses full of cold hard coins – as much money as they had ever seen in their lives and would ever see again unless they miraculously produced more beautiful offspring. An unspoiled, virile youth such as the one she had found for herself on this profitable journey was rare. She licked her lips, unpleasantly dry from the wind and the dust of the road, and smiled to herself knowing he was riding behind her now. The servants were crowded together on bumpy carts while the young bodies she and the Count intended to use for their pleasure were treated more kindly.

Eventually the rhythm of the horse trotting beneath her ceased to beat erotic images into her mind, and no matter how much she resent-ed it, she had no choice but to succumb to her body's languid exhaus-tion. She surrendered herself instead to the more innocent pleasure of admiring the majesty of the dusky blue mountain ranges, rising to meet velvety black clouds with luminous silver borders woven by the sun setting behind them. Her eyes wandered contentedly to her lover's stern profile (for they always rode side-by-side) and then back again to the undulating landscape of fertile fields fringed by dark forests.

The spires of Brasov's church came into view first. Serban and Erika smiled at each other. The sun-bleached stone glowed pure white against the brooding sky, and gazing upon it one could almost forget that its foundations were crawling with vermin. They had to be careful when they were staying in a city, but the danger was a thrill in itself, and Erika was determined not to waste how much the sword-quenching rite had aroused her. A shaft of sunlight thrust through a sudden break in the clouds, illuminating the fields in front of the city walls so the grass shown like a precious stone. It was across this welcoming carpet of light that the Count and his bride galloped, racing each other and leaving their armed attendants, servants and slaves far behind. They would visit the church first as a courtesy, and by the time they were through charming the silly priest, everything would be ready for them when they arrived at the Inn.

* * *

'You must strive to contain your murderous lust until we are safely home, my love,' Serban said fondly, pouring them both more wine from a silver flagon.

'No, my lord, I will not be denied tonight.' She gazed challengingly into his eyes.

'Yes, I am your lord, and your master,' he reminded her quietly, rising out of the richly cushioned chair. 'If you do not obey me, I will be forced to punish you.'

She tossed her head back to look up at him as he loomed over her, bracing himself with both hands on the carved back of her chair. She continued defiantly holding his dark eyes, the hard line of his mouth exciting her by reminding her of the sword he had plunged into a man's bowels only hours ago. She felt her breasts threatening to swell out of her tightly laced bodice as she took a trembling breath, as always afraid of what he might do to her even as she craved his cruelty.

'Please, my lord,' she begged softly, 'my body is tired from our long journey, but my soul is hungry, terribly so!'

'You wish to watch me, my lady?'

'Yes, my lord, it would give me great pleasure.'

'You know I can deny you nothing, my love.' Still bracing himself on the ornately carved chair with one hand, he clutched her slender white throat with the other. He moved too swiftly for her to have a chance to catch her breath, and her black lashes fluttered with a submissive ecstasy as he began strangling the life out of her. He watched her face intently, the bulge in his leggings growing more pronounced as her full lips parted, her eyes narrowed, and her hands clutched his arm without, however, trying to push it away. The hot discomfort blooming in her chest was as nothing compared to the delicious warmth smoldering between her legs. The more cruelly his hard fingers dug into her soft throat the more her sex wept, not with fear but with a lust more powerful even than her desire to breathe. She was aware of her hands falling into the lap of her dress as black suns began rising in the corners of her eyes... Suddenly, he ripped open her bodice, relaxing the grip of his hand just enough to let her take a desperate breath, watching her breasts heave from the strain before turning her bosom to stone again by putting even more vicious strength into the hand throttling her.

'I could kill you now, Erika, you know that,' he whispered, 'and one night I *will* kill you, my love, I swear it on my sword!'

The tears of fear and pain that should have been shining in her eyes were instead burning between her legs and trickling down the insides of her thighs as she gazed worshipfully up at him. The black suns swimming in the corners of her eyes merged with the shadows cast by the candles and the crackling fire… his black-clad body looming over hers was an embodiment of the darkness to which she was willingly offering not only her body but her very soul…

He waited until the instant before her eyes closed as she lost consciousness to remove the pressure from her throat, quickly forcing his own breath down her bruised neck by way of a savage kiss. He savored the flavor of her cry as he gripped her hard nipples between his thumb and forefinger, pulling on them cruelly, stretching her lovely round breasts into agonizing peaks. Then, just as abruptly, he let go of her and straightened up.

Erika watched him with the mindless eyes of a cat, aware only of how beautiful she looked to him with the signs of his ownership branded into her flesh, her aureoles a fiery rose around the darker towers of her nipples powerless to defend themselves against his possessiveness. She would be forced to wear a high collar tomorrow as they rode out of the city, and knowledge of the discomfort she would experience then only stoked the perverse excitement his dangerous cruelty always filled her with. The pain in her neck and chest and breasts was not important; all that mattered was the aching, bottomless yearning between her legs.

She watched with a hunger that consumed her very soul as he untied the leather flap over his crotch, and freed the erection forged by her submissive brush with death at his hands. She waited until his rigid penis was aimed at her like the sword he had held that afternoon before pushing herself up out of the chair. She did not care that her legs were almost too weak to support her because all she wanted was to kneel at his feet. In her mind's eye she saw the slave crouching before him, saw him plunge the red-hot blade into his body as he thrust the full, hard length of his penis into her mouth, ramming it down her ravaged throat. She clung to his leggings as he gripped her skull with both hands to bury her beautiful face against his body, brutally stuffing her orifice to the hilt with his pulsing erection. Once more relentlessly cutting off her breath, he stimulated himself in this way for much longer than he ever had before, testing and tormenting her; bruising the inside of her neck now with his cock until she thought she would die from the excruciating effort she had to make not to gag and wretch all over him. Whenever she did not gracefully fulfill his violent desires he punished her afterwards; punished her so severely it was black magic that pleasure not only survived but flourished deep inside her coupled with the hot, hauntingly luminous sensation of pure pain.

The Count did not satisfy himself in his wife's mouth. Leaving her a gasping heap on the hard wooden floor boards, he quickly laced his leggings closed again and left the room.

Erika knew she had only moments to compose herself, and how intensely aroused she was gave her the strength she needed to gain her feet. It was more difficult controlling the trembling of her fingers as she made a vain effort to lace her bodice closed, but he had torn the threads beyond repair so she abandoned the effort and sat back down in the chair, her lovely breasts exposed to the cold room and the warm licks of the fire. She hoped he would choose the least comely of the peasant girls they had collected and save the special ones to be more enjoyably disposed of at the Castle. For this quick, secret sport at a public Inn they needed only a young and reasonably attractive body, virginal or not.

As usual, her husband did not disappoint her. When he returned she saw he had gone so far as to not even deplete their personal stock at all. He brought with him a local wench undoubtedly procured for them by their steward. All along he had meant to enjoy more than a fine meal and a flagon of wine at the Inn and had said nothing to her so he could also relish the pleasure of hearing her beg, and then punish her for it.

He shoved his prize into the room and barred the door behind him. Erika smiled as the girl stumbled, and then gasped when she saw a beautiful woman sitting half naked by the fire, the marks of her husband's fingers branded into the fine skin of her neck. If the whore had not been frightened before, she was now. Erika saw it in her eyes – the realization that a man who shared his pleasures with his wife would not be easily and quickly satisfied. It was too soon for her to be afraid, after all the noble couple in whose rented chamber she was standing was strikingly attractive, and there was nothing threatening about the way Serban walked over to his wife and kissed her affectionately on the cheek while idly caressing her breasts, as gentle with her then as he had been vicious only moments ago.

'Do you like her?' he whispered in her ear.

'She will do,' Erika replied shortly. 'What is important, my lord, is that you like her.'

'You know she is of no consequence, my love.' He spoke in his normal voice as he straightened up. 'It is you I will be looking at and who will be pleasing me as you touch yourself watching us.'

The young woman was clutching her cloak protectively around her, and the uncertainty in her jaded eyes made her look attractively innocent in the flickering light.

'Remove that,' he commanded, and the rough cloth immediately fainted to her feet as if frightened by the tone of his voice.

Erika stood up long enough to lift her heavy skirt up around her hips, bunching the rich material around her waist as she perched on the edge of the chair. Her dark-red stockings clung to the tender white flesh of her slender thighs as she spread them wide, the gems in her gilded slippers flashing in the firelight as with one heavily ringed hand she held up her dress, slipping the other between her legs.

The girl stared at Erika as though she had never seen another woman's sex before, and perhaps she never had seen one shaved smooth as alabaster suffused a lovely rose color by the warmth of her blood.

'My wife is beautiful, is she not?' Serban asked the girl as he began unlacing her plain black bodice.

'Yes, very beautiful!' she replied obediently and, it seemed, sincerely.

Erika pressed down on her clitoris with three fingertips, moving them slowly and lightly back and forth, biting her lip as she struggled not to climax right away. She wanted to savor the anticipation of her first blindingly pleasurable release before allowing herself as many more orgasms as her lord saw fit to indulge her with. She would wait for the exciting vision of his long, thick dick plunging in and out of the other woman's body, yet she was scarcely able to bear the suspense of wondering which orifice he would choose to possess first.

The girl stepped out of her skirt and stood naked in the center of the fire lit room except for gray stockings and worn leather shoes. Her breasts were large, beginning to sag a little from their own voluptuous weight, and her waist was that of a peasant unaccustomed to tight, shaping corsets, but her hips were unusually slender (they could never be called childbearing) and her legs were nearly as long as Erika's although not quite as shapely. Apparently, her long blonde hair was not artifice for her bush glimmered a dark-gold as Serban grabbed it roughly, growling and then laughing as she cried out in fear. Erika furiously stroked herself, but then quickly lifted her hand away from her sex as her husband released the girl. His watching bride was panting, her breasts heaving as she struggled not to come. Her excitement was a divine blade stabbing her between the legs and cutting straight up through her body into the almost painfully sharp points of her erect nipples. Sometimes he asked her which hole she preferred he start with, but that night they were both too weary from long days on the road and impatient for gratification. He simply took the girl by the hand, pulled her over to the chair beside Erika's, and bent her face-down over it, offering his wife a close-up view of her quivering buttocks as he smacked them. He spanked her until her cheeks were red, priming her for his cock, which he quickly freed from his leggings again and pushed into her anus with cruel suddenness, ignoring her shrieks of pain.

Erika was scarcely aware of her hand working between her thighs as she watched the Count's rending erection rising in and out of the girl's tight little hole. The wanton fool was sobbing as he reamed her heartlessly, and the sight of a muscle in her thighs quivering as she struggled to brace herself against his agonizingly violent thrusts filled Erika with a pleasure so exquisite, so fine, it cut through her ability to resist the searing climax that had been building inside her ever since she watched her lover plunge his sword into a man's body. She did not take her eyes off his pumping hips and stabbing penis until the intensity of the pleasure blinded her and she collapsed into the hard arms of the chair. When she opened her eyes again the first thing she saw was his smile.

'That was only the first of many, my love,' he remarked at once indulgently and proudly.

'Oh, yes, my lord, thank you...'

'But I think we must find a way to make her quiet.' He grabbed the girl by the hair and yanked her around towards her.

For an enticing moment a woman's full breasts dangled before Erika, inspiring her to reach out and caress the slack, tender mounds, until her husband forced the sniveling creature down onto her hands and knees, his cock still lodged deep in her ass very effectively eliciting her whimpering compliance.

'Lick my beautiful wife's slit, you noisy whore!' he commanded.

Erika gently smoothed stray hairs out of the girl's tear-streaked face to make it easier for her to obey, but then all thoughts of kindness vanished as she threaded her fingers possessively through the sleek golden strands and pressed the pain-contorted features against her hotly juicing sex. She positioned the firm bridge of the whore's nose just where she wanted it so her clitoris could ride it fast and hard; selfishly following the sharp trail of the pleasure cutting up through her body and once again devastating her as she watched her husband's hips beating faster and harder against the girl's quivering buttocks.

By the time the young woman was kneeling before the fire licking her own blood off the Count's undying erection, Erika had lost track of how many times she died to her surroundings in the throes of a pleasure so intense it sacrilegiously rivaled a saint's mystic ecstasy with its transcendent power. By then she was so tired she barely remembers the girl hastily dressing herself, and then limping as quickly as she could from the room. The next thing she was clearly aware of was the milky rain of her husband's fulfillment cooling her flushed face and flickering star-like in her eyelashes. Afterwards, he stroked her long black hair like a cat's back before leaving her in the care of her personal maid, who knew never to ask questions as she undressed her mistress, and then wiped her face clean with a damp cloth before helping her up into the bed. Erika was asleep by the time her husband joined her; she did not feel his gentle kiss on her forehead or hear him whisper, 'I love you more than anything!'

* * *

The Count and Countess slept late the following morning and hence did not arrive at their Castle that evening. The sun was already low in the sky when they reached the bottom of the mountain pass, and when it was too dark for the horses to see, they stopped and struck camp beneath the stars. Servants immediately scrambled off the carts and set about their respective chores, the most important one being to quickly kindle a fire for their Master and Mistress to relax beside on embroidered cushions hastily strewn across a clear expanse of the rocky ground. In a matter of minutes a covered pavilion where they would sleep rivaled the rising moon with the flowing white purity of drapes capturing the starlight in gilded borders.

Erika loved the mountains. She experienced a thrill deeper even than sexual excitement when the horses took their first steps up the steep slope, and when they reached an open vista she and her husband paused as one to admire the view. She had sought in vain to have material dyed for her dresses that captured the deep, beautiful greens and blues of the Carpathian mountain ranges when they were not buried beneath a shroud of snow. It both angered and pleased her that no cloth merchant could match God's handiwork. She and her husband had enjoyed many a stimulating conversation over wine during which they agreed that challenging the Supreme Being was so arousing because He was worthy of their best efforts to shock and defy him.

A young lamb was being roasted for their dinner as servants took the edge off their hunger by offering them a fine red wine accompanied by delicate pastries stuffed with beef and pork sausage. When Erika shivered, the Count immediately ordered a blanket unpacked from his wife's chest, and he himself draped it gently over her shoulders before offering her another goblet of wine to help warm her. She smiled into his fire-lit eyes, enjoying the sinister play of shadows across his face which made her wonder, with a stimulating touch of fear, how well she truly knew this man she loved as much as life itself, perhaps even more.

'Is not the comely young man you are bringing home as a pet also a *Cobzar*?' he asked, waving aside a servant for the pleasure of stoking the fire himself and in the process gaining them a measure of privacy.

She gazed up at the pulsing multitude of stars, imagining them as the sharp tips of swords wielded by Lucifer's fiercely beautiful angels as they fought against God's pathetically pure power. 'Yes, he is,' she replied with a gratified smile. 'It was the sensitive and highly skilled way his fingers strummed and plucked his instrument, and the way he rested it on his lap and cradled it in his arms, that made me want him.'

'You are hoping his fingers will prove as talented between your thighs?' He smiled.

'Yes, but if I am disappointed, making him suffer will give me even greater pleasure.'

He motioned for a servant. 'Tell the *Cobzar* we want a song,' he said, and the woman bowed without meeting his eyes before quickly running to fulfill his desire.

Erika sat up attentively as the young man stepped proudly forward. She was so intent on getting her fill of his splendid beauty she did not notice the way her husband was staring at her face. Even in captivity the youth possessed a carriage and dignity most nobles would envy as much as his height, his broad shoulders, and the unblemished skin made even more desirably delicate by the pitch-black hair framing it. On his lean physique the rough, homespun gray shirt, threadbare black leggings and worn leather boots went unnoticed as they only served to enhance the appeal of his firm muscles flexing beneath them. He seated himself on the stool provided for him, facing the man and woman who now owned him, cradling the wooden lyre against his chest. The long, slender fingers of his right hand strummed it once, commanding their attention as he announced in a voice that seemed to arrest even the fickle flickering of the stars, 'This is the song of He That Betrayeth Not...'*

> *I gave my heart to him that betrayeth not.*
> *He said, "Come back in a hundred years again,*
> *And you shall find it safe beneath my mantel still."*
> *Yet in a hundred years we both shall be but dust,*
> *how can I ask him then to give me back my heart?*
> *He that betrayeth not, he loved me,*
> *and happier am I than the first spring days.*
> *But he is never happy, for he hath seen the world,*
> *and knows that life is like a nest in the winter;*
> *the heart of man is always cold therein.*
> *Therefore he took my heart to keep for a hundred years,*
> *even in the dust.*

Nor will he suffer death to touch it, nor the earth
to quicken it.
But he will say to death and earth, "This is her heart,
that I in a hundred years promised to give her back."
Then death and earth will wonder at him that betrayeth not.
And my heart will sleep, there in the dust of thy hand,
there, in thy hand of dust.

'Well, that certainly was uplifting,' Serban remarked when the youth's voice faded away, leaving in its melancholy wake only the mysteriously eloquent crackling of the fire.

Erika concealed her annoyance. 'The sentiment was certainly inspiring.'

A slight tilt of his head and the *Cobzar* was immediately led away. 'Do you truly believe love can transcend death?'

'I do not know, my lord. Certainly *our* love could never survive in heaven.'

'And in hell?'

She shivered and wrapped the cloak more securely around her. 'No, it would not be comfortable enough for us!'

He laughed, gripping her chin and tilting her face up towards his. 'Perhaps we will be together forever in the grave,' he whispered.

'You have my heart, my lord...'

'And in a hundred years, when we are stripped naked down to our bones in the crypt, I will give it back to you.' He kissed her soft, warm lips.

'I never want it back!'

'Then I swear you will die by my hand, Erika.' He stroked her high cheekbones with the balls of his thumbs. 'It is I who will rape the soul from your flesh, not God!' He thrust his tongue into her mouth, making it impossible for her to respond.

* * *

S erban smiled. 'It certainly is good to be home again.'

'I suspect this poor creature is wishing she was home right now as well,' Erika's voice was full of mock sympathy as she caressed the girl's hair.

A thick course rope hung from a rafter in the high vaulted ceiling. A naked girl was suspended from it by her wrists, her toes barely touching a dark-red and black hand-woven rug covering the stone floor. At first she had tried to clutch the rope in a desperate effort to take some of the agonizing pressure off her wrists, but they had been bound too tightly and it was not long before she ceased her struggles as her hands went numb. All the muscles in her young body were strained exquisitely taut, and to Erika there was no more arousing sight. A woman's naked body was even more beautiful with the skin smoothed out and mysteriously polished by stress, the tender mounds of her breasts flattened against a chest through which the ribs were clearly visible – the fleshly cage in which her immortal soul was so sweetly, so briefly imprisoned. Erika intended to find out what it would feel like to set the girl free completely. She wanted to feel the slave's heart beating wildly in her hands as her mistress savored the darkest of all climaxes – that ineffable moment when the soul left the body behind and it became an empty, suddenly undesirable shell. She never tired of the way suspension made a girl's nipples thrust out even more vulnerably defined from the snowy mounds of her breasts. The Count's pleasure slaves were fed only enough to keep them alive. It was he who had taught Erika to relish feeling the individual bones of their skeleton straining against their flesh as if rising up to meet his warm caress. It was at once impossible and all too easy to imagine the lovely young body hanging in the middle of their bedchamber as slender bones buried deep in the earth, where their owner could at last rest from the torments so unjustly inflicted upon her innocent beauty. This particular young woman's terrifying discomforts had only just begun, however.

'I am feeling cruel tonight, my lord.' Erika pressed herself against his tall body, possessively caressing his firm chest. He had stripped off his shirt, leaving on his breeches and boots. She was wearing only the long black hair waving down her back, jeweled high-heeled slippers, and the ruby choker he had given her on their first anniversary.

'Good.' He pressed her against him while idly fondling the other girl's sex. 'I love it when you are feeling cruel, my love.'

The creature suspended before them might have had something to say about this were it not for the gag stuffed between her lips. The black cloth was wet with her saliva and from the tears streaming down her face.

Erika watched breathlessly as her lover thrust two fingers up into the girl's dry, resistant cleft. In one hand she was eagerly holding the instrument of pleasure the Count had had especially carved for her from a black piece of wood taken from a tree after it was struck by lightning. Her favorite toy was much thicker than a real cock and curved like a bow with smooth, arrow-like shapes crowning both ends. She positioned one of these cold heads between the suspended girl's legs while her husband stepped behind the miserably writhing body, gruffly clutching the insides of her thighs to lift them up and open. Erika sank to one knee to get a better view of the little pink slit fully exposed by the sharp edge of the knife that had shaved away her bush, leaving only glistening clean skin in its wake. This slave was no longer a virgin; the Count had made thorough use of all her orifices on more than one occasion. Erika knew from watching his expression as he fucked the girl that she was pleasingly tight on the inside, and suppressed jealousy gave her the angry energy she needed to thrust one end of the wooden phallus into her helplessly gaping hole. She relished the feel of the girl's innermost flesh resisting, and tasted a faint trace of the pleasure a man must experience as he stabs himself into a silky, clinging sheath. The sight of her husband's fingers digging into the tender flesh of her thighs as he held them up and open excited her as much as shoving the ribbed and unyielding rod up into the girl's body. She pushed it in remorselessly, until its exciting evil crescent was at the right height for her to stand up and eagerly impale herself on it as well. She moaned from the fierce fulfillment as the unnaturally large erection opened her up completely, filling her up to the point where she almost couldn't breathe for a frightening instant. Yet she couldn't resist stabbing herself even more deeply, and the more she was sure she could not bear it, the more she craved the glorious discomfort of the lightning-struck wood rending her open; bringing her body closer and closer to the other woman's until their nipples kissed, and the delicate sensation was such a stimulating contrast to the powerful one between her thighs that she nearly climaxed.

The Count let go of the girl's legs so they fell closed around the shaft impaling her, and a muffled wail escaped the gagging cloth as he stepped quickly around the joined women. Standing behind his wife now, he grasped her hips hungrily with both hands. Her ass had already been prepared for him with a special scented oil imported from the Orient.

'Oh, yes, my lord, fill me up!' she begged. 'Fill me up until I cannot bear it, until I feel as if I must die from it!'

He silently granted her request by lodging the engorged head of his erection in her tight sphincter, pushing it through her darkly devoted ring, and then pausing to let her savor the threat of his full length about to plunge into her buttocks.

'Oh, yes, yes!' she gasped, fiercely pressing the girl's suspended body against hers as she began riding the wooden cock impaling them both. She drove the helpless hips hard against hers in order to shove the unnaturally thick phallus as deep inside both their bodies as possible while her husband's equally excruciating penis stuffed her other hole.

'Oh, Erika, you are so tight...' He rammed his erection into her ass, cruelly clutching her hips as she in turn gripped the girl's bony pelvis, moving in rhythm with him so both cocks thrust in and out of her at once causing her an agony of pleasure; a torment of fulfillment she could not endure another second yet which she never wished to end.

'Oh, yes, yes, come in me, my lord!' she gasped, viciously sinking her teeth into the girl's neck as she imagined there were two men inside her both ejaculating at once and drenching her insides with their cum.

Afterwards, they left the girl hanging from the rafters while they refreshed themselves with more wine, but not until Erika had wiped her lord's penis clean with a cloth she dipped in a basin of water kept warm by the fire. She had not climaxed as she fucked the girl and herself; she was saving her orgasms for the night's more sinister sport.

When they had finished their wine, she presented her husband with one of his many knives. 'I wish you to cut her, my lord,' she said sweetly. 'I wish to see her blood flowing in delicate streams down her skin like the map of a river seen from heaven. I wish to sip the horror in her eyes like the finest vintage.'

He asked very quietly, 'You wish me to kill her?'

'Yes, my lord, but slowly, so very, very slowly… I want to hear the first birds begin to sing before her life finally sets in your hands.'

'First I will move the rug,' he said, walking purposefully towards their victim. 'We do not wish to spoil it.'

Erika's eyes closed beneath a stab of love for him so intense she was surprised it did not kill *her*. She went and stood by his side, once more pressing her body up against his as he raised the dagger and gently traced the skin beneath the tender swell of one of the girl's breasts with the sharp edge. For a magical instant a bright-red crescent shone against her pale flesh, before the blood began flowing in fine threads slowly unraveling her life. Erika watched the girl's face contort with pain as she thrashed from side-to-side, jerking her hips back and forth and kicking violently out with her legs.

'Bind her ankles,' the Count commanded, and she promptly obeyed him as he effortlessly forced the slave to hold still by resting the edge of the blade threateningly against her throat.

Some time later the suspended girl had stopped looking down in horror at her ravaged body; her eyes had glazed over as if the shock and the pain were too great to comprehend.

'She might still live,' Serban remarked, observing his handiwork. 'If we took her down and had her wounds tended, she would be scarred for life, but she might live.'

'Do you do not think she has lost too much blood to survive?' Erika asked curiously.

'Perhaps, perhaps not,' he sounded only mildly interested.

'Well, in any case, a scarred slave is of no use to us, my lord, and you promised to give me her life before the sun rose.'

'I did not promise, my lady.' He looked hard into her eyes. 'You said you wished me to give it to you, but I did not, in fact, promise that I would.'

She sank to her knees before him, wrapping her arms around his thighs and pressing her cheek against his crotch. 'Please, my lord, as a gift...'

'Stand up!' he commanded.

A thrill of fear once more tugged on her clitoris despite the fact that during the course of the night it had dissolved with pleasure more times than she could remember. The demonic vision of the girl's convulsing body as he delicately cut her flesh over and over again from her breasts down to her sex had aroused Erika to the point where orgasm after orgasm was not enough to satisfy the dark lust blooming so deep inside her nothing could seem to reach and fulfill it. Now the young body hanging from the center of their bedchamber was so drenched in blood it was no more appealing than a hunted animal's carcass hanging in the larder, except for the haunting gleam of the soul staring almost calmly out through her eyes as though untouched by her body's nightmarish plight. It angered Erika that she no longer seemed aware of them, but instead gazed straight ahead of her as if she could see through the stone walls of the Castle to another world entirely.

The Count shifted the knife in his hand, getting a firm grip on the handle. 'Wrap your fingers around mine,' he instructed suddenly.

Glancing gratefully up into his eyes, she did as he said.

'I want you to feel the thrust, my love. I want you to feel her flesh resist at first, and then yield to my penetration. I want her agony to be part of us both and unite us like the most sublime pleasure, a pleasure known only to God, and to those who dare claim his power of life and death as their own.' He reached up abruptly with his free hand and wrenched the gag out of the girl's mouth, flinging it away. The gesture seemed to rouse her from her stupor, and Erika's sex juiced in response as the stricken eyes once more looked down at her dying body. At that moment he plunged the dagger deep into her belly, and on that cold morning, in those breathless moments just before dawn, it was not the innocent music of birds but a woman's agonized scream that heralded the sunrise.

'One day I will do this to you, my love,' he promised, forcing Erika to climax a final time around his stabbing fingers, and despite the fear his promise aroused in her she would much rather her soul belonged to him forever than to God, who would deny her all the pleasures just one intense man could give her.

* * *

The Count and Countess slept for most of the day, and that evening Erika commanded her handsome *Cobzar* to sing them a song while she and Serban dined together in the privacy of their rooms, after which both men played her body between them until her cries filled the night with their carnal music.

*The Comforters**

He who sleeps by the fire doth dream,
Doth dream that his heart is warm,
But when he awakes, his heart
Is afraid for the bitter cold.
Dids't thou mark how the swallows flew, how they flew away
from hence?
My father is dead – and his cap is mine,
His cap of fur and his leathern belt –
Mine, too, his knives.

guilty pleasures

When I fall asleep, when I slumb'ring lie,
Then the knives spring forth, from their sheaths they fly,
And roam the fields.
I know not whither the knives have strayed –
But when morning dawns, at my window-pane
I hear a tapping – I fling it wide,
And there are my knives come home again.
"Where have ye been?" I ask them then,
And they make reply: "In the hearts of men!
There was one so sick for love, and torn –
We healed its wound;
And another was weary and travel-worn –
We gave it rest.
For dear to us are the hearts of men,
And dear their blood;
We drink it as furrows drink the rain,
Then, tapping, come to thy window-pane:
Make way for thy knives – they have done their work.
Now wipe the blood with thy sleeve away –
Thy sleeve with the dusk-red embroidered flowers –
And wash the sleeve in the river clean,
Then thrust us once more our sheaths between,
The sheaths on the leathern belt.

*From The Bard of the Dimbovitza – Romanian Folk Songs
Collected From The Peasants by Helene Vacaresco, translated by
Carmen Sylva and Alma Strettell, London and New York Harper
& Brothers, 1914

Secret Societies

Florence, Italy 1500

For my Master

The Italian people have always had a fascination with intricate and mysterious social constructs. There have been a plethora of secret societies in Italy since before Roman times and many of these same societies still thrive, hidden deep down in the social fabric of the country. All have their symbols and ceremonies, and some even have their own elaborate languages that have evolved in secrecy for millennia, with libraries of ancient as well as modern literature, decipherable only by the members. Many cultures have sophisticated social hierarchies and networks, and in Italy these are only the window dressings that limit voyeurism into the ancient heart of Italian political and social interaction – the secret societies.

Her husband's body had been lying in the family crypt for nine months when the letter arrived, delivered by a handsome nobleman Laura remembered often seeing in the late Vittorio's company. She had caught only glimpses of her spouse's mysterious guest, his tall figure bent over books resting open on large tables in the fire-lit library, and once she had seen him from behind walking down a statue-lined hallway on his way out of the Villa, a black leather cape flowing down to his ankles from shoulders too broad for her not to notice. His hair had ceased to be fashionably long and become a defiantly decadent statement of virile power, the curled tip of his dark-brown mane – pulled back with a vivid red leather sash –

resting against the small of his back as he strode down the corridor of her memory more than once. After her husband's death she had never expected to see him again, yet there he was sitting across from her in the large drawing room that had become her ponderous possession along with the rest of the Villa. His aura was not that of a humble messenger delivering a secret missive the contents of which he was unfamiliar with. He watched in silence as she broke the wax seal carefully, almost reverently with a jeweled penknife, for what she held in her ringed hands was a posthumous message from her lover. Never again would she hold his feelings in her hands or listen attentively as he spoke to her, silently this one last time. As she read, her bodice felt increasingly tight, and she was more acutely aware of different sensory impressions than she ever had been in her life. She was looking down at the elegant script covering the heavy paper in controlled serpentine coils, but she was aware of Sandro's eyes resting on the deep line of her cleavage as if he found it more eloquent than any which could ever be written with a feather quill dipped in ink. A fire was burning in the stone hearth across from them, and never had its quiet crackling sounded so urgently significant; she had never truly heard the flames' voice until then when she seemed to feel them licking up between her legs even through the heavy black material of her dress. The muted rattle of a carriage passing by on the street outside was no longer a harmless, normal sound as she felt it mysteriously taking her soul somewhere she was not at all sure it was safe and right to go. The subtle rustle of the stiff parchment as she slipped the first page behind the second and continued reading struck her as profoundly loud in the ensuing stillness. She schooled her expression to reveal nothing, but she could not conceal the swelling of her bosom as she found herself unable to control her breathing. The stiff paper suddenly put her in mind of her husband's dead skin from which the suppleness of life had vanished in the haunting blink of an eye. His decaying hand, the bones already showing luminous through the bloodless flesh, was reaching out to her from the grave and clutching her heart so it beat faster in fervent defense of her life, threatened even more radically now than after he died.

At last her dark eyes came to the end of the impossible letter and she rested it gently in her lap, staring into the shadows as if merely pondering an invitation to dinner. When she spoke, her voice was soft and unusually deep for a woman's, 'I must confess, Signor, that I cannot find words to express how I feel about the shocking thoughts and ideas entertained by a man whose soul I had thought safely entrusted into the Virgin's hands.'

'It is understandable,' he replied, his voice as quiet as hers.

She turned her head and met his eyes, which were an inscrutable dark-gray in the firelight. 'I begin to understand why my husband valued your friendship, for surely you never bored him with idle chatter.'

He smiled faintly, and directed the invisible blade of his intent stare harmlessly towards the hearth. 'You are not alone in wondering if perhaps the letter in your hands should not simply be burned and forgotten.'

'You insult not only me but your immortal friend, Signor. Do you think Vittorio would have married a woman who would so blithely disregard his desires?'

'I sought merely to reassure you that the traitorous possibility had crossed all our minds, Signora.'

'I am made breathless by how suddenly my inferior feminine nature and intellect finds itself in such illustrious company.'

'Your husband was always disappointed with Aristotle's reasoning, which he considered inferior to Plato's more inspired and comprehensive wisdom.' Without moving his head – poised calmly and beautifully as a statue's contemplating the fire – his eyes shifted slightly in their hooded alcoves to meet hers again. 'The world is changing, Laura, and it appears your husband does not wish you left behind in his grave, through which there are only two doors you can escape back into life again.'

'Yes I know,' she calmly folded the letter closed, 'the convent, which is not much warmer than a crypt, or a wealthy husband I do not wish.'

He was silent. His hands rested on the chair's wooden arms, and his fingers curling languidly around the carved ends kept drawing her eyes towards them because they were such a contrast to how tense she felt.

'There are many questions a vow of silence makes it impossible for me to ask,' she pointed out as matter-of-factly as she could manage.

'The questions to which you refer are best not asked with words for the answers can only be experienced to be true, and for that you must dare to be curious with every part of you.'

'Even if I did not recognize my husband's handwriting, still I would not be tempted to consider this an elaborate hoax for it would mean foolishly putting myself, and my rather wilted charms, at the center of everything. Therefore, I must conclude that what I have just read does not describe a sinful dream from which I will rudely awaken to the world's harsh judgment once it is played out in darkness.'

'I cannot pretend to know how he expressed his thoughts to you, but I am confident he commanded you to trust me with your life, Laura, and since I am not a man of the Cloth, I do not consider your modesty a virtue. Surely you know the languid confidence of a rose in full bloom serves only to make its sensual abandon more strikingly beautiful by contrast with less complex flowers, whose eager charms last but one sunny afternoon or two.'

'Yet in this secret world we cannot speak of, Sandro, what is even more vital than complexity is my inability to bear children by some misfortune, or perhaps by some mysterious fortune, of nature. My barrenness gives me the same freedom as a man, whom one would never compare to a flower already doomed to fade the moment you pluck it to adorn a ballroom or a grave.'

'You had Vittorio's confidence. I am sure he made you aware of the fact that less pious and more flexible ancient attitudes are increasingly respected in our beautiful city by decree of the Medici.'

'Yet surely the equality to which I must aspire in order to fulfill my late husband's desire would taste unacceptably extreme even to Lorenzo's worldly palette?'

He lowered his voice, 'The Society's cellars are very deep, Laura, and the wine it drinks in secret comes from vintages so old their roots extend to the beginning of time, when men and women were first conceived in God's mind. Such wine is never drunk in public; its intoxicating powers are known only two a select few who can truly appreciate them.'

'Even though they risk losing their heads?'

He continued steadily holding her eyes. 'Life is dangerous.'

'As all women who risk dying in childbirth know only too well.'

'Vittorio often spoke of you to me.'

She picked up the silver bell resting on the small table between them and rang it more imperiously than she intended, obeying the rhythm of her pulse speeding up in response to the sudden hard intimacy in his voice. 'Please join me in a glass of wine, Sandro.'

'It would be my pleasure, Laura.'

She instructed the servant who appeared to bring them a bottle of

Chianti from the cellar, and when the woman left to fetch it, she swallowed all her doubts and fears as she stated, 'We shall drink to my husband, who has honored me with the depth of his love and with his trust in the equality of my spirit, both of which inspired him to leave me in the care of his closest friends so they might strive to fill the emptiness inside me created by his passing.'

He leaned forward to grasp her left hand. 'Such a toast spoken by such a woman,' his firm lips warmed her skin as he kissed her, 'is a pleasure worth risking everything for, Signora.'

* * *

The carriage arrived at sunset. The driver did not dismount; he did not even glance at her as she walked down the front steps of the Villa. The hems of her cloak and dress rustled against the flagstones in a secret whisper of cloth, defying the pious stillness of twilight when all virtuous women are closing their windows and doors against the dangers of the night. Laura managed to step up into the carriage without assistance. She had barely settled her skirt around her when the horses bolted, eager to be on their way again, and she felt the motion directly in her chest where her heart was beating so fast she literally feared for her life. She was still clad in mourning black, but her somber dress was only a façade for beneath it she was wearing nothing at all. Her personal maid had remained discreetly silent as she tightened her mistress' bodice directly against her naked skin and breasts. Christina had been with her for years, and it was she who would inform the staff the Signora had received an urgent message to visit a sick cousin outside the city. Why she had taken no servants and luggage with her would be an entertaining topic of speculation for her servants Laura sincerely hoped would not spread to neighboring households.

Where she was going had not been revealed to her, in fact, nothing had. She was exercising more faith in her late husband's good intentions than she ever had in God. But ever since she received his letter from beyond the grave she was able to taste life again, and if the acidity of fear was mixed in with the intoxicating warmth of returning sensation, then so be it. Having had her life mapped out for her since the moment she was born, not knowing what was going to happen to her was as refreshing and exciting as it was terrifying. Relentlessly schooled in virtue, what her body suspected lay in store for her senses was inconceivable to her mentally. Such images as she had allowed herself to paint in her mind during the long three days and nights since Sandro's visit seemed impossible and therefore unreal, like the medieval fresco of hell adorning a small alcove in her villa's private chapel. She wondered why Vittorio never had it painted over, until she examined the faces of the eternally suffering sinners and realized they were all smiling. Looking closely at the nature of their punishments, she had been shocked by the suspicion they were enjoying them.

When the carriage abruptly came to a stop her heart followed suit for a breathless instant. The door on the other side of the cushioned seat opened, and a tall man entered the small space with her. His gloves, his cloak, his boots and his hair, all were black, as was the mask that revealed only sinuous lips and dark-blue eyes. They regarded her steadily for a moment before he leaned intimately towards her and covered her own eyes with a soft red cloth, robbing her of sight as he tied it securely behind her head.

Laura bit her lip to stop herself from whimpering like a frightened child. If she lost her courage before anything even happened she would only be serving to prove women were indeed inferior, and worse, that they could not be trusted to keep their word. When the nameless man forcibly gripped one of her arms, it was harder for her not to make a helpless sound, but she somehow managed to sustain a dignified silence as he bound her wrists together in her lap.

As the carriage continued on its way again she found herself praying he would speak to her, that he would say her name, at least, reassuring her he was a friend of Sandro's, but he remained silent and she experienced the curious sensation of questions crowding her throat until it felt hot with the urge to weep and beg to be taken home. Sitting perfectly still and silent with her hands clasped tensely in her lap took all the willpower she possessed, and it filled her with despair how quickly she had squandered her strength. She wondered if the last thing she would ever see was a man's sinisterly masked face. She sensed him looking at her, yet of course she could not be sure she wasn't merely imagining his intent regard, his invisible presence mysteriously growing in warmth and dangerous power the longer he remained silent.

The carriage came to a stop a second time. Laura clenched her hands even more tightly as she heard a door open and felt her companion step out of the carriage. Then the door beside her also opened and a hand possessively grasped her arm. She clutched the combined folds of her cloak and skirt, lifting them to avoid tripping as she turned in the seat and searched blindly with on of her high-heels for the steps leading down out of the compartment. The hand bracing her offered her no other assistance, and she was proud when she made it to the ground without stumbling. Immediately a second hand grasped her free arm, and suddenly it did not seem so important she could not see were she was going. Her blindness was a weakness, but a curiously pleasant one as her steps were confidently directed. All she had to do was trust the strong presences surrounding her. She felt both protected by them and at their mercy, a combination her feminine soul found perilously intoxicating.

'There are nine steps before you,' a man announced quietly.

Glad of the warning, and inordinately grateful for the sound of his voice, she managed to ascend calmly between them. So far her regal behavior was worthy of her husband's faith in her. It was not until the brisk night air gave way to the closer warmth of a candlelit interior that anxiety began flickering its painfully hot flame so deep inside her no reassuring thoughts could quench it.

'There are now thirteen steps before you.'

She raised a high-heel and felt herself falling into a void. Her two guides steadied her without comment as she realized the stairwell lead downwards. The air grew noticeably colder as they descended and she heard again Sandro's voice in her head saying, 'The society's cellars are very deep, Laura…'

At the bottom of the steps her arms were released and she was left standing alone at the center of nothingness, yet the inner darkness imposed by the blindfold was illuminated by brilliantly colorful memories… Her husband's body lying stiffly across a cold stone bed deep in the family crypt, his rich clothing defying the dull lace of ancient cobwebs embracing the naked bones of his ancestors… Sandro's intensely handsome face and the look in his eyes when he raised her hand to his lips… She stood poised at the dark heart of the experience that for three long days and nights she had both dreaded and desired… at the symbolic instant of death when she would find out if her soul truly could rise above whatever happened to her flesh…

Her wrists were untied so swiftly she barely had time to appreciate their freedom before a pair of strong arms swept her up against a hard chest, and then spread her gently back across a soft surface. It was amazingly easy to cross a forbidden threshold – the death of her old life happened in the few seconds it took the man to cradle her in his arms and lay her down again. Warm, ungloved hands slipped up her skirt, lifting it out of their way while other hands impatiently opened her cloak and still more hands carelessly ripped open her bodice. Her arms were forced up over her head, her shoes were removed, and a loud ripping sound satisfied her desire to cry out as the heavy black dress she had worn for nine months was in that many seconds destroyed, exposing all the soft, pale flesh buried beneath it.

In a desperate effort to stop herself from being afraid, Laura concentrated on trying to determine how many men were present. She distinctly felt two masculine hands sharing her breasts, yet she could not be sure those were not the lips of a third man, and the tongue of a fourth, savoring her nipples. She quickly gave up; there were too many hands stroking her legs to make sense of, especially when her thoughts slipped strangely out of her grasp as her legs were spread. Fingertips massaged a slick, warm oil across her labial lips before insinuating themselves into her clinging, resistant sex, yet so much more was happening to her body at the same time she was stunned into a silence that seemed shamefully to scream her willingness to be so used. A cry of protest perched on the tip of her tongue, yet it never took flight in defense of her virtue as she writhed shamelessly against the divan in response to a man's big strong hand opening her up. Then suddenly a thumb was thrust into her mouth and the rising guilt urging her to cry out for mercy was effortlessly crushed. She found herself sucking fervently on the man's slightly salty hardness, grateful he had saved her from the tense temptation to resist being relentlessly penetrated at both ends as fingers slid swiftly in and out of her pussy while a second thumb thrust into her mouth, demanding her tongue evenly divide its attentions.

The hand between her legs fucked her until her back arched in response, then it slipped away and another set of breathtakingly skilled fingers slipped deep inside her. She could feel they belonged to a different man; there were subtle but vital differences in the way they forced her open and stroked her, and the more sensations she was aware of, the more they all came together inside her as one overwhelming pleasure. Two other thumbs insinuated themselves between her lips, coaxing her tongue to beg for them, and the more wantonly she opened her mouth to hungrily suck and lick, the more her innermost flesh yielded to the thrust of fingers exploring the shape and texture and tightness of her sex; roughly pointing out how wet and deep and ready she was for much more. Hands clutching her wrists held her arms up over her head while two other hands gripped her ankles and kept her legs spread. She did not need to see in order to sense – to suffer the knowledge – that she was surrounded by men. The darkness behind her eyelids had assumed the exhilarating form of beautiful masked noblemen, one of whom she knew (she fervently hoped) was Sandro. But none of them spoke; not one offered her the slightest clue to his identity. She would never look at a man's thumbs the same way again. They were everywhere, and the way they worked on her forced the men stationed at her feet to hold her ankles more tightly as she struggled to close her legs against the painfully sharp delight cutting up through her body. The thumbs dancing with her tongue were breathtakingly allied to the one brushing the top of her mound and to the ones rubbing her nipples until they were so hard they hurt. Smoldering in response to the relentless stimulation, her clitoris radiated a rapturous blaze of feeling up her body into the burning peaks of her breasts, her twirling tongue stirring her senses up into a frenzy of impressions deliciously possessing her. She could not see, but she could taste and feel and hear and smell everything intensely... the uniquely desirable flavor of male flesh... every imaginable quality of touch, gentle and rough, squeezing and caressing... the embarrassingly distinct sound of her juicing sex parting around two, three, and even four thrusting fingers... the delicate yet heady perfume of her arousal scenting the air mingling with the mysterious musk of men's growing lust... robbed of sight, her remaining senses were sharpened almost unbearably, so that it came as a shock and yet as no surprise when she climaxed.

The thumbs slipped out of her mouth as if their owners wished to relish her cries as countless hands continued caressing and pinning her down until she completely relaxed against the velvet divan, then they all slipped away at once. She was left alone again, but this time she did not feel poised at the center of nothingness – her body was the heart of tantalizing possibilities. Whatever happened now, her willingness had been established beyond a shadow of a doubt. The searing ecstasy she was capable of experiencing was a light in the darkness showing her the path she had to take for the rest of the night, or for however long her initiation might last. Her body grasped the key before her mind did – that she must submit absolutely. She was utterly naked, a condition she suddenly felt applied not just to her flesh but to her very soul. No gold rings claimed her fingers, no heavy gemstones weighed down her earlobes, and no necklaces burdened her heart with their precious weight. She was purely herself clad only in the gifts God had wrapped her spirit in when she was born – lustrous black hair flowing down to her waist and flesh so smooth and cool to the touch on the outside yet so warm and wet on the inside.

When two hands firmly grasped hers, Laura sensed they belonged to one man as she obeyed their silent command to sit up. But that was not enough; apparently, he wanted her on her feet, so she slipped her legs off the edge of the divan and stood up, grateful for his bracing grip. Then it slipped away and once more two hands grasped her upper arms, guiding her forward between them. She walked tentatively in her bare feet across the cold stone floor, increasingly afraid of bumping into something sinister, and how large the space was where she found herself blind and lost began making her nervous again. Finally her escorts stopped and raised her arms over her head, spreading them open as they had her legs. The unmistakable feel of supple leather embraced both her wrists, and she suppressed a whimper of terror hearing the cold clink of chains hanging above her. A moment later, her ankles suffered the same fate as her legs were forced open as far as possible while still enabling her to stand. She had suppressed all sounds of weakness until then, but she could not stop herself from gasping when her blindfold was yanked off. Blinking against the light that seemed bright after so much darkness, after a moment she was able to make out torches burning in sconces on dark stone walls. She closed her eyes again for an instant, returning to the safety of not knowing how many masked strangers her loving husband had willed her to.

Before her stood three men, and turning her head from side-to-side she glimpsed four more men flanking her even as she sensed even more men standing behind her. Yet all that truly mattered was the fact that Sandro was one of the tall figures her erect nipples were pointing towards with shocking eagerness. Like his companions he was dressed entirely in black, but his mask was slightly different, rimmed in a glimmering thread flashing a deep violet in the torchlight. She was so profoundly relieved to see him it was a moment before she noticed he was holding something. Once, when she was a little girl, she had witnessed a man being flogged in public, and she had never forgotten the sight of his bare back ravaged by vividly bleeding welts. She could not believe her husband's friends meant to hurt her in such a terrible way, leaving her permanently scarred, yet it was definitely a flogger she saw resting menacingly in Sandro's gloved hand. She would have said something then – she would have begged for his mercy as a surge of visceral panic broke the sophisticated damn of her control – but a tightly wound cloth was suddenly forced between her lips, gagging her and making it impossible for her to speak. What she experienced then had to be dread, but the feeling had a disturbingly similar affect on her as the pleasure which only moments ago had blinded her; her heart began beating so fast her knees weakened as if they were actually running to keep up.

Sandro stepped forward. She prayed he would speak to her, that he would have the good grace to offer a civilized explanation for why he was about to brutalize her, but a faint whistling sound immediately followed by a resounding smack was all she heard before the silent scream of her flesh. She discovered a flogger was like a brood of serpents all biting her at once, and it amazed her how much of the perversely invigorating venom of pain she could absorb without fainting. The elegance of Sandro's movements mesmerized her as he walked slowly around her, making sure to strike every inch of her body from her breasts all the way down to her thighs. She was not bleeding; the wide leather bands did not break her skin. How much she suffered beneath each lash was excruciatingly real, but it appeared she would not be scarred. She reminded herself she was not a condemned prisoner being publicly humiliated. She was a beautiful woman being privately initiated... a beautiful woman being challenged and aroused by a group of noblemen mysteriously instructing her in the dark, secret ways of her flesh thrilling to the brutal kiss of leather with an even deeper excitement than to a tender caress. Her pussy became so wet she was mortified to feel its juices trickling down the insides of her legs... making her think of tears shed by the mother of Christ witnessing what no moral woman could possibly desire much less enjoy. Then the tips of the flogger deliberately bit one of her nipples and real tears filled her eyes as she turned her head to gaze beseechingly at her tormenter. He ignored her silent plea and stepped behind her, where he devoted himself to lashing her back and buttocks until her sex felt hot enough to light another torch with.

She had ceased to believe the ordeal would ever end when three things suddenly happened at once. A man knelt and placed a dark-red pillow at her feet as the sodden gag was wrenched from between her lips and a grinding sound told her the chains attached to her wrists were being lowered so they would continue holding her up as she sank to her knees. In a haunting way the flogging had rendered her even more naked than she already was. Men surrounded her, but she had eyes only for the darkly desirable space of Sandro's crotch looming directly in front of her face. She watched with a ravenous, blasphemous reverence as he opened his leggings, pulled out his cock, and slipped it between her lips. It was impossible to explain why being beaten exquisitely enhanced her senses, and she had no wish to; all she wanted was to worship his erection and to suffer his head blessing her throat with its profoundly selfish caress. She moaned in despair when he stepped back and another man's rigid penis filled her mouth. It was a true test of her oral skills that she was allowed to use only her lips and tongue and throat to stimulate one man after another, and it proved a revelation to her how differ-

171

ent they all felt and tasted; she was able to distinguish subtle yet vital nuances in all their pulsing presences.

At long last her mouth was emptied and, vaguely, Laura realized her wrists were being freed as someone pulled her roughly to her feet. A moment later she found herself on her knees again, only this time she was bent forward, her wrists and neck resting in leather-cushioned slots, then the top half of the stock was brought down again, pinning her in place. Her breasts and belly, and especially her ass and thighs, burning from the relentless flogging had made her pussy deeply jealous, and while her mouth received all the thrusting attention it craved her feminine wound had become even more desperately hungry for attention. She had never been more ready for a cock in her life as she was then with her head separated from her body.

She got what she longed for – what she needed more than anything – when an erection surged into her sex, gloriously filling her belly. She could not see around the black curtain of her hair, but she did not really care who the man was penetrating her as he gripped her hips and made her accept his full length from beginning to end over and over again. Then strong fingers wove themselves through her hair and lifted her head. What she had earlier experienced with hands and thumbs was nothing to how she felt a moment later with a man driving himself deeper and deeper between her thighs while another man pumped his hips in a gentler rhythm riding her face.

When the stranger fucking her from behind pulled out of her pussy and rubbed his threateningly thick head against her other, much tighter hole, the man stroking himself with her throat emptied her mouth and let her head fall. Strangely enough it was more of a strain on her neck when his fingers weren't threaded possessively through her hair. She wanted another man to hold her heavy skull up as he used one of the three vulnerable orifices God had blessed her with… that was truly how she felt then, that her woman's body was a supreme blessing, not an inferior curse. She was being possessed by countless men, and by the sense of what a perfect vessel her body was for her soul, which was more fearlessly passionate than she had ever been allowed to realize.

Very soon her lips and throat and the muscles of her jaw were sore from performing the art of fellatio, unlike her pussy which had been designed especially to welcome the arrogantly demanding guest of an erection in its silky-soft space. After the flogging the only thing that made her sex hurt was the absence of a hard cock, and she groaned from the loss when her dripping sex was ignored as a finger slid slowly into her anus, greasing her sphincter with a shockingly cold liquid. Vittorio had buried himself between her ass cheeks more than once, she was not a virgin to being sodomized; nevertheless, she could not help but dread the thought of more than one man using her that way. The finger withdrew and she felt something inexorably harder than a penis force her buttocks open around it. The wooden plug was thankfully no longer than a finger but it felt twice as thick, preparing her for the coming trial. The members of the secret society of which her husband had been the leader were doing everything in their power to enable her to enjoy the fierce desires her beautifully submissive body aroused in them. She barely had time to reconcile herself to the stiff presence in her bowels before the same man penetrated her pussy again. The pleasure was almost unbearable, and yet she knew it was nothing compared to what awaited her. It was a relief when another man grabbed a handful of her hair and took the strain off her neck again by thrusting his dick between her lips, secure in the knowledge she would do everything in her power to accommodate him; indeed, the swift confidence with which he filled her mouth was flattering.

Laura knew aristocrats who prided themselves on how many animals they killed hunting, and in a similar vein she found herself counting how many men expired violently inside her. Six men possessed her, two and two and two more, until she forgot she had ever been anywhere except on her knees in a torch-lit cellar. It was awful how hard they used her because she knew it would end; because she knew that once they finished pumping their essence down her throat and into her womb they would slip away and abandon her dissolute soul to an eternal hunger for more. The overwhelming experience was sacredly fulfilling instead of terribly sinful because there was a priest-like figure officiating. Sandro's presence had the power to make the impious acts forced upon her feel like an infinitely exciting sensual martyrdom, for each time a man spent himself in her mouth he washed the bittersweet taste of cum from her tongue by gently lifting her head and giving her a wonderful red wine to sip, wine that must have been spiced with mysterious herbs for it made her feel totally relaxed and prepared to remain on her knees forever.

When after a private eternity the time came to move on to yet another station of the erotic cross, Laura was freed from the stocks and helped her to feet. For a wonderful moment Sandro allowed her to rest her cheek against his chest, and she would gladly have remained there, but he pushed her gently away and another man effortlessly lifted her slender body up in his arms. He did not lower her onto the divan, for it was already occupied by another man lying naked across it except for the black mask framing his brilliant blue eyes. All her other lovers were still fully dressed, and the unexpected vision of a man's smooth bare skin and towering cock came as a glorious shock. It was the first real good look she got of the weapon God had armed all men with, and she was in awe of how many such splendid erections had already stabbed her into feeling more alive than ever. He offered her his hand, and she touched his fingertips tentatively with hers before allowing him help her onto the divan. After kneeling for so long in the stocks she moved a bit stiffly, afraid the wooden plug in her anus would slip ignominiously out of her, but it remained lodged deep between her ass cheeks as she straddled the naked youth. Planting her hands on his hairless chest, she looked up at Sandro – at his intense masked eyes and unsmiling lips – as she willingly stabbed herself with another man's dick. She felt a second man kneel on the divan behind her and moaned with trepidation, lowering her head and shyly hiding her face behind the curtain of her hair while he drew the wooden rod out of her buttocks. Her sphincter was more receptive now, yet she still experienced a burning misery as he slowly stuffed her little hole with his much larger and longer penis that seemed to reach dangerously deep into her bowels. Gradually the agony dimmed to a tolerable discomfort as her two partners began moving in rhythm, one of them holding on to her narrow waist, the other one gripping her tender hips as they moved her up and down between them. She became excruciatingly aware of the thin wall of flesh separating her bowels from her womb as the two erections caressed her, pushing and sliding against each other with only the delicate veil of her innermost flesh separating them. And then it got even worse or even better, she could not tell and she did not care, for already the night had taught both her body and her soul not only to accept this overwhelming paradox but to thrive on it. Another man stepped up to the head of the divan and, firmly holding her chin with one hand, slipped his cock between her lips as Sandro caressed the hair away from her face, giving his friend smooth passage into her mouth and throat. Three men relentlessly drove themselves into oblivion inside her, and afterwards, when they all pulled out of her at once, a fourth man caught her in his arms as she collapsed.

Laura opened her eyes when she was laid across an even softer surface... she was resting on a bed with torches burning in sconces on the wall behind it clearly illuminating Sandro's masked face as he joined her. *I can die now*, she thought, and it seemed her silent surrender was hauntingly audible because two men kneeling on either side of her head wrapped a black leather strap around her neck, one of them lifting her hair out of the way as the other one remorselessly tightened it. Then they each pulled on one end of the leash as two other men positioned at her feet raised her legs and spread them wide. Her breath was cut off as Sandro penetrated her, the rhythm of her lungs replaced by that of his cock sliding in and out of her as he stared down into her eyes, his hands resting on either side of her naked breasts, for her arms were also spread helplessly open, her wrists firmly in the grip of yet two other men. He watched her face as he fucked her, banging her more and more brutally as no plea for mercy – as no sound or word of protest whatsoever – emerged from her submissively parted lips, her ecstatically narrowed eyes gazing steadily up into his. She was overcome with respect and gratitude for her late husband's wisdom because naturally she would never have imagined that being strangled as a man penetrated her would feel like touching the face of God... which had become, which *was*, Sandro's... she could feel her awareness ebbing in rhythm with his erection swelling, her pulse fluttering as his penis began pulsing... he pulled off his mask, the pressure around her neck was relaxed, and the breath she took was full of their pleasure's mysterious life as they climaxed, together.

* * *

Her husband's final wish had been fulfilled – Laura was initiated and took her place beside his successor as the head of Italy's oldest and most secret society.

Lady of the Lake

England, Dark Ages, 12th Century

One spring twilight a young woman was swimming in a lake set like a shining broach at the heart of a forest's dark cloak. Lilly lived for the caress of contrasting sensations; intense or subtle, she loved them all. As she broke through the surface of the water the dark drumming in her ears surrendered to cheerful bird songs. She blinked dozens of tiny liquid suns from her lashes, laughing at how long she had managed to remain sitting at the bottom of the lake. She had held herself motionless as a queen on an invisible throne, basking in the absolute silence which seemed mysteriously to observe her presence as she kept her eyes open, searching the shadowy depths for any subjects swimming her way. The pressure in her chest was strangely exciting; an invisible opponent she was challenging with her calm endurance. Her only regret (which she did not admit to her mum lest she fear for her daughter's soul) was that she had been born a human and not one of the enchanted creatures who lived in the woods. The fact that magically beautiful men and women truly existed Lilly did not doubt for an instant. Their hidden presence was the reason she tested herself at the bottom of the lake on the evening of every full moon in the spring and summer hoping they would notice how she always strove to live on the edge of her dull mortality. There was always the chance a prince of the Fairy would fall in love with her and take her away with him into his hidden kingdom, where the limitations of her flesh would dissolve like mist and she would be free as only her laughter was now.

Shaking the last of the twilight-jeweled water drops from her lashes, Lilly smoothed her long hair away from her face enjoying how the sun setting behind her gently warmed her bare shoulders with its fine crimson cloak. The trees around the lake were as familiar to her as the back of her hands, and sucking in a quick breath she plunged her whole body except for her eyes back into the water, staring with a confused depth of hope and terror at the figure standing on the shore almost directly across from her. The sun was shining directly in the man's eyes; she did not think he had seen her. That he was not a local farmer or woodsman she discerned at once from the sword in his hand, and everything else about him. His hair waved freely down to his broad shoulders and the dying light glimmered on the silk threads of his tunic. The embroidered dragon rearing against his chest was all she could clearly see of him, his silhouette hard to distinguish from the tall trees behind him. He raised his arm, and fear made it easy to keep holding her breath as he flung the sword straight at her into the lake.

She dove towards the soft, safe bottom, and saw the blade plunge like a silver fish into the dark depths before her. She swam towards it, grateful for the precious stones adorning the handle which made it easier to see in the murky gloom. She grasped the thick hilt, and an urgent need to breathe gave her the strength she needed to kick swiftly to the surface thrusting the heavy weapon straight up out of the water ahead of her. She did all this without thinking, and by then it was too late to wonder how the man would feel about having his sword returned to him by a girl after he had discarded it so passionately. Quickly blinking the water out of her eyes, she saw him sink to its knees. She lowered the sword, resting the flat of the blade in one open palm and the jeweled hilt in the other. The manner in which the knight had clasped his hands against the dragon emblazoned on chest reassured her she need not fear his anger. Perhaps he had lost his faith in the Crusades and she was doing his immortal soul a favor by returning to him the weapon with which he had fought for Christ in the Holy Land.

The deepening darkness offered her bare breasts some protective cover, but she could not prevent her naked body being gilded by the fading light as it gradually emerged from the water. She could not see his eyes, but the intense reverence with which he watched her approach him thrilled her as nothing else ever had. Her dream had come true – she had become an enchanted creature of the woods. The birds had stopped singing; water splashing gently around her ankles was the only sound in the world as all the spirits of the forest watched a naked young woman holding a sword walk out of the lake towards the knight waiting for her on his knees. Before her feet emerged from the water she paused, stretching her arms out towards him. He unclasped his hands, rising to accept the sword from her, and suddenly fear made her aware of the cold breeze caressing her skin. Standing vulnerably unclothed in front of an armed man, Lilly understood that an aura of supernatural peace was her only defense. Silently, she turned away from him and began walking as slowly as she had risen from it back into the lake. She did not know what she would do if he spoke to her, but he remained profoundly silent behind her as she dove back into the water's protective darkness. When she surfaced again night had fallen and the man and his sword were gone.

* * *

The flour was kneaded and the bread was baking; the hens had been fed and the eggs they had lain collected; the pigs were nudging each other noisily over their trough; her father and brothers were out in the field; mum was mending shirts, and Lilly was free for a while to do what she loved best – roam the woods in search of herbs, wild berries and roots. A whole moon had passed since she rose shamelessly naked from the lake to offer a nobleman his sword, yet not a day passed that she did not return to the place on the shore where he had knelt. There was a growing ache in her chest which felt strangely like holding her breath, but it was different in that it never went away and made her unusually restless. Her dream of meeting an enchanted prince of the forest had vanished like dew at sunrise as she waited for the real possibility of the mysterious knight emerging again from between the trees surrounding the lake, but every evening she was disappointed when only promising shadows populated the woods around the suspenseful stillness of the water.

The day was still young when, sitting on the grass plucking blueberries from a bush and tossing them into a cloth resting open on her lap, Lilly heard a rustling in the foliage made by something larger than a fox or any of the other woodland creatures she knew of. She had woven a garland of Bloody Cranes-bills to crown herself with before setting about the more mundane task of collecting berries for a pie, and she was glad of this small adornment when she looked up and saw her knight walking between the trees towards her. The dragon had flown from his chest and he was dressed more casually, but his clothing was still the finest she had ever seen. He could easily have killed her that night, yet for some reason she was more afraid of him now with sunlight streaming in sword-like shafts between the leaves and clearly illuminating all the lovely little Violets, Petty Whins and Creeping Lady's-tresses he was crushing beneath his black boots as he walked. She thought of abandoning the painstakingly picked fruits filling her lap and running away, but she could not seem to move, like a rabbit spotted by a hawk. He stopped a body's length away from her, and despite the fact that she could not even see the lake she felt breathless looking up at him.

'Are you real?' he asked quietly.

She licked her lips, tasting the deep timber of his voice as she struggled to get her tongue to stop playing dead in her mouth. If she did not answer him he would think her an ignorant peasant possessed by demons who had robbed her of speech... or perhaps he would continue to regard her as a magical creature who had risen naked from the bottom of the lake with his sword in her hands... but surely he could hear her human heart beating... 'Yes, my lord, I am real.'

He took three more steps, and crouched down before her. 'What is your name?'

'Lilly.'

'Why did you return my sword to me, Lilly?'

She glanced down at his hands where they rested on his knees. His fingers were slender, but they looked strong, and she had never seen such fine skin on a man. 'I do not know, my lord... it felt like the right thing to do.'

'I thought you were the Lady of the Lake,' he whispered as if afraid to speak the words out loud.

'I was… for you…'

'You have cast a spell on me, Lilly,' he confessed.

She said nothing, looking shyly down at her lap.

'Since that evening I have been able to think of nothing but you,' he went on quietly. 'Even my dreams are haunted by your beauty.'

'My lord,' she dared glance up into his eyes again, 'please forgive me, I meant no harm…'

'There is a way,' he reached over and lightly touched one of the flowers wilting against her reddish-gold hair, 'for you to free me from this spell.'

'I am yours to command, my lord.'

'I passed a small farm on my way here. Is that where you live?'

'Yes, my lord.'

'On the morrow I will send my man to tell your parents I have chosen to honor you with a position in my household.' He stood up. 'Bring nothing with you; I will provide all you need.'

She stared up at him, stunned. Whenever she imagined a prince of the Fairy taking her away with him it was always deeper into the woods they went. 'My lord, I will die if I leave the forest!' she exclaimed.

'You said you were real…' he murmured, doubt softening his determined expression for an instant that gave her the courage to defy him.

'I am, my lord, but I have no wish to leave here.'

'It is enough that *I* wish it.'

The tone of his voice made her forget all about the berries in her lap as she leapt to her feet, meaning to run away, but she too had thought of nothing but him since that evening at the lake, and she found herself unable to resist when he grabbed her by the wrist and pulled her beneath an oak tree.

She was not surprised by how swiftly and impatiently he stripped off her clothes; the coarse and dirt-stained material undoubtedly offended him. Once more she stood naked before him, only this time he pulled her roughly into his arms. The weapon he had sheathed in his leggings in no way resembled a sword or a dagger, nevertheless she discovered it had the power to hurt her and make her bleed when he shoved her back against the tree, lifted one of her legs up against him, and stabbed her with it. She cried out, digging her fingers into his shoulders, bracing herself against the intense pain caused by his thrusting hips. She was vividly aware of the soft material of his shirt beneath her hands, such a soothing contrast to the hot agony where he was forcing his manhood deeper and deeper into her body. When he suddenly clutched her other thigh, lifting her off the ground, she cried out again, but a mysterious note of elation rang in her protest.

'Ride me!' he commanded, and even though she had never been on a horse before she sensed what he wanted.

It was like sitting under water as she moved slowly back and forth, concentrating on ignoring the intense discomfort between her legs the way she did the pressure in her chest when she was holding her breath at the bottom of the lake. She had taught herself to sit weightless, and pretending his arms were strong currents holding her up – the kind of currents that had almost swept her away when she dared try and swim in the river after the spring rains – she managed to obey him well enough that he breathed her name, 'Oh, Lilly!' as though he was in church praying to a blessed saint. She did not question how something that hurt her so much could please him; she was content to be rewarded by the tender, almost worshipful note in his voice and by a wealth of contrasting sensations such as she had never dreamed of. Beneath his wondrously soft shirt his shoulders were tense and hard as tree roots, and unlike her father's his cheek was smooth, tender as a woman's. The thick limbs of the oak cast black shadows across their entwined bodies, and one of these bands of darkness masked his eyes so she could not tell what he was thinking, but it didn't matter as she caught a glimpse of a fine, almost pleasant sensation spinning a delicate web around his burning penetrations... a feeling as mysterious as a spider quivering in a shaft of sunlight. The forest was so silent around them that the whimpering sounds she could not stop herself from making excited her, as if another woodland creature had always been living secretly inside her. When he abruptly sank to his knees she moaned and clung to him, afraid he would drop her, but he spread her back across the grass and beat his body even more violently against hers.

'Spread your legs, Lilly, and do not fight me. The pain will be but a memory soon, trust me.'

'I am not fighting you, my lord!' she gasped even as she realized it was true – she was making the hole in her flesh painfully tighter by hugging his erection in a desperate effort to get him to slow his driving rhythm. She concentrated on the crisp sensation of blades of grass cutting gently into her palms as she clung to the ground on either side of her, biting her lip to keep from whimpering pitifully as she obeyed him and spread her legs open a little farther.

'Oh, Lilly!' he breathed again as if praying.

She suspected God was punishing her for all her pagan fantasies, but the fierce penance felt worthwhile hearing her name spoken with such passionate reverence. He was still fully dressed, and as she found herself wondering what his naked skin would feel like something happened deep inside her... a stubbornly budding pleasure was clinging tenaciously as a wildflower to the rock-hard length of his manhood digging into her... She focused on this dawning feeling and on the hot storm of his breathing in her ear making her feel hauntingly powerful despite her helplessness. Then at last he lay still against her.

Before she could be sure it was over, he was on his feet again looking down at her. 'You will become a member of my household,' he stated as he closed his leggings and sheathed the part of his body that had so dramatically devastated hers. 'Be ready when my man comes for you tomorrow.'

Blood gleaming darkly on the pale skin of her inner thighs, the mouth between her legs burning as though tasting a glimpse of what the fires of hell would feel like for sinners such as her, she said, 'Yes, my lord' her whisper nearly lost in a soothing rustle of leaves as she resigned herself to her fate whatever it might turn out to be.

She spent the rest of the afternoon swimming in the lake, basking in its pure, cold embrace long after the water forever washed away her virgin blood.

Sea Lion Soles

The Aleutian Islands,
the present & 1,000 years ago

t all started with the stone penis she couldn't date. Dana had tied her blonde hair back as usual, but the wind insisted on running passionate fingers through it from all directions and inevitably the Aleutian-style bun at the nape of her neck surrendered to the insistently fierce caress. Streaks of solid light slashed across her lips and eyes but her dirt-encrusted gloves forced her to ignore them. Any spirits haunting the excavation site would have been drawn to her hair as if to the ghost of the sun, which for days had remained buried behind funereal clouds massed on the horizon as waves filled with life crashed in growing frustration against the shore. She used the back of her hand in vain attempts to free her features from the luminous net of her wildly blowing hair, but it was only a subconscious gesture; all she was truly aware of was the incredible find rising out of the earth around her reverently caressing fingers. The rueful smile with which she first greeted the

Sea Lion Soles

emerging discovery had long since vanished beneath an expression of rapt concentration. It wasn't her neglected libido imagining that the smooth end of the stone object resembled the head of a man's penis. Months of celibacy were hard to bear but they did not have the power to conjure objects from thin air.

Her partner was working on the other side of the rocky outcropping; the discovery was all hers for the moment and she savored a curiously intimate thrill as she unearthed what resembled a centuries-old sex toy. Whether the stone phallus had been used as part of a native ceremony or whether it had been brought to the island by Japanese or Russian traders was impossible to tell. *Because you can't date a stone penis*, she thought, and by the end of the intensely uncomfortable but deeply gratifying day, Dana regarded the find as an apt symbol for her love life. She was blonde and beautiful, but there were no men to date her on this remote shore. The islands she loved so much were treeless, windswept, foggy and volcanic, yet the ocean's once boundless wealth had made them a very desirable place to live. She couldn't see all the riches hidden in the deep anymore than she could see where her love-life was going, but if people had been able to create a sensually rich culture in such a stressful environment, then there was a chance she too could find whatever it was she was looking for. The Aleutian culture had taught her that places and circumstances are never as barren as they might appear. Everything she cared about was here on these harsh coasts still rich in edible plants and animals, seaweeds, shellfish, birds, fish, sea otters, seals and whales. The interior of the islands were essentially useless to the Aleutians, much like landlocked Iowa was to her even though the university where she taught was theoretically much richer in datable men. She only spent eight weeks a year working on the islands, yet the rest of the time went by quickly in the pleasure of cataloging and writing about her discoveries while planning another season of digging.

That night Dana lay awake on her cot for a long time as the emotional stimulation of her discovery vied with her body's exhaustion. It wasn't easy sleeping in a place where the wind never stopped blowing. In the Aleutians the wind didn't howl like in Gothic novels around the gables of haunted houses; the sound was much rawer, much more forceful than the wailing of one trapped and lonely spirit. In her mind the wind seemed to blow across the islands as if from another dimension altogether, exposing humans to a pure and relentless, untamed power. The constant, sometimes gale-force winds made archeological work brutally difficult, especially when coupled with stinging rain and wet earth. To the untrained eye the coastline where her team was excavating that season appeared utterly hostile to the human body and all its subtle, sensual needs, but in reality its complexity offered up many of the most expensive delicacies served in gourmet restaurants thousands of miles farther south. Protected bays were rich in a variety of fish the Aleuts relied on during storms when hunting could not be done on the open sea; seals and sea lions were hauled up in rookeries on offshore islands; tasty sea urchins, succulent octopus and nourishing seaweeds were collected on reefs exposed by low tides; a variety of shellfish was abundant in tidal pools and lagoons which were also alive with ducks; fat salmon rose to spawn in lakes emptied by freshwater streams, and halibut could be found in deeper waters.

As Dana lay in the lee of the tent (as she liked to think of it) trying to catch sleep like an elusive deep-water fish slipping between the tireless fingers of her thoughts (which kept her awake the harder she struggled to drown her consciousness for the night) the wind dropped. In the sudden silence the darkness of the tent was so profound she might have been at the bottom of the sea. And she must have drifted off then because suddenly her eyes are open and her senses are being wonderfully assaulted by the colorful sight of meadows in bloom, by the lazy droning of bees, and by the invigorating sound of thousands of birds singing. It must be August in her dream because the temperature feels a balmy 65°. From her position at the base of the cliff where she found the stone penis yesterday far away in the future she can sea kayaks cutting through the water in front of a small village. Her archaeologist's eye distinguishes the houses buried beneath flowering grasses, and because the sun is actually shining she has to shield her eyes with her hand to look up at seagulls noisily circling a group of women on the beach busy cleaning fish and innocently tormenting the hungry birds with the smell of fresh entrails. The wind is blowing as always, but a dream wind is different… this wind is like a lover caressing her the way she has always longed to be caressed, so that her hair never gets in her eyes or in her mouth but instead blows behind her in a golden banner expressing freedom from all cares and concerns… the wind in her dream is the breath of a Goddess who really does exist inside her…

Two young women carrying baskets full of birds' eggs walk right by Dana without greeting her, which doesn't seem strange even though she knows one of them… or rather she *is* that girl because she suddenly finds herself protected from the vigorous wind by a garment bright with feathers, her feet comfortably snug in seal esophagus boots with sea lion slipper soles. There are many tasty eggs in her basket but they are not the source of the vibrant contentment enfolding her, or of the feelings spreading an exciting fissure in the smoothly rounded routine of her life. She is dreaming of outgrowing the comfortable warmth of her family's nest and setting off on her own with the young hunter whose penetrating stare seems to reach deeper inside her every time he casts it her way like his spear sinking into a doomed whale. There is a sweet poison in the sharp sensations that have stricken her deep in her belly because part of her is afraid, yet another part of her has no desire to resist the inevitable pull towards the safe and enduring harbor of a strong man's arms. Her grandmother – who seems to see everything even more clearly since her eyesight began failing – has already begun preparing a separate cubicle for her in their *barabara*. She both dreads and cannot wait for the night when she will first lie all alone in her cradle awaiting her suitor's first visit, after which she will know what it is like to be a vulnerably naked creature being speared by a powerful hunter in the life-filled wound between her thighs were she is most vulnerable. But even though she is almost painfully aware of his presence in the small summer village, his father has not yet approached her headman, and every day she is increasingly afraid that they are still hunting for another more suitable young woman. Yet, whenever she finds herself the object of his piercing glances, they make her feel weak in the knees as though she was not bound properly when she became a woman. In the forty days of her first endless confinement she wove a special charm belt of sinew and grass stems, and during the long, warm days of summer as she helps gather berries and eggs, salmon and roots, she fantasizes about offering him her belt to protect him from the dangers of hunting on the open sea... Her companion is laughing and saying something, her smooth cheeks polished to a rosy hue by the salty breeze. Her friend's words are as unintelligible as the cries of the seagulls and yet she says something in response even as she feels herself rising above the scene as if her soul is a bird confident of the invisible meaning and the bracing beauty of everything without needing to understand or define it...

Sea Lion Soles

'Hey, you alive in there, D?'

Words she unfortunately understood yanked her warm and colorful dream from around her, leaving her feeling stiff as a mummy with no desire to rise and face another dreary, rainy day. She managed to dig her voice up out of her throat to say, 'I'm only getting up if you've already made coffee!'

* * *

If the only female member of a small archaeological team suddenly starts talking about her dreams, especially right after she unearthed a stone penis, the results would be uncomfortable, to say the least, so Dana keeps to herself. She doesn't mention the fact that she is collecting colorful dreams like stones from the seashore she doesn't quite know what to do with except hoard them silently in her tent even as they begin weighing her down, because she doesn't have any place to keep them in her rational psyche. At first she treats the strikingly vivid images like the Disney cartoons of her anthropological subconscious, until the ratings begin to change, then she is forced to consider the annoying notion that in this case PG stands for Psychiatric Guidance needed as a result of too many days spent out in the wind and rain and no nights spent in a man's warm embrace. And the R rating doesn't mean Restricted, it stands for Realistic. The details in her dreams are so amazing that by the second week she ceases to care what is producing them; all she cares about is the drama unfolding inside her made hauntingly believable by the fact that she can't control or direct it as she does all her waking fantasies.

No one living in the 21st century, Dana muses as she cleans and catalogues her finds for the day inside the main tent, *can really grasp what it feels like to be surrounded by people bound to you in a web of relationships that make the borders of your flesh feel like a pleasure shared by everyone instead of an isolated burden.* She sits gazing up at the whalebone rafters of the *barabara* as her mother combs her jet-black hair and ties it into a knot as hard and yet as tender as the bud of her virginity growing deep between her legs. Everything she has come to own as a young woman – a stone lamp, a lamp stand, matting, three grass baskets, two dishes carved of driftwood, and several boxes containing all her sewing equipment – are now in her own private cubicle, where she will soon be receiving her strong young suitor. He arrives and the formal greeting ceremony feels interminable, but at last she finds herself alone in her private space gazing at a man's naked body by the light of her lamp. He is firm and sleek all over and his skin is a texture her fingertips revel in. His flesh is a wonderful change from slick salmon bodies, cold fish and greasy seals. Even though her cradle has been enlarged to make room for his body lying beside hers, it is still barely big enough to hold them both, but she doesn't mind lying pressed tightly up against him, and she giggles thinking they must resemble two plucked ducks in a basket to the god hanging above them. But then the way he looks at her makes her feel that naked together they are much more beautiful than any animal she has ever seen. His mouth is pierced on both ends, the labrets marking the border of exciting, unexplored territory as his tongue thrusts aggressively between her lips. He seems to be seeking some special delicacy deep in the cave formed by the hollow of her mouth and throat, and what an ardent hunter he is with different parts of his body makes her weak with gratitude that she was chosen to be his wife. He lies on his side caressing her, and she experiences a breathtaking sensation like the impatient spirits of all the strong babies who will be born to them warming up her womb as he suckles one of her nipples and then the other. She gasps in wonder at his hunger for her. This strong young hunter who already has two whales to his name seems utterly content with the soft feast of her breasts even though they offer him no milk. And the more he savors the stiff tips of her bosom like the most delicious berries, the more urgent her need becomes to give him everything she has no words for. One of his hands finds the gill-like folds between her thighs, and she whimpers in deepening discomfort as two of his fingers begin probing her insides. She feels there must be something wrong with her because surely the opening in her body is too tight and shallow to survive the thick length of his flesh spear. She is flattered that caressing her has honed his manhood to such a hard length, but she is a little afraid of her strange craving to feel him bury it deep in her belly. She knows her mother and grandmother and aunts and sisters have all been killed by a man in this mysterious way that doubles the power of a woman's life, yet his desire feels so painfully big as it enters her she has to close her eyes and bite her lip to keep from crying out. Pain, hot and strangely glorious, swells inside her like a rising tide as he beats his powerful body against the softer shore of her flesh. She prays to the little ivory figure hanging above her head to give her strength, and the god hears her because the pain slowly begins to ebb...

* * *

'Did you sleep okay, D?' Ted asks as they're having coffee together in the main tent.

'What?' She looks at him over the rim of her cup trying to focus on his scruffy beard and wire-rimmed glasses. She can't seem to stop seeing the young hunter's strong brown body, and the memory of his erect penis (bigger than the stone artifact she found) sinking slowly into her body is still embarrassingly vivid. Her pussy was hot and wet for him, but not with virginal blood. She was touching herself when she woke up on the verge of an orgasm which made the noise of the tent flapping in the wind an erotic echo of his heavy balls slapping against her and of the slick sound of his cock gutting her, opening her up, laying bare all her most base and primitive desires. She didn't need to speak his language or know his name, she didn't need to love him, hell she didn't even need to live in the same time and place to get off on the force of his thrusts...

'I asked you if you slept okay, Dana.'

'Oh, yeah, fine, thanks.'

'Your eyes are a little bright. The weather's been miserable. Do you think you're coming down with a fever?'

'No,' she replies firmly, downing the last of the vile tasting brew in her cup. 'Whoever invented powdered cream should be shot,' she adds in disgust, and glances around the tent searching for the basket of fresh eggs she collected the other day... the other night... in her dream... She sets her empty cup down, gets up off the camp stool trying not to feel self-conscious about the way her panties are sticking to her labia, and pulls on her windbreaker.

'You sure you're feeling okay?' Ted insists. 'Maybe you should take it easy today.'

'There's not enough time. We only have a few days left and I want to get as much done as possible, you know that.'

'Right, just don't make yourself sick over it.'

If feeling more sexually aroused than she ever has in her life is considered being sick then she has to admit it might just be the best thing for everyone's health. Yet it isn't totally sane of her to miss the intimate warmth of a *barabara's* cubicle... and the flickering flame of a lamp casting shadows over an ivory figurine hanging above a cradle causing its face to come alive with intense expressions all directed down at two lovers… at a man's perspiring back, shining beneath the naked flame, rising and falling powerful as a whale surfacing and diving into the warm, wet depths between the woman's legs… She misses the bright colors of berries, hard as her nipples between his fingertips, filling her grass basket. She misses the strangely deep pleasure of digging for roots that all remind her of the one she has the power to make grow between his strong thighs every night so she can savor it hungrily stirring up the life-filled stew of her sexual juices. She misses the feel of the bone needle in her hands penetrating lustrous animal skins and the colors of soft birds' feathers beneath her fingertips. She misses the cozy warmth of the *barabara's* main room and the bodies surrounding her a reassuring continuation of her own flesh and blood…

Rain baptizes her face when she steps out of the tent. She misses the life in her dreams as if it was real. Her work is fulfilling – the site is rich in valuable artifacts – but this time when she returns to Iowa she will be taking home more than what she can pack into crates.

Dana walks to the outcropping were she was digging yesterday and stands looking out to sea. The clouds are lifting. A determined shaft of sunlight sparkles on the water as a humpback whale surfaces for air. She holds her breath watching the massive glossy back rising from the deep and plunging back in again… like the memories surfacing from her subconscious depths in the form of dreams as vividly sensual and yet as out of reach as the whale's flowing dimension… Because of the dreams that have haunted her for weeks, she experiences the whale as the profound weight of time and space to her soul's subconscious currents rich with memories of other lives and loves suddenly surfacing from untapped depths in her mind.

She stands watching the whale until it swims back out to sea and leaves her feeling utterly alone on the pounding shore. But she isn't alone, it only feels that way for a chilling moment, until she looks deeper inside herself and somehow senses the countless souls surrounding her like the bodies of her relatives in the *barabara* all silently occupied in some vital task... her father making a lamp, her mother sewing feathers on a parka... and now the daughter of their humanity is digging up the tools they once used, hauntingly making her part of their life again. It doesn't matter that she can't see where the world is going, that she's sick at heart because much of the marine life still so abundant in her dreams is now in danger of becoming extinct, giving way to an arid world of powdered cream and chemically processed coffee beans desperately needed to artificially recapture the stimulation of salty air and open sea while hunting and gathering to fulfill all ones needs. The lovers in their grass-cushioned cradle still live inside her, she is their child born centuries later, not just in a different time but in a different place thousands of miles away, and yet she made her way back somehow. Her soul was like a whale speared by the spirits of Aleutian hunters the first time she read about the islands, and eventually she found her way to these shores where the last thing she expected was to be met by memories of a man she once desired – by dreams more intensely real and vibrantly alive than anything she had ever imagined her brain cells capable of.

Maybe the gene pool is deeper than scientists believe, she thinks. *Maybe we all have the power to reach deep inside ourselves and catch hold of memories and feelings in the form of dreams sustaining the part of us that believes everything isn't just coming to an ignoble end. Maybe earth is just one coastline on the brink of an infinitely rich universe we'll have the power to go hunting in one day and discover wonders to forever keep nourishing us, body and soul.*

Shiva and Parvati

Mahabalipuram, India 7th Century

*"The Sanskrit term 'kama' in a wide sense refers to
all the desires of a human being. It denotes love as well as lust.
Kama refers to sex, the means to get physical and mental
pleasure...In ancient India, many treatises were written
on kama describing the ways and means of deriving maximum
enjoyment from sex. The authors of these works were
Munis and Rishis...revered sages. They accepted that the correct
practice of kama made both men and women happy."*
Dr. Raj Brahmbhatt

F or almost as long as I can remember, I wanted to be like the women carved on the temples. I never knew my mother, for when she spread her legs – opening them wide like the doors of a sacred shrine to let the divine energy of my spirit into the world – part of her caught a glimpse of the blissful reality in which we are all conceived and her Kama was not strong enough to keep her rooted in Maya. As I grew older, I concluded that she must not have loved my father very much, for if she had she would have stayed with us. Yet even though it was not my mother who held me as I suckled at her breast, my family members seemed numerous as the gods and goddesses so I do not believe I missed her that much. I shared the warm engulfing tenderness of my first meals on earth with a distant cousin who could not have been closer. The first thing I clearly remember seeing is the smooth golden gleam of his naked skull rising beside mine where we hovered hungrily over the hills of two naked breasts. I was never lonely for Shiva was always with me. We did everything together; he struck out first on adventures, and I followed him afraid of being left alone. When he first straightened out his body and walked away from me, I was terrified of being left on all fours like a dumb animal while he asserted a divine power, ascending into the lofty realm of adult gods and goddesses who scooped him up in their arms and joyfully praised him. Then I, too, defiantly balanced myself on just two tiny naked feet, and suddenly instead of just the ground and the roots of my fingers I saw Shiva running happily towards me with his arms open wide, and from that moment on his embrace defined the horizon of our wondrously growing world.

Later in life I learned that Shiva's mother had also died in childbirth one moon before I was born. We both arrived in the world with the same fiery intensity that fatally burned the flesh of the women who offered their bodies as doorways for our spirits. I thought it was because from the beginning everyone recognized the bond between us that we were suckled together, but eventually I learned it was because there was only one woman of our caste whose breasts could give us the milk we needed. What I do know for certain is that I was never alone and that I was always happy. I could not seem to tell the difference between Shiva's tongue and mine as we stretched them out as far as we could to see what a ray of sunshine pouring into the nursery tasted like. The dark and thunderous monsoons were never frightening or dreary for there were always fascinating corners of our vast home to be explored filled with smiling servants who fed us sweets and seemed to savor the flavor of our forbidden adventures as much as we did. Shiva and I were not brother and sister yet we were treated as such and more often than not left alone to our own devices. I would have been happy to keep sucking my thumb, but he was already crawling so I had no choice but to empty my mouth and follow him. I thought it a singularly bad idea when he decided to let the hard, cruel mountains of teeth rise on the smooth horizon of his gums, but how proudly he showed them off made me so angry that I promptly grew a whole row of snow-covered peaks just to spite him. We were one soul, so I could not understand why our bodies were not completely the same. It did not seem important at first that he had curious flesh-colored fruit growing between his thighs, whereas the slit between my legs made me wonder if, while my body was being shaped, heaven had trembled with a passion that left a long crack in my flesh like the one that formed on the wall of my bedroom once when the earth shook. Shiva put one eye to this dark rift between my thighs and declared he could not see into my insides, which was disappointing for us both, but we soon forgot about it as there were so many other things to explore.

As usual we were together when we first visited the temple by the sea. Shiva loved the entrances guarded by the carved heads of lions and elephants, while I had eyes only for the miniature supple figures of people rising with their colorfully painted limbs entwined up into the profoundly blue sky. These men and women looked as happy together and as familiar with each other as Shiva and I, and suddenly I could not wait for the time when I would have a body like that – tall and slender and yet also full and curving where it was still disappointingly straight and flat. Shiva would simply have to grow taller to be even more handsome than the gods carved on the temple walls. It did not seem fair that my flesh would have to do so much more mysterious work than his before I could claim to be an embodiment of all the goddesses on earth, yet how much I loved him made any effort necessary to please him feel worthwhile. As he stood beside me gazing up at the dancing stone figures, I stole a glance at his profile. The distinct way his features carved themselves against whatever was behind him always somehow told me what he was feeling even before I looked into his eyes – dark liquid pools that managed to look deeper than the ocean at night and were filled with infinite glimmering thoughts like the star-filled sky.

'What do you suppose they are doing?' he asked me curiously.

'I do not know, but I have never seen any real adults having so much fun together.'

'When we are grown-up, we shall be like them,' he said firmly.

'I hope so!'

* * *

I did not taste the bitterness of loneliness until I was nine-years-old. One moon before Shiva went away, our family made a pilgrimage to Pakshi-tirtha* and the summit of Mount Veda-giri to watch the two Eagles take the *prasadam* of lord Shiva from the hand of a priest. I could not eat, for it was as if I had swallowed a black stone that sat in the middle of my chest where my heart charka used to be. I could still feel it beating, but surely its steady pulse would flounder like a cripple with one leg and come hopelessly to a stop when the boy who was the other half of my life went away. Only how impossible his absence was to imagine protected me from a bottomless despair as we made our way up the steep mountain slope hand-in-hand, the only two people in the world who realized it was coming to an end.

'I will come back for you,' he promised me when we found out he was being sent away to further his education. 'We will not be alone forever.'

'But we have never been apart, not even for one single day, much less for years!' I exclaimed, wondering at how good my miserable tears tasted as they flowed down my cheeks into my mouth.

Yet for a few moments I managed to forget the crushing loneliness looming like a chasm before me as together we gazed down at the city and the temple by the sea. We were still together looking down from the heaven of our perfect oneness on the world where we loved to play.

'I do not think I can live without you, Shiva,' I confessed so quietly only he could possibly have heard me.

'You must!' He spoke almost angrily. 'Like the temple, your body must be here when I return so I can bring your spirit proof of my eternal devotion.'

Gazing down at the tiny figures moving about in the city and on the temple walkways, and further out still at the miniature ships docked in the harbor, I felt like a goddess who had swallowed a monsoon trapped in her throat making it impossible to put into words the terrifying tempest of emotions raging inside me. Only in my mind was I screaming, 'But what if you never return? What if we never see each other again? How can I survive endlessly long days and nights without the light and comfort of your company? How long will you be gone? How many years must my heart run from the pain in my soul that can only be assuaged by looking into your eyes and feeling your hand in mine?'

'Look, it is time!' he declared, and the excitement in his voice effortlessly turned my body around to face the summit of the mountain where the Brahmin priest sat in his humble robes with one arm outstretched and his palm open to the sky, where two eagles soared side by side. A hush fell over the crowd, and the silence was so deep the flapping of the eagles' wings was louder than my own pulse in my ear as I heard Shiva whisper, 'That is you and I, Parvati, together forever!' and I said nothing so as not to betray my shameful lack of faith in the power of our love. The birds plunged as one to pluck the bread from the monk's hand, and I felt the danger of their sharp beaks through the pain in my heart, followed by the mysterious hope and joy of witnessing the divine principle incarnate on earth as Shiva squeezed my hand so hard it hurt.

* * *

My father – who was more of a stranger to me than the smiling statues of Bodhisattvas – suddenly took an interest in me five years after Shiva and I were separated. I did not dare be angry at the gods and goddesses, for they were my only hope of ever seeing him again, but that did not prevent me from being disgusted with people, none of whom were as beautiful and daring and wise and wonderful as my Shiva. More than once I saw a servant make the sign of the evil eye when I walked by; their caste seemed more aware than mine of the hole in my soul through which demons could pour into the world unchecked since the boy who was my brother and so much more went away. And perhaps because I felt so empty inside my body strove to comfort me by outwardly shaping itself in ways it knew would please me. More and more my breasts and hips, my slender arms and legs, and my long black hair resembled the figures of the goddesses carved into the temple Shiva and I had stood gazing upon what seemed so long ago.

When my father called me into his presence, I felt no more than an idle curiosity as to what this old yet still handsome stranger wanted from me.

'You have grown very beautiful, my daughter,' he said by way of greeting.

'It brings me great happiness that I please you, father,' I lied, gazing impassively over one of his crimson shoulders.

'Your teachers are pleased with your skill in letters, for which I am very proud of you, but you are a woman now, Parvati. It is time for you to learn the thousand names of Shakti and to listen to your body as it begins teaching you the meaning of words.'**

Despite the profound indifference Shiva's absence had filled me with for everything except the hope of his return, I could not help but be intrigued. 'You mean like the goddesses on the temple walls?' I asked with an eagerness I saw no reason to conceal.

'Yes, just so,' he replied, a smile softening his firm mouth even as his eyes remained inscrutably dark.

* * *

Concentrating on my studies had given me the excuse I need-ed to avoid my family as much as possible, but the lessons my father would now have me take could not be learned alone with an old man. Hence I found myself attending my first birthing, held in a large room open to an inner garden crawling with women, their colorful Saris and long black hair making me think contemptuous-ly of fruit covered with flies buzzing meaningless conversations. I held myself apart in a corner, as far away from the pregnant woman as I could get, but as she was the center of attention it was hard to prevent my eyes from straying in her direction. She in turn was intently watching the three women dancing around her, their naked bellies undulating in a way I could not help but find fascinating. They had discarded their Saris and were wearing only a tight shirt that ended just below their breasts, and they had tied their skirts as far down their hips as possible. I glanced down at my own saffron-colored Sari wondering if I could learn to make my belly ripple like water. The woman whose body was on that day serving as a bridge between the worlds was squatting over the birthing cloth. Her belly was grotesquely distended, yet she seemed to be finding some comfort watching the slender, undulating dancers.

'They are urging her to relax her innermost muscles and make it easier for the baby to slide out of her,' a languid voice explained. 'By reflecting the waves of her contractions they are magically encouraging the child to leave the sea of eternity and swim safely into life between the harbors of his mother's thighs.'

I turned my head and found myself looking into eyes the color of a peacock's proud feathers.

'My name is Saraswati,' the woman said, smiling.

'Parvati,' I replied shortly.

Her laughter was soft and deep. 'Yes, Parvati, inseparable from Shiva. You must miss him terribly.'

Her words and the quality of her expression intrigued me. A woman had never looked at me that way before; in a way that made me wonder what she was thinking.

'Is this your first birthing, Parvati?' She was standing so close to me that her shoulder brushed mine when she turned her body to watch the glistening crack between the pregnant woman's thighs as it suddenly began expanding. I, too, watched in rapt horror as the mysterious mouth opened wider and wider around a dark little skull. So must Shiva's head have appeared as he struggled to free himself from his mother's confining embrace, and surely this woman would also die for I did not see how she could possibly survive the selfish way the baby she desired so much was rending her open. Suddenly, I felt Saraswati slip her fingers between mine and grasp my hand as no one but Shiva ever had. 'Do not be distressed.' She spoke gently. 'The gods are being kind today.'

I gasped when the baby suddenly slid out of his mother swift as a Cobra's tongue flicking a dark and gleaming red. The dancers made way for three older women, one of whom was holding a knife with which she cut the cord still connecting the newborn soul to the divine even as another woman held the baby upside down by the ankles and slapped its slimy little bottom three times. 'It is a boy!' she announced, and I did not blame him for letting out an indignant scream.

'Come and share some refreshments with me, Parvati.' Saraswati led me away.

* * *

It was Saraswati who taught me that I would not be betraying my love for Shiva by opening my heart to other friendships even if they could not compare to the bond I shared with him.

'When he returns, do you wish him to find a dull and sullen child or a beautiful young woman skilled in the arts of pleasing the man he will be?'

I had to admit this was one of the most relevant questions anyone had ever asked me. Her astute wisdom gained my confidence, and because I was not yet fully a woman I was not jealous of her beauty. I was still a girl and saw in her the promise of all I could become. I did not question what she saw in me; Shiva loved me therefore I felt worthy of everyone's attention. My father seemed to approve of my budding friendship with Saraswati for I was allowed to visit her home regularly. I never saw her husband, nor did I meet any of her female relatives or friends during my afternoon visits, during which only servants came and went as silently as ghosts across colorful rugs. She always received me in a courtyard planted with trees so heavy with fruit that the drumming of ripe mangos hitting the ground was occasionally added to the delicate music of stone fountains and the singing of caged birds. The delicate sound my hostess' jewelry made whenever she moved was also soothingly musical to my ears, as was the throaty laughter that had impressed me on our first meeting. I did not once see her wear the same necklace – wide collars set with precious and semi-precious stones in the shape of flowering vines with a different pendant hanging from each one into her cleavage – and each magnificent creation was always accompanied by long matching earrings. When I awoke in the morning, the sinking feeling in the pit of my stomach when I remembered that I would not be seeing Shiva for another long day was acute as ever, but I also had a morsel of comfort to savor in the knowledge that I would once again be spending the afternoon in Saraswati's relaxing yet also pleasantly demanding company. One day she declared she was going to teach me to dance the way the women had at the birthing, and we both discarded our Saris so she could demonstrate what she wanted me to do before helping me emulate the undulating motions of her torso by stroking me with her ringed fingers. My body responded naturally to her hand caressing my belly while her other soft yet firm palm pressed down on my spine, urging it to curve inwards and making me intensely conscious of the part of my body she was touching.

'Keep your arms raised gracefully over your head. I will tell you what to do with them later. Now shake your hips, swiftly.'

I did as she said, and a strange new sensation awoke between my legs that made me feel flushed and more breathless than the physical exercise demanded.

'Mm, very good,' she murmured, grasping my hips firmly with both hands and pressing her naked belly and the tops of her thighs hard against mine. 'Now do that again.'

Once more I obeyed her, and experienced again that strangely luminous flash of sensation almost like a tongue moving deep inside the forever enigmatically silent mouth between my legs. I felt as though my body was trying to tell me something, speaking without words as my father had described.

'Let us dance together, Parvati.' She raised her arms gracefully over her head, reflecting my posture like an image in a pool. 'Shake your hips again and do not stop until I tell you to.'

For a moment I forgot to obey her, distracted by the feel of her full breasts grazing my smaller bosom, and the contact intensified the silent yet urgent message rising up through my body from between my thighs. Her eyes were very close to mine and shining a proud challenge like the peacock's tail they had first reminded me of. I glanced down at her mouth and it looked softer and more welcoming than any bed I had ever rested on.

'Yes, Parvati, press your hips forward and keep shaking them against mine.'

'I am growing tired,' I protested reluctantly.

'Is that all you feel?' she whispered.

'No,' I confessed just as softly.

'Tell me what you are feeling.'

'I do not know… I think I have truly found one of my chakras… it is as though a fire has been kindled deep inside me and is growing steadily stronger, sucking my breath down as fuel and making me feel strangely hot and weak… and yet also as beautiful and excited as flames leaping…'

'Oh Parvati!' She grasped my face and kissed me, thrusting her tongue between my lips and forcing mine to dance with it. I lowered my arms, intending to push her away, but my hands were more honest than my thoughts as they surrendered to a curiosity I had not dared to admit by hungrily caressing her long, sleek hair while moving down to her bosom. We clutched each other's breasts through our blouses, and the sensation in my belly became sharp as a divine knife stabbing me.

'I have told the servants we are not to be disturbed, Parvati. Do you truly wish to please Shiva on your wedding night?'

Her certainty that he would return made me feel both intensely grateful and vulnerable; more afraid than I ever had been of the possibility that even though I thought of him every day he had already forgotten me. 'Why are you so sure he will come for me?' I asked.

She took my hand and led me over to a bed of cushions coolly shadowed by flowering trees. 'I am going to teach you to see yourself as others do, Parvati, for you do not realize yet how beautiful you are and will be.' She removed her blouse, exposing her breasts, and I thought no goddess could possibly possess as perfect and delectable a bosom. I watched, uncertain yet entranced, as she untied her skirt and let it fall to her jeweled ankles. She spread herself gracefully back across the crimson cushions. 'To truly please a man, you must love your body.' She smiled up at me.

I stood looking down at her feeling as though I was gazing into a magical pool showing me my future reflection – the voluptuous, confident, sensual woman alive inside the tight seed of my girl's flesh.

She cupped her breasts with both hands, making me even more conscious of their heavy fullness as she pushed them up and together, her thumbs caressing her large, soft nipples which quickly hardened, becoming deliciously prominent. Then she spread her legs, enticing me to gaze upon the mysterious cleft in her flesh which I also possessed, but could never see as clearly as I studied hers then. *This is how Shiva will see me*, I thought, and giggled remembering how he had once innocently put his eye to that darkly listening hole between my thighs.

Saraswati's smile deepened. 'Does our beauty please you?' she asked.

'Yes,' I replied sincerely. 'You are more beautiful even than the goddesses carved on the temple walls!'

'*We* are more beautiful, Parvati. Remove your clothes and come lie with me. I will teach you how to caress yourself. If you cannot bring pleasure to your own body no man will be able to fulfill you, and if he senses he is not pleasing you a real man will never be completely satisfied himself.'

The mere thought of being responsible for Shiva's unhappiness in any form prompted me to strip off my clothes without wondering what anyone else might think, for no one but Shiva truly mattered, and Saraswati was special because she knew and understood this. I had not been naked with anyone since Shiva and I were very young, so perhaps that was why I giggled again like a little girl as I spread myself down beside her. She took me in her arms, holding my naked body tightly against hers. My small breasts rested so comfortably against her engulfing bosom I wondered why my nipples tensed as if in protest. Then that breathless feeling I had become aware of when we were dancing together overwhelmed me as she wrapped one of her long legs around mine, pressing her tender belly even harder against me.

'Oh, Saraswati, my chakras are spinning!' I whispered, clinging to her and to the sensation smoldering in my womb as though the gods had kindled their divine fire there and intended to use my limbs as fuel. When she released me and rolled onto her back, I did the same, embarrassed by my outburst.

'Watch me, Parvati.' She, too, sounded breathless.

I sat up, my eyes drawn to the way her wrist and hand were working between her open thighs. She was fingering her sex as though she had hidden a very special jewel within its complex silky folds and was trying to find it. I watched two of her ringed fingers slide into her hole, and I caught my breath when her hand clutched the dusky bloom of her vulva with such force that her back arched. 'My fingers cannot reach as deep as a man's penis, which is thicker and longer and harder.' She withdrew her fingers – shining with her inner juices as if she had just plunged them into a succulent fruit – and reaching up grasped my right hand. 'Place your fingertips here… yes, there… Do you feel it, Parvati, the tiny gem, the priceless treasure, all women are born with?'

'I am not sure, but there does some seem to be something firm cushioned in your softness…'

'Rub it… rub it for me, Parvati…'

I caressed the summit of her mound tentatively, until she grasped my wrist and made my fingertips move more swiftly and firmly against her.

'Yes… now let us caress ourselves together.'

I fell willingly onto my back beside her again, but even though I seemed to sense the area where my fleshly gem was hidden, I could not find it, until Saraswati suddenly spread my legs, crouched between them, flicked the tip of her long, pointed tongue just beneath my fingertips, and there it was – a fiery jewel sending luminous facets of sensation flashing through my body. I looked down the length of my body and saw her vivid blue eyes gazing back at me. I imagined it was Shiva's tongue licking me like that… Shiva's eyes looking so intently into mine as he buried the rest of his handsome features hungrily between my thighs… A terrible joy full of glorious certainty that I would see him again made me cry out so loudly I was afraid servants would come running to see what was wrong.

Saraswati taught me to love my body, and then she made sure I would suffer no pain on my wedding night by taking my virginity with a penis carved from ivory. Had she not gagged me I would most certainly have screamed when she thrust the god-like erection up into my body. Tears blinded me as the painfully thick tusk rammed me; stabbing me over and over again with such force it lifted my hips off the cushions. I thought the agony would kill me as I felt my hot blood flowing around it and was very glad Shiva was not there to watch me sobbing and writhing in misery.

Afterwards, my beautiful teacher allowed me to revenge myself on her, and as I pushed the ivory cock deep into her belly, relishing the way her rosy sex gaped wantonly open around it, I suffered an irresistible urge to reach over with my other hand and clutch her throat. The chakra between my legs became the burning center of the universe as I watched her breasts quivering from the impact of my clenched fist banging her as I clutched the end of the brutally hard shaft, and how delicate her neck was in my other hand made me feel uncontrollably fierce. I expected her to clutch my wrists to stop me from hurting her, but she kept her arms flung open submissively as I violently penetrated and strangled her until her body went tense, her hips and back rising rigidly off the bed as if levitating. Only then did I let go of the ivory penis, leaving it lodged between her thighs as I unwrapped my talon-like fingers from around her throat. I collapsed beside her, for a darkly gratifying moment imagining I had killed her, but of course I was glad when she turned her head and smiled at me languidly.

* * *

On a bright cold day in winter – the time of year when the sun is passionately in love with all colors and forgets to be cruel – nine peacocks arrived, three resplendent males and six modest pea hens to keep them happy.

'They are a gift for the Lady Parvati,' the man who delivered them said proudly.

'It appears you have a suitor,' my father remarked.

'Who has honored me with such a splendid gift?' I asked indifferently, for I was sure I knew.

'My lady, I was commanded not to tell you.'

I thanked and dismissed him. Saraswati had sent me the birds. I had only to look at the males strutting across the courtyard to see her deep-blue irises and the black holes of her pupils, and for a disturbing moment I seemed to glimpse the eyes of a goddess challenging me from behind the mask of exotic plumage.

The following day a loud commotion in the entrance courtyard lured me from my room. It was not my imagination; I had indeed heard the trumpeting of an elephant annoyed by all the people milling around it, servants and family members calling happy greetings to the rider perched on the sedan chair – a young man resplendent in white and silver. Everyone was clamoring for his attention, yet the moment I stepped out of the shadows his head turned my way as though he sensed my presence. Our eyes met, and it seemed impossible to find myself awake and standing in the sunlight, for I was dreaming… Shiva was smiling down at me and it was as if he had gone away only yesterday and everything that had happened since then was the dream immediately forgotten in the reality of our love. Years had passed, our bodies had changed, but I was still, and always would be, the girl who had wept with her arms around his neck when he left and who wept again now, this time with relief that the ordeal of our separation was finally ended as he quickly dismounted and took me in his arms.

'Oh, Shiva, Shiva, you have come back! You are truly here!'

'I promised you I would return,' he said almost sternly, holding me at arm's-length to look into my eyes. 'Did you ever doubt me, Parvati?'

'No, of course I never doubted you, Shiva, but I *did* doubt the world and all the Maya that might keep you from me.'

'Then I must teach you to have more faith in the power of our love, Parvati.'

* * *

My father accepted Shiva's proposal as though he had always expected us to marry, and for the first time it occurred to me that the brother of my heart had been sent away for a reason, and not just to torment me. Because I was happy I had the energy to realize there was much I had yet to learn, but instead of frightening and annoying me, the prospect was exciting because once again Shiva and I would be exploring and growing together.

Saraswati was an honored guest at our wedding. I was afraid Shiva would be angry when I told him I had not saved my virginity for him. We had been together for a full moon before I was able to confess this secret to him, anxiously explaining the reasons why I had given a woman what rightfully belonged to him. He listened to me in silence, his eyes reflecting the moonlight in their bottomless black pools where we sat in a garden at night even though it was cold because we could be alone there. 'I wanted to please you on our wedding night, Shiva,' I whispered desperately, wishing he would look at me and say something even if his words were angry, for anything was better than the silent concentration he was directing away from me.

'I believe you did it to please me, Parvati,' he spoke finally, 'and you are so beautiful I cannot be angry with you for wanting to explore your body.'

223

'But it would have meant nothing to me if I had not been imagining it was you looking at me; if I had not been thinking about you caressing me as she did, and as I did her. It was as if in those moments I became you and was no longer alone, but instead I was one with the pleasure I knew you would take in my woman's body, so different from the body of the girl you left, when we were at last together again.'

Abruptly, he grasped my hand and rested it on the firm swelling between his legs. 'I am not angry with you, Parvati. How can I be angry when I am becoming aroused imagining you kissing and caressing another woman? Saraswati shall visit us when we are married, and you can show me then all the things you did with her while you dreamed of me.'

'Would that please you, my beloved?' I asked fervently, desiring his smile more than I did eternal salvation.

'Yes,' he caressed my cheek and kissed my lips, 'it would please me very much, my Parvati.'

* * *

Nine moons after our wedding, Shiva and I traveled back to our infancy, defeating time and completely forgetting what loneliness tasted like as once again we suckled together at a woman's breasts, one of Saraswati's nipples in his mouth and the other in mine, only this time it was the divine milk of pure pleasure we were hungrily seeking together.

*Pakshi-tirtha in Tirukkalukundram is famous and considered a holy place for several reasons, the foremost of which is that every day for the past 5,000 years or more two eagles have come to the summit of the mountain called Veda-giri to take the prasadam of Lord Siva from the hand of a Brahmin. These two birds have been coming daily for thousands of years and hundreds of pilgrims have gathered at the summit of Veda-giri to witness the event. To verify the antiquity of the daily arrival of these two eagles there is a stone pillar in the temple courtyard which bears a carving of the two birds. As of 1998, however, the two eagles have not visited Veda-giri to take prasadam. This event that occurred for thousands of years and was witnessed by millions of people has mysteriously come to an end.

**The Sanskrit word "shakti" means "power", but it can also be used as "the meaning of words".

Theron and Rhodopis

Athens, Greece 5th Century B.C.

*'The wife for our house and honor, the
Hetaera for our solace and delight.'*
Demosthenes

R hodopis was nine-years-old when she first saw a man's fully
erect penis.

Rhodopis was named after the famous Greek slave girl who married a Pharaoh and became his queen.* The odds – the gods – were
seriously against her namesake ever having one of her slippers stolen
by a falcon and dropped in a king's lap. This one particular little Ionian
orphan was still too young to take part in philosophical arguments
concerning Fate vs. chance, and even though she was forced to obey
the laws of the mortal gods who ran the household where she grew up,
she was never in awe of them, or of their authority over her, not even
when she was still so small she had to crane her neck to look up at
them. All adults are as tall as Olympians to a small child, a fact her
developing rational faculties latched onto as profoundly significant

since she liked the way it made her feel.

Rhodopis was in her first day of a new class and so far it was making her favorite course on the use and preparation of herbs and other plants seem dull by comparison. She had seen many scantily clad and even naked men and women before – the Atrium of the school in which she lived was proud with statues – but they were made of marble not flesh-and-blood, and they certainly never interacted in such a breathtakingly violent way that was also as controlled and choreographed as a sacred dance. Some of her classmates were giggling helplessly, although their wide eyes looked more shocked than amused, Rhodopis was quick to note. As for herself, she remained respectfully silent, her hands clasped in the lap of her tunic. She was old enough to understand she was witnessing the mysterious heart of her future profession. A young man and woman occupied the center of the room. At the beginning of the presentation they seemed as casually familiar with each other as brother and sister, yet by the end of the class they struck Rhodopis as the most the passionate of adversaries relentlessly seeking out each other's weaknesses to the violent glory of them both. Somehow each one emerged victorious from the sensual struggle, and Rhodopis felt they should have been awarded a crown of laurels as they stepped down off the couch placed in the center of the room to serve as a stage for life's most important drama. This was the sort of play respectable Greek women were not allowed to witness, much less study in detail, but Rhodopis was an Ionian in the care of Athen's infamous Hetaeras.

The young man's bare chest was glistening with perspiration and rising and falling in a way that made it difficult for Rhodopis to catch her own breath. She was disappointed when he slipped his modest *chiton* back on and concealed his manhood, which was much larger than any she had ever seen carved in stone. His lovely partner's sexual organs were less overt, yet they were a strangely complex personal revelation Rhodopis took serious note of. The woman hired to demonstrate the erotic arts was herself, naturally, a Hetaera. The young man, also not surprisingly, was an unpaid volunteer. Rhodopis thought she recognized his face; he looked like one of the slaves who tended the villa's lavish gardens, hard won from the dry Attic soil (and who were also rumored to tend to the still healthy erotic appetites of the old Hetaera who had founded the school.) When he removed his *chiton* at the beginning of class her first wild thought was that his erect male organ resembled a very large mushroom with an abnormally long stem and a cylindrical head rising from it. It looked much firmer than a mushroom, however, and Rhodopis knew the Hetaera kneeling at his feet was not eating it as she did bread and cheese even though she *was* licking it, and then slipping it hungrily into her mouth in a way that made it appear much more delectable than any of the food Rhodopis had ever been served. During this part of the demonstration many of her fellow students had to be commanded to keep their eyes open, their shocked and even revolted gasps impatiently silenced by the instructor.

'There is nothing frightening or distasteful about the art of fellatio,' she said sternly, 'it is, in fact, a Hetaera's most important skill. If you fail to excel in this supreme erotic act you will have only shriveled old men for company!'

This dire prophecy had the desired effect, and the wet sucking sounds made by the experienced Hetaera showing off her skills sounded even more significantly loud in the strained silence. She had not paused in her dedicated performance when the instructor chastised her audience, and the man smiling down at her bobbing

Theron and Rhodopis

head seemed unaware of anything else. Rhodopis made note of the fact that fellatio appeared to be a very good way of getting a man's full and undivided attention, but since it was impossible to speak with her mouth full, she would have to come up with other, creative ways of expressing what she wanted. After a while the Hetaera moved her hands from his thighs and began playing his erection like a flute, except the only sounds she produced were deep groans that escaped his lips as his eyes closed. His own fingers responded to her subtle skills by roughly threading themselves through her fiery red hair. *No doubt the result of regular applications of red powder,* Rhodopis thought, biting her lip as she watched the Hetaera cup the man's scrotum in one hand, as reverently as she probably did the drachmae-filled silk pouches awarded her by satisfied male friends. Her head and mouth and hands all worked in rhythm as her partner's tall body swayed slightly in response to the silent music she was making with his flesh.

As a general rule Rhodopis did not get on with her classmates and kept mostly to herself, but she too was aghast when the man suddenly gripped the Hetaera's head and pushed his rampant column of flesh all the way into her mouth, shoving it determinedly down into her white throat. Yet unlike most of the young girls in the room, Rhodopis did not suddenly find herself dreading the profession into which she had been dedicated when she was still too young to remember. For her the brutally refined demonstration posed a fascinating challenge. She did not merely see a man's penis violently invading a woman's defenseless mouth – she saw a woman in complete control of her body mysteriously defeating the force seeking to conquer her by absorbing and accepting it, and in the end winning something intangible and yet also very real for herself. At first what she got for her efforts appeared even worse as the man pulled her to her feet, unwound her *chiton*, and urged her back across the couch so he could spread himself on top of her and stab his fleshly weapon into her yielding body over and over again. Rhodopis thought he must surely be hurting her, yet the gratified little smile on the Hetaera's face, not to mention the very willing way she spread her legs, seemed to say otherwise.

* * *

Rhodopis made one good friend named Athenia. She was still a virgin, of course – the chastity of every girl at the school was guarded like the treasure it was to those who would profit from its sale. On the surface virginity was all Athenia seemed to have in common with her namesake, but Rhodopis could sense, and was drawn to, a willpower sharper than the goddess' spear. Athenia was single-mindedly vain, but that was a virtue in a future Hetaera. The girls were rarely allowed out of the school – except for visits to different temples on festival days lined up in a pretty procession as they made offerings of fruit and flowers to the god or goddess – but they were aware of the fact that respectable young women their age led very different lives. Free-born girls were brought up to be wives and to bear children, not to entertain men and converse with them as their intellectual equals, the only reason Rhodopis and Athenia were receiving such a thorough education. They were also not allowed on the other side of the plethora of land where many of the school's former students now lived and worked, each afforded the luxury of her own private rooms where she received one or more men almost every night. Nevertheless, Rhodopis and Athenia sometimes dared to break the rules. Late at night they snuck out of the school and spied on the festivities in the adjoining villa that always began after sunset. Athenia seemed to feel nothing but a rapt admiration for the women with their painted faces, elaborately dressed hair and embroidered tunics. Rhodopis, on the other hand, wondered what they were really thinking behind their bright red smiles and kohl-blackened eyes as they caressed and conversed with handsome young athletes, dignified statesmen, old philosophers and dark foreign princes... the list went on, for a Hetaera's sensual and mentally stimulating company was sought by all men, even those who preferred boys. They could distinguish the more popular Hetaeras from the number of bracelets clinging to their soft arms and shining enviably in the lamplight.

'Oh, look at that one's *pharos*!' Athenia whispered. 'I have never seen one so beautiful! It has little silver stars embroidered on it!'

'It *is* lovely,' Rhodopis agreed, even as she wondered how many weights the Hetaera in question had put into the hem of her *chiton* so that it draped like mist over her naked breasts and made her rouged nipples clearly visible through the fine weave.

'That will be us one day!'

Rhodopis was silent. *If we are not married off to a rich Libyan,* she thought, *or kidnapped by Carthaginian traders eager to feed their masters' hunger for fair-skinned slaves.* Only the most beautiful of the school's educated Hetaera were offered up for marriage for one-hundred or more *minae* of silver, and perhaps that was why Rhodopis excelled in Literature and Philosophy but applied herself to the art of personal grooming only halfheartedly – because the thought of leaving Greece and ending up in a barbaric part of the world terrified her. Athenia seemed blithely unaware of any dangerous possibilities and spent endless amounts of time practicing the cosmetic arts on her smiling face, as well as on her friend's more serious countenance. When she shaded her upper lid with a reddish-brown color, then applied a jade-green tone to the lower edge of her bone above it, her grey irises made Rhodopis think of full moons reflected in the small polished bronze mirror, one of the few items they possessed along with their *chitons* and leather sandals. As they grew older, Athenia even seemed to enjoy the excruciating process of depilating the delicate flesh around her sex. Rhodopis couldn't help staring at her where she sat with her legs spread open. This part of a woman's body made her think of a soft, spiraling little seashell echoing all the mysteries of the deep.

They were instructed on all the different ointments, pomades and oils they could rub all over their bodies. Rhodopis hated applying a meal pack to her face at night and was very glad to wash it off in the morning with milk. They were taught how to make cosmetics out of goose fat and butter, how to properly clean their teeth, and how to scrub their skin with a *strigil* after bathing. Athenia's hair was a lifeless brown, and as soon as she was permitted she mixed a special ointment of yellow flowers. She massaged it into her damp air, and then sat out in the sun while her curls dried a deep golden color. Rhodopis writhed restlessly on a stool as her friend tried to teach her the art of creating the perfect ringlet. She bound Rhodopis' long, natural reddish-brown hair with ribbons, or combed it back and looped it over of a filet after smoothing it to a lustrous sheen with a variety of oils she loved the smell of. Rhodopis had seen kitchen slaves picking bunches of mint, marjoram and thyme for the cook to put in her stews, but future Hetaeras were taught how to make essences from these herbs to use as scents to provide some variety from the indispensable vial of perfume distilled from violets.

Theron and Rhodopis

* * *

A tension Rhodopis had lived with for so many years she believed the constant stiffness in her neck and shoulders a natural part of her was massaged away by circumstances when one of the school's working Hetaeras became wealthy enough to set up her own household and Rhodopis was elected to take her place. Not, however, until her virginity had been sold for a flattering sum applied to the cost of her upbringing and education. The man who ruptured her hymen was a renowned physician. He could have been a Cyclops for all she cared; all that mattered was that she would be remaining in Greece for the rest of her life free of the fear of being married off to a rich barbarian.

The first man to explore the delights of her soft young body had once helped nurse Pericles through a severe fever brought on by prawns that had apparently sat too long in the sun. Feeling benevolent towards him simply because he was a civilized Greek, Rhodopis hid her amusement at his claim to fame. She had been warned to expect pain the first time she lay with a man, and indeed, the experience *was* rather torturous, mainly because the illustrious doctor had a difficult time getting his modest member hard enough to penetrate her. She called upon all the dissembling arts she had been taught to make him believe the frustrated pounding of his bony hips between her tender thighs was the most exciting thing she had ever experienced. She did not need to feign her relief, however, when his meager battering ram at last succeeded in breaking down the wall separating her childhood from the rest of her life. In her mind they were like two adjoining City States; there would always be mental and emotional commerce between them since she was, after all, still the same person she had been before the good doctor forced her to bleed around his dull little scalpel.

guilty pleasures

The following morning, Rhodopis moved into her new rooms. She tried not to think of Athenia as she examined the meager furnishings she had inherited from the departing Hetaera. She would have to supplement them with purchases of her own once she could afford them. Athenia... who had so long dreamed of the day when she and Rhodopis could embark together on the road to fame and fortune as the city's most beautiful and sought-after Hetaeras... if the gods, to whom all mortals belonged, did not claim one of their lives first. Whether the divine Athena was displeased about sharing her name with a girl dedicated to Aphrodite, or whether jealous Hera had seen a future problem in the beautiful, strong-willed young woman, the results were bleakly the same for Rhodopis. Two years ago she had lost her only friend to an outbreak of plague brought by a ship from Carthage. She was not even allowed to care for Athenia, or to be there in the crucial moment when her Shade left her lovely body. The infected members of the household had all been herded under one roof and (Rhodopis was repeatedly assured) well cared for until the end. She kept her doubts about this to herself. The plague had not touched her, proving she was not as beloved of the gods as Athenia had been, to her eternal misfortune. Or perhaps, Rhodopis mused as she surveyed her new rooms, light-hearted Athenia had been mysteriously much more fortunate than her serious-minded friend, who now faced a lonely life of men such as the illustrious physician operating blindly between her legs.

Rhodopis was awarded a personal slave who, ironically, was named Atalanta, for she could never run from her fate, and she was lucky to occasionally enjoy a fresh apple much less a golden one. Atalanta's previous owner must have possessed a perverse sense of humor, for whereas the legendary maiden warrior was long-legged and tall with

237

flowing golden hair, her namesake was short and dark and powerless. A Hetaera's personal slave was invariably renowned for her plainness, which made her mistress appear even more beautiful by comparison. Rhodopis had never been sure if the hawk-like glances of the school's founding mother had indicated approval of her auburn-haired chic or the hostile intention of kicking her out of the nest as soon as possible. Athenia had repeatedly assured her that she was beautiful, but Rhodopis felt different enough inside not to be sure what her outside appearance conveyed to others, especially men.

* * *

Rhodopis' second client was an aging statesman with coal-black hair and cold dark eyes who quickly made her aware of a serious gap in her education. She was forced to build an improvisational bridge over it with just a few moments notice, for to displease one of the first men who paid for her company could prove disastrous to her career and maybe even get her shipped off to Phoenicia after all. Roughly – and for a breathtakingly long time – he obliged her to prove her untried skills in the art of fellatio without revealing whether he was pleased with them or not, except of course through the undiminished firmness of his thankfully slender and unimposing member. Her knees had grown stiff by the time he yanked her to her feet and slapped her cheek with such force she suddenly found herself sprawled across the tile floor surrounded by broken perfume vials, an expense her modest fee as a novice would scarcely cover. After that he was a bit gentler with her, yet not because he repented his action; she could tell it had aroused him to hit her by the gratified glint in his disturbingly black eyes. It was obvious from his use of her other, even more painfully tight hole that he either

preferred boys or very young girls, and as she grit her teeth, struggling to relax her burning bowels around his agonizing thrusts, she
found herself fervently pitying all the young slaves in his household.

Rhodopis did not expect the two orifices she had in common with
boys to be the ones he preferred, but of course she knew what she
expected did not truly matter to men, much less to the gods.
Sometimes she was pleasantly surprised by a guest's undemanding
gentleness and charming conversation. At other times she achieved
levels of discomfort worthy of an Olympic athlete. During such visits she sought to distract and amuse herself by envisioning a compe-
tition of Hetaera sanctioned by Pericles himself, whose infamous
lover, Aspasia, was a Hetaera. Most of the time, however, she was
simply bored.

* * *

Rhodopis had been a working Hetaera for six long cycles of the
moon when one evening she entertained the youngest son of a
prominent Athenian family. Theron was strikingly handsome of
face and form. His broad shoulders, well-developed arms and muscular legs implied he was an athlete, but the keen intelligence in his
dark-grey eyes was not what she had come to expect from men who
spent the better part of their lives in the gymnasium. Rhodopis
received him alone in her rooms. The most pleasant feature of her
new accommodations was a portico made private by a curtain
Atalanta pulled open to reveal the perfumed garden, and above it
the splendid colors of the twilight, on that particular evening bold
crimson streaks reflecting a Hetaera's lips. Rhodopis did not use the
white clay foundation favored by many of her class, especially those
past their prime who wished in vain to conceal how many years they

had been entertaining men, the evidence of which was written on their skins in wordless but sadly eloquent lines. Rhodopis subscribed to the radical opinion that her flesh was much happier if it could breathe, and indeed, she considered her soft, flawless skin one of her best features, perhaps because it was the part of her she was most familiar with; her face remained a rather blurred stranger in all the mirrors now at her disposal. She wore less make-up than other Hetaeras, and preferred to entertain one man at a time alone in her rooms rather than to attend the nightly parties she and Athenia had once spied upon.

Atalanta served Rhodopis and her illustrious guest a selection of choice dishes accompanied by a fine red wine from Etruria. Arranged on a three-legged bronze table placed between the two couches was a small platter of smoked eel and asparagus spears delicately seasoned with oregano; a bowl of creased black olives with goat cheese; a plate of shrimps sautéed in vinegar and honey and decorated with cauliflower; and (Rhodopis' personal favorite) cuttlefish cooked in their own ink with pine kernels and barley and freshly baked bread for dipping.

She was still feeling a bit tender in certain places from the attentions of her most recent guest and was hoping this handsome young aristocrat possessed more natural tastes. She was also curious. Now that her virginal discomforts had vanished completely she wondered if she might begin to feel something else during the erotic act... something the Hetaera she had watched nearly ten years ago seemed to be feeling while the virile young gardener dug his tool deeper and deeper into her hole, causing the lips on her face to bloom in a secret smile that haunted her...

'Twilight has always been my favorite time of the day,' she commented, smiling at the intensely attractive man paying for her company as they sipped their wine.

'And why is that?' he asked from where he reclined on the couch facing hers. He was close enough, however, to reach out and cup one of her delicate breasts through her *chiton*.

She was expected to give a clever answer, but the truth rose more easily to her lips beneath his caress. 'Because everything is so much softer in the evenings… Apollo has shed his blindingly polished armor and laid his golden head to rest for the night while other more subtle and mysterious gods like Dionysus slip on their black capes and walk amongst us in the shadows… rousing the sweetest perfumes from the most delicate flowers as we feel their caress in the gentle breeze heralding the descent of night, and all the divine pleasures to be found in its deep embrace…'

'You are a poet, sweet Rhodopis.' He slipped his hand into her *chiton* and grasped one of her long nipples between his thumb and forefinger, pinching it as he spoke. 'Tell me more.'

'You make it most difficult for me to concentrate, dear Theron,' she protested flirtatiously, her cheeks dimpling and her dark-blue eyes narrowing as she gazed up at him from beneath full and naturally black lashes.

'Who is your favorite god?' he demanded, pulling on her nipple and squeezing it even harder so her other breast perked up sympathetically beneath the fine, nearly transparent sea-green *chiton* she had bought only last week.

Her response was delayed for a moment by a confused awareness of two contrasting sensations – one of hot discomfort approaching pain in her nipple, and another more subtle smoldering deep in her womb sparked by the friction of his thumb and forefinger… and suddenly the look in his eyes fanned the oddly breathtaking warmth in her belly into that mythical blaze of desire she had never truly believed possible though she sometimes dared dream of it. 'How can you ask me that?' she said at last. 'Surely you know the name of the deity my profession demands I honor above all others.'

'If you tell me Aphrodite is your favorite god I will be very disappointed in you, Rhodopis.' He released her nipple.

The sudden loss of his touch, uncomfortable though a part of her had found it, dismayed her, and this in turn astonished her. She had not expected to ever truly crave a man's attentions, much less suspected that his idle caress could threaten the self-control she had valued above all else for as long as she could remember. 'Prometheus is the god I am most fond of,' she confessed, 'for surely he cares more for us than any Olympian who has never suffered what it means to have your spirit confined by flesh and blood.'

When he smiled it was with both his lips and his eyes. 'Surely such a lovely body as yours is not such a terrible trial to bear, Rhodopis.'

'No...' She thought of Athenia dying of the plague. 'But sometimes my spirit resents being subject to its needs.'

'But are not these needs also pleasures, for example, the delectable dishes we are even now partaking of, and this fine wine that helps elevate our minds as well as pleasing our senses? Perhaps the spirit, as you call it, desires to be embraced and confined by your lovely limbs and finds the living grave between your thighs at once a safe and stimulating place to be.'

'What a marvelous concept!' she exclaimed, and the smile she bestowed upon him then was admiringly genuine. Her mirrors were in the bedroom, but for the first time Rhodopis saw how beautiful she was reflected back at her in a man's eyes. His teasing smile vanished, replaced by an expression almost like anger, and she savored her first intoxicating taste of what it felt like to be wanted by a man she also desired.

'I feel I understand, but perhaps you could explain to me what exactly you mean by your spirit?' he requested soberly, downing the wine left in his cup.

'I do not know *exactly*...' She gazed past him at the sky which had darkened to the luminous gray of all the Shades in Hades... including lovely, laughing Athenia, her painstakingly achieved golden curls eternally concealed beneath a black cowl...

Atalanta returned, and with modestly downcast eyes asked them if they desired more wine.

'Yes,' Theron said. 'Dionysus is *my* favorite god.'

Rhodopis laughed as she had sometimes laughed with Athenia, and hearing the unfamiliar sound stopped herself. 'Please close the curtains, Attie,' she commanded gently.

* * *

Theron left when the first bird began to sing, heralding the approach of Apollo's chariot on the horizon. 'This is no ordinary day dawning,' he whispered in her ear, caressing her hair which for most of the night had flowed like cool flames through his hands in the lamplight. Her small room had been transformed into the sanctuary of a temple where Rhodopis almost found herself believing in the gods with a man who made her feel like a goddess herself. None of Aphrodite's statues could ever have received such skilled and reverent handling. The tricks of her profession fell away from her like seeds and left only the vulnerable flower of a pleasure she had never before experienced. She tried not to let herself forget that the magic between them was destined to vanish with the sun. He would leave, another man would take his place later that evening, and she would once again be in control of her destiny. The physical act was the same with Theron as with all her other guests and yet felt totally different. After ritually divesting him of his clothing, she slowly unwrapped herself as he watched. She spread their garments across her painted wooden chest, and then, without his having to ask, she sank to her knees before him.

'Oh, sweet Rhodopis...' he murmured, fingering the violet ribbons Attie had wound through her hair. 'How do I get these off?' he demanded.

She reluctantly emptied her mouth of his penis to respond. 'I fear they are as great a mystery to me as they are to you.' She smiled up him, and what she saw made her heart beat faster in wonder. Apollo himself could not be more magnificent. His ribbed stomach muscles were pale and firm as marble in the lamplight, and his shoulders were broad enough to become the horizon of a woman's world. But what excited her most – what had aroused her from the instant she saw him – was the expression in his eyes, as penetratingly serious as his hair was soft and light. The vision of him towering over her like the statue of a god inspired her to skip several steps in the act of fellatio and immediately offer him the ultimate sacrifice of her breath by filling her slender neck with his erection. She surrendered her throat to his tender helmet, her hands gripping the hard columns of his thighs urging him to lean over her so she could get every bit of his thick length into her devoted orifice.

'By the gods!' he breathed, and yet only a moment later slipped out of her mouth and pulled her to her feet.

'Was I not pleasing you?' she gasped, anxious and confused because for once it was more than money and her reputation she cared about.

'You were pleasing me more than you will ever know, Rhodopis, but there is another even sweeter realm I am aching to explore.' He held her hand as she stepped onto the stool and spread herself across the couch Attie had decorated for the evening with a fine violet cloth embroidered with green flowering vines. 'You are the most beautiful woman in Athena,' he said quietly, and she hid her disappointment at the trite compliment even while mentally chastising herself for expecting more from a client. 'I can see you do not believe me,' he added, 'so perhaps I should express it differently… it is as if the gods fashioned your face and form especially to please me… turn around,' he commanded, and she obeyed him willingly, resting on her side as he spread himself behind her, and it excited her how much taller and stronger he was. He thrust his hand between her thighs and lifted one of her legs to expose her sex. His erection pressed demandingly into her back and a sweeter threat she had never known. 'Move up a little,' he whispered into her hair, and once again she obeyed him eagerly. Gymnastics had always been a part of her life growing up, and she still stretched regularly as part of her beauty regimen, which made her able to gracefully hold her leg straight up in the air while his fingertips gently explored the petals of her sex as though searching for something. It made her realize how naturally wet and slick she had become without the aid of scented oils, and she moaned when he pressed his fingertips into the top of her mound. He was the first man to reveal any knowledge of that sweet spot in her flesh, and she wondered with a sudden thrill if he was an initiate of the Eleusinian mysteries, which would explain his casual disdain of popular mythology. Then she stopped thinking altogether when the thick head of his penis lodged itself in the heart of her flesh and slowly began spearing her. He kept caressing her in that special place as his other hand smoothed the hair away from her neck so he could bite her gently but possessively.

'Oh, Theron!' she breathed. When her leg became tired she reached up and grasped her ankle to hold it up, opening herself for him completely, not because he had paid her to but because his slow, deep penetrations felt so unbelievably good. He was making her so wet the sent of her sex seemed to fill the small space like a sacred incense, the soft wet sounds of his erection sliding in and out of her body more meaningful than any animal's noisy sacrifice. For the first time Rhodopis longed to feel the hot libation of a virile man's seed deep inside her, but it was not to be, at least not for a very long time… not until he had taken her in a variety of positions, two of which she had never even been taught…

'I want you to be all mine for a time,' he said to her before he left that dawn. 'Do you understand?'

'Yes, I understand, Theron.' She gazed down at his turquoise-studded leather sandals. 'For a time…'

He gripped her arms with an urgency that made her gasp in surprise and look up into his eyes again. 'We never know what the gods have in store for us, Rhodopis. A short time may be all we are fated to have together in this life.'

* * *

It became rumored in Athena that the youngest son of one of its most renowned citizens was enamored of a Hetaera. This was not good news or bad, simply a choice tidbit of gossip to enjoy with Egyptian beer at a tavern or with wine from the island of Chios in wealthy households. Everyone knew it would not interfere with Theron's arranged marriage, in fact, enjoying the company of a Hetaera was considered an admirable and traditional part of his life.

Theron had not forbidden Rhodopis to see other men, but it was understood between them that she was exclusively his 'for a time', and she certainly had no need to entertain other clients. The evidence of how wealthy her lover's family was everywhere surrounded her. The two small rooms and portico she called her own were barely large enough to contain all his gifts. There were jewels – gold and turquoise earrings and filets along with a variety of silver arm bands – folded in amongst the growing number of finely woven and intricately embroidered *peplos'* and *chitons* in her chest together with the quinces hidden amongst her garments to keep them fresh, and she had been forced to buy a larger coffer in which to store her growing horde of drachmae. So it was difficult to explain why with every passing day Rhodopis felt more and more bereft. She was the envy of her class, an honor to her school, and the talk of the city. Her name was on the lips of the most venerable Athenians, and it was possible Pericles himself had heard of her. That her name was also in the foul mouths of dock hands and the whores who serviced them was of no consequence. Her knowledge of philosophy and history, the expensive weave of her tunics, the quality of the oils with which she scented her body and conditioned her hair, all these things and more raised her above common prostitutes. A wealthy man's passionate patronage was a bonus she had not expected or prepared herself for.

Rhodopis grew increasingly despondent dreading the day when Theron would begin to grow weary of her charms. She did not allow herself to hope (even if the thought did keep irresistibly crossing her mind) that she could be as blessed as Aspasia by a man's undying love. She consoled herself by imagining how proud Athenia would have been of her. Athenia would not have been so

Theron and Rhodopis

foolish as to allow herself to be devastated by the loss of one man who had already given her so much. Rhodopis was not afraid of once more plying her trade, what terrified her was how much she would miss Theron's presence; how much she would wish it was him conversing with her as they dined and not some other lesser man; how much she would hunger for the feel of him inside her and all around her and for the warmth of his breath whispering wonderful things in her ear she could easily believe were true while he was caressing her. Already he had made her a wealthy woman with his generous gifts. After less than a year she was closer to setting up her own household sooner than she would have thought possible. But nothing she possessed now or could ever possess would be able to console her for the loss of Theron's uniquely stimulating company. He assured her that even when he had a wife nothing would change between them, and she smiled and kissed his firm lips pretending to believe him. Yet it was increasingly difficult to keep her true feelings from him, for the harder he thrust himself into her body the deeper her sadness became. Not only had she lost control of her life, she no longer cared that she had; all that mattered was the time she spent with him and her fear that it would soon be coming to an end. She had become addicted to the happiness she felt when they were together, and even though her daily routine did not change all she could think about as she exercised and bathed, as Attie oiled and massaged her and dressed her hair, as she applied her make-up and selected the evening's food and wine, as she rode in a hired litter to the marketplace or to the temple of Aphrodite where she was expected to make regular offerings, all she cared about as she did these things was that she would be seeing Theron again that evening.

* * *

He pounded into her, furiously stabbing his erection deep into her belly as if she was a mortal enemy, but even as he conquered her with his passionate strength it was he who was surrendering control over himself for the timeless space during which the tight, warm borders of her innermost flesh surrounded him. Technically it was only his penis her clinging need for him had so much power over, but when his manhood was rampant with lust it thrust straight out from his body like the ambassador of his feelings, which journeyed on their own into her exotic depths where the rule of his mind was powerless, and where the most superficial and yet also the deepest part of him was mysteriously hers to command. It was a comfortable pleasure for Rhodopis to rest on her back with him spread on top of her; he was usually fond of more strenuous positions. He shifted her body slightly and reached down to capture one of her bottom cheeks in a talonlike grip. She cried out from the intensity of the pleasure his ramming strokes suffused her with when he slipped a finger up into her anus, pinning her between his thrusting hips and clutching hand as he stimulated himself with the feel of both her very different orifices. She knew from glorious experience that he could not long resist the rich offering of sensations plundering her in this way awarded him. She moaned beneath his increasingly violent penetrations, his face buried in the side of her neck, his breath a storm in her ear worthy of Zeus himself. It was almost unbearable how much she loved the experience of his erection swelling and pulsing inside her until it was impossible for it to grow any bigger and his noble sperm crashed in a foaming wave against the lifeless shore of her womb. (One of Attie's most important duties was to every day prepare the special tea that would keep her mistress barren.)

Theron and Rhodopis

Afterwards, he lay breathing heavily, as if mortally wounded, across her couch while she stepped lightly down onto the stool and the cool floor. He had stripped off her *chiton* and *peplos* the instant he entered her room and possessed her without bothering to undress himself. The food and wine Attie had laid out for them on the portico was still untouched, and Rhodopis picked up her discarded clothing looking forward to drawing the curtains and watching the sunset while they ate and conversed. Perhaps she would even tell Attie to play the *Kithara* for them softly in the background...

'I did not give you permission to dress,' Theron spoke abruptly, and the tone of his voice caused her to drop her *peplos* in surprise. 'I am to be married on the next full moon,' he announced.

All the cold darkness of Hades suddenly seemed to fill her chest. 'I will make an offering to Hymen in the temple for your happiness,' she said.

He leapt off the couch without bothering with the stepping stool, anger wafting from him like the charged heaviness of the air before lightning strikes. He cupped her breasts roughly in his hands and stared down at them as he spoke. 'Several moons after the ceremony, after I have had sufficient time to consummate my marriage,' he squeezed her soft mounds cruelly, yet the pain in her heart was already so great she scarcely noticed, 'I will be leaving Athena as ambassador to Syracuse.'

And I will be cutting off all my hair longing for the day when I may join Athenia in a numb and thoughtless darkness where I pray I might not be able to remember that I did not wish to live without you. She could not meet his eyes because he had not paid for the burden of her tears; all his gifts and drachmae were an honor she would betray by not always making her company as pleasurable for him as possible.

'Look at me, Rhodopis.'

A lump in her throat as terrible as the piece of pomegranate Persephone foolishly swallowed – as she had even more foolishly allowed herself to hope deep inside that she and Theron would be together forever – she desperately batted her lashes and gazed up at his face, her eyes the sparkling blue of the sea at sunrise, her salty tears evidence of a sorrow whose depth she dared not reveal to him.

'My wife will remain here in Athena,' he added quietly, 'but you will be traveling with me.'

She laughed.

He let go of her and stepped back. 'Do I amuse you?'

'No, Theron, please forgive me, it as I who amuse myself! All my life I thought the only thing I would ever truly care about was never being forced to leave Greece, but now I see that the gods are more subtle than I believed. They have played a trick on me, for I will gladly journey to the ends of the earth and beyond, to lands Odysseus never even dreamed of, if it means being with you.'

'And so you might.' He smiled and drew her into the loving harbor of his arms.

*Considered one of the oldest versions of the Cinderella story. It was first recorded by the Roman historian Strabo in the first century B.C.

PRINCE MAJ-RA

Ancient Egypt, New Kingdom, ca. 1,000 B.C.

*'That which was divided has been made whole, and
that which was lost has been found... Even as the child is
born of two parents, so shall that peace you have not known
alone, that wisdom you have not yet experienced,
that power which has not yet found you as its channel,
come forth from you at this uniting of your spirit...'*
Joan Grant, Eyes of Horus

Nefra sought to understand what it was about Prince Maj-Ra that made him so different. She carefully weighed his qualities on the scales of her heart and mind, yet she could not trust the result because desire is not Maat's feather of truth. Desire is heavy as a lion's pelt, and acts as swiftly as a cat pouncing on an unsuspecting mouse, which in a mysterious way is what happened to her the moment she met him in her father's courtyard. No doubt the Forty-Two Assessors would reveal his character to be as full of flaws as an old barge, yet Nefra felt he had beauty enough to easily win his way into Nepthy's heart. Set's sensual consort standing behind Osiris' throne in the Judgment Room could not help but love Maj-Ra's form, and her shining sister, Isis, would be caught in the charmed net of his wisdom and wit.

Nefra knew there was nothing the daughter of a minor noble could do to escape what her sisters envied her as they chattered away about the royal city's glorious pleasures. It saddened and confused her to listen to them because she had no desire to go there. She would gladly have transferred this joy to one of her sisters, yet for some reason the Prince had chosen her. His eyes were a startling light-blue – his grandmother had been a foreign princess – and at first Nefra thought they were all that made him different from other men. When he stared at her she felt even more luminously reflected than in her polished bronze mirror. Alone in her bedroom she found herself curiously caressing her delicate breasts. They felt lovelier and more mysteriously special than fruit ripening in the mist that softly embraced the Prince's first morning as a guest in her home. After a few days, when he genuinely seemed to be enjoying her father's humble hospitality, she began to suspect that Maj-Ra's eyes were special because his Ka was.

Nefra did not wish to be a concubine in the royal city, yet she could not stop her heart from beating into Maj-Ra's hands. She was frightened as a wild fowl of his cat-like slenderness, yet she was also irresistibly drawn to the way he walked so gracefully taut with an invisible strength of purpose. He was pharaoh's favorite younger son and had never been refused anything, which made it strange he did not seem angry when he asked her mother for her and Nefra refused him. He was silent, his clear eyes as innocently wide as his favorite dog. They both looked at her as if she had just commanded them to fly away but, naturally, they could not obey. Nefra was discreetly pulled out of the chamber and explained the great honor of the situation, but she had not listened remembering the way his brown hair curled around his expression when she denied him. He did not like to wear ceremonial wigs and let his hair grow down almost to his shoulders.

As preliminary gifts – since most of his treasures were in the royal city – Maj-Ra gave Nefra a crown of infinitely fine golden vines twining around each other as if truly alive and blooming with lapis-lazuli flowers; a girdle made of little golden fish to swim devotedly around her hips over a semi-transparent dress of water-blue linen; a large wooden chest inlaid with gold that came full of colorful faience bracelets and floral collars; and an ebony box containing jars of unguents as well as black kohl and malachite for her eyes.

In return Nefra presented to Maj-Ra a small ivory coffer in which to keep his gold rings, and a white alabaster lamp in the shape of three lotus flowers for his bedroom.

The morning after the festive exchange, Nefra left her father's house accompanied by her favorite servant, shyly hiding behind the curtains of her litter which protected her from the hot sun and the blinding amount of gold shining on Maj-Ra's barge. At the crowded dock everyone quickly made way for the royal son's entourage. The treasures of his life flowed in procession between the brown banks of sailor's shoulders, bathing the watching crowd with the refreshing, reassuring sense of divinity's cool ease as the tips of his bodyguards' lances rippled sharp and bright as the Nile on that windy dawn.

On the slender vessel, Nefra was not visited by her new lord all day long, a fact that both relieved and upset her. She sat beneath a leopard skin canopy fanned with an ostrich feather by a tall Nubian servant who otherwise remained motionless as a statue, his strong black chest glistening with a sweat that made it mysteriously much more valuable in her eyes than ebony. She watched Ra playing on the water – eager and full of energy as a child in the morning, penetratingly intense at noon, and shining softly, meditatively in the afternoon. Then, as the sun god's barge began its journey through the Underworld, Maj-Ra's barge pulled up to the Western bank.

Trembling in the evening's passionate sighs about the night to come, Nefra was escorted by the dark servant to a large tent. A lamp was burning behind the white linen so it seemed to glow with all her pure expectations. The Nubian lifted the curtain aside and she saw Maj-Ra sitting straight-backed within like a young god.

He rose, smiling, when she entered. 'Nefra…' He always spoke softly to her.

'My lord…'

'For you I am Maj-Ra now.'

'You are both,' she dared correct him. 'However, I have no desire to be your concubine any more than I wish to be eaten piece by piece by a crocodile every night until you grow sated and seek fresh game.'

'Sister!' he laughed. 'I have dreamed with you so many times! When you refused to become my wife I rejoiced, for you are always delightfully willful when we are asleep together.'

Nefra concentrated on the pectoral of Horus grasping eternity's red sun and blue horizon in both its claws against the prince's chest. The god's jeweled wings were spread open, and in the uncertain lamplight she thought she saw them beating a reflection of his heart's steadfast force. 'I do not remember these dreams, Maj-Ra,' she whispered.

'I know, Nefra, you told me you did not remember our meetings after you awoke, but I have been searching for you. You are the reason I have always accepted the hospitality of a nobleman with daughters.'

'But how did you know I was not a servant or a-'

'Because you told me once that you like to walk through your garden before Ra awakens, and the first morning in your father's house, when I looked out my window and saw you pacing restlessly through the mist as if confused and saddened by the fact that you could not remember your dreams, I knew I could finally show you.' He touched her hands, which were clutching a linen cloak tightly around her. 'You have nothing to hide from me, Sister…'

His tone relaxed her and she allowed the cloak to fall onto a blue rug darting with colorful fish.

'I know everything, Nefra…'

She could avoid his eyes no longer and held her breath to brave their luminous depths. She floated joyously in his loving gaze for a moment, but then she seemed to see the flailing, drowning arms of all his other women and she slipped away from him as he bent to kiss her. 'My Ba will die in your harem's cage,' she warned him.

'Nefra, I did not search all of Egypt for another concubine. They are happy with their gardens and pet monkeys, but you are my Sister, for whom I have already built a house by the Nile far from the palace. Is this pleasing to your heart, beloved?'

'Oh, yes, my lord…'

'Then share your joy with me, for I have had a hard time searching for you.' He smiled when she suddenly knelt before him and gazed gratefully up at him. He held her face gently in his hands. 'Do you not desire to see *all* of your lord?' he whispered, and she obediently began removing his golden belt made up of ten ankhs linked together embracing his hips with their life energy. She was going to rise to fold his loincloth carefully over a stool, and to avoid his royal phallus which frightened her, but he flung the gilded linen away carelessly and held her down facing his god-like manhood.

'My lord,' she murmured, tentatively kissing the tip of his fleshly scepter, but then she became a little more confident when she felt the understanding tenderness beneath the strong certainty demanding her obeisance. 'My lord,' she repeated, 'Prince of Kam, Maj-Ra… you are…' She licked him curiously, hesitantly, for she had never wor-

Prince Maj-Ra

shipped Min so personally; all she had ever done was offer his statue baskets of grain after the harvest along with everyone else. 'You are... you are lord of all...' She took him boldly into her mouth and sucked on him with a hunger that amazed her. His hands fell like a blessing on her head as he stood tall and straight as a god above her, the soothing way he caressed her hair assuring her that she was not being unforgivably selfish... on the contrary, she sensed him experiencing the pleasure of his divine generosity through her worshipful mouth... until he crooked her in his strong arm and raised her from beneath his wonderful flail.

'Please forgive me, my lord!' she gasped. 'It was just that I suddenly understood why cats... why they...'

He laughed. 'That was the sweetest bath I have ever had, my kitten, but look at all the linen you have become entangled in. Let me help free you...' He drew her deeper into the tent where Hathor's lovely cow's head rose from the shadows, the lunar disc resting between her delicate golden horns, his bed formed by her slender body.

Slowly, Prince Maj-Ra unwrapped Nefra's dress, the white gazelles embroidered on the light-green linen no longer corralled by her hips seeming to run into the shadows when he flung them away, and their hooves beat wildly in her heart as he pulled her against him. She cried out when he bit the side of her neck like a serpent, but then – firm and knowledgeable as shaven priests – his fingers began performing a magical service in the sealed shrine hidden between her thighs only the lord of her heart was allowed to enter.

'Oh, my lord, my lord!' She clung to his broad shoulders.

He didn't let go of her as his breath gently crushed the luminous lotuses she had given him. After he had put out the lamp, he lifted her slender body effortlessly in his sun-browned arms.

Hathor's cool back rose against hers as his warmth descended over her. Then suddenly it was as if Hapi, the black bull of Osiris, was ramming his horns between her thighs. She couldn't help feeling profoundly blessed despite the agony as the Prince rode the god's fierce power between her open legs.

'Oh, Maj-Ra, help me!' she gasped. 'Hapi is here and he is killing me!'

'Sister, I am here,' he whispered, and she almost forgot her torment in his deep, soothing kiss, until Hapi thrust his divine horn even deeper inside her as though longing to be forever corralled by her hips.

'Oh, my lord, free him, please!' she begged.

'No, you must sacrifice him slowly and reverently, as the embodiment of Osiris, who eternally rises through your love, my sweet Isis.'

The Double Axe

Ancient Crete, Knossos, ca.3,000 B.C.

Sunshine laughs silently off wet rocks as Lyra runs across the grass. She hurries past the cold black caves of the dead gaping toothless grins at the warm spring morning. Yellow butterflies seem to rise from her hot body like sparks as she senses the spirits buried in the earth aching to rise through her naked feet and live again, but this morning the world is hers alone. She leaves the dead behind in the rocky hills, her eyes avidly searching the meadows above and below her for the young goatherd she met the other day. She wants to see again the cocoon-like shape hanging between his legs from which he said his soul could take flight. He offered to let her hold his intriguingly large chrysalis in the warm wet shaft between her thighs, from where he said she would be able to feel his soul ascending. She had run like a frightened animal from the crook of his smile, but ever since then she had thought only of his mysterious power. She knows that butterfly cocoons require safe places to unfold the colorful splendor latent within them, and apparently his fleshly cocoon also needs a special nourishment found only inside her. And the more she thought about it, the more she feared that if she did not help him release his soul it would die inside him, so now she is running back to the place where she last saw him.

He is sitting in a tree gazing out at the sea.

'Give it to me!' Lyra commands in the firm voice of the temple priestess she will one day be. 'I want to see your soul break free... unless...' Her voice trips over his smile as he leaps down from the flowering branch. 'Unless you fear to lose it...'

'Silly girl.' He laughs. 'It always flies back down to its master.'

'I am not silly! Go and find another cave to hatch in!' She starts to run away but he catches her, and rocks warn her sharply about his intentions as he makes her lie on her back on the hard ground.

'At first you will feel helpless and angry as a fledgling struggling to use its wings,' he whispers in her ear, 'but after that I promise we will soar like hawks together!'

Everything he said comes true, so Lyra meets him in the hills almost every day, until she is sent to the Temple and no longer allowed to roam free. Her days grow dark even though the sun shines as always, and the moon only stares down at her coldly when she prays to see him again. Then at last one evening – after she has hungrily harvested her memories of him for three long years – he is brought to her relaxed and smiling. The male attendant lays him in a stone basin while she and eight other young women form a circle around him. Lyra dutifully raises the ceremonial vase, but she cannot bring herself to pour out the water that will help his soul flow through the hole in the rock and back into the Mother's womb. She sees heads turning in the living sphere inside which his stiff body lies. Her attendants are wondering why she is hesitating, and curiosity causes them to close admiringly around the young man's potent spirit.

'Stay back!' she commands, and they obey her reluctantly. Slowly, she tips the vase and water pours in a thin, clear thread around his sex, causing a frightening warmth to come alive between her legs. The water flows down his thighs and she follows it, entranced, before she spills what remains in the vase over his chest, the splashing sound echoed by shocked gasps because she left his face dry, but she refuses to let his features crumble back into the soil where the Goddess can selfishly embrace him forever. She grasps the cold reality of life and death like snakes and defies the poisonous fact that she can never hold his living body in her arms again.

One of her attendants takes the black-and-white vase from her hands and she claps them loudly six times. The priestesses' – their long black hair coiling over their naked breasts all the way down to their multi-colored skirts – file silently out of the shadowy room as the male attendant returns. He lifts the body up in his strong arms again and follows the women into a space alive with paintings. Blue dolphins leap happily on their left, birds of red-and-gold plumage forever fly on their right, and smooth crimson columns rimmed in black at both ends support the room's dimensions just as blood flowing through the body creates the soul's abode. The male attendant carefully sets the deceased on the gilded throne and from behind it takes a golden chalice which he hands to Lyra. Then everyone except the high priestess leaves the room again through a small black door, their procession moving so swiftly they evoke a huge snake slithering away.

Lyra stands before the enthroned body and raises the chalice. Its stem is forged in the shape of two entwined serpents and a bird's open wings form the cup. She drinks the contents so quickly that she sways slightly as she offers the now empty vessel to the dead youth, the gold feathers enfolding a final symbolic drop of his blood's power. She should call the other priestesses back now, but instead she dips her finger between the wings and gently spreads the remaining wine over his lips so that for an instant they shine as if with life. She bends to set the goblet down and her knees graze his. She quickly grips his shoulders, terrified he will fall, and when his head tilts to one side she feels him asking her if he is really gone forever.

'Yes, but I am coining with you,' she tells him, and dares to kiss his lips. They are cold and unyielding as stone to her breath's warm breeze, but her tongue is a lithe and stubborn little animal squeezing through their tight crevice to wander over smooth rocks and a cold, sandy floor. She moans and closes her eyes as his throat's dark shaft begins luring her deeper inside him... she feels herself falling into a bottomless darkness...

Lyra straightens up and slowly raises the long golden dagger she keeps sheathed in the petals of her skirt. She hesitates for a heartbeat, but then with a cry like a hawk soaring high above the earth she follows his soul, the moon-white path between the hills of her breasts suddenly flooded red by the setting sun of her life.

Star Crossed

Another Solar System – Date Unknown

I n linear time every second is crushed by the next, emotions the scent
of moments falling away like petals. The human spine is a stem from
which feelings blossom with as much beauty as the attending gardener of the brain permits.

Siriana was morbidly fascinated by the three-fold nature of humans
– by the way thought, emotion and will worked independently within
them like the three points of the empty pyramid they used in their
favorite pastime. One of her first memories was watching them
engaged in an activity they called 'pool' during which they gathered up
the colorful spheres of planets, and then made them explode into a
whole new galaxy just for the pleasure of conquering each one again.
The tables on which they played had looked like vast green plains
from the vantage point of her father's shoulder. She had watched,
breathless with fear and fascination, as the alien men casually knocked

worlds around, three of the balls they used the same luminous tones of
the planets that rolled swiftly up into the sky at night.

During the long days, the eyes of her world's unforgiving lord
sparkled off the Webs spun between rocks and plant life, dewing the
hot violet air with cool prisms. Humans could not breathe this fluid
atmosphere; they lived in structures like massive eggs half buried in
the rosy sand. Tunnels branching from one to another connected
them all to the Space Port, and it was this ponderous web that caught
Siriana more and more often as a result of her father's dealings with
the Star Merchants.

* * *

It wasn't until she had turned eight in Arachnoid years (a human
term) that she realized her sire was engaged in illegal activities.
The knowledge literally came to her between one inhalation and
the next.

Watching a man as he bent over a pool table she caught her breath,
let it out in a sigh as he broke the pyramid of planets with a musical
sound, and nothing was ever the same again. Suddenly, she understood
that the voluminous cape her father always wore was different from
others, and that the pockets sewn into its inner lining had been especially designed to conceal the vials he sold to the humans.

When inside the Port she always wore a protective veil of her
world's atmosphere, and she had to take a long, steady mouthful in
order to assimilate this new awareness concerning her sire's activities.
She dared to take it a breath farther wondering what was in those vials,
and two anxious gasps brought her the answer... Distilled air!

She tried to stop breathing after that, because she had no desire to
face the fact that her own father was breaking the law.

The air outside the Port was an element the humans could not define in their terms, and her own people were not inclined towards scientific dissection; to them the atmosphere was simply everything. Not only did it sustain their flesh form, it was their very awareness, the scope of which developed ever so slightly with every breath they took.

After her realization, Siriana began wearing several layers of air-veils into the Port; she was finding herself shorter and shorter of breath there.

* * *

Sitting in the dark corner of a bar waiting for her father to conclude his business in another room, Siriana concentrated on one particular man. She liked to watch the heart beating in his chest, and the way his nerves were strung on his spine like a sacred Web or the strings of an Imager's instrument.

He glanced into the shadows at her violet-veiled form, and unexpectedly broke his orbit around the table where brilliant spheres moved in carefully controlled ellipses.

She experienced a strange sort of blindness as he approached her in which all she could see were his eyes.

'Simon, keep away from that little mermaid,' another man urged quietly. 'Daddy shark's in the back room.'

Her air veils were infinitely soft and sheer, and swelled gently with her breaths.

'And talk about jail-bate,' another man added, studying what remained of the solar system they were methodically destroying. (She suspected the black world was theirs, because they always saved it until the end.)

'She *looks* old enough.' The man called Simon came so close to her living veils that they swelled gently towards his strong gravity. He was much taller and broader than her father, who cut a formidable figure amongst his own people, and his skin was lighter. 'She's at least sixteen in earth years. What's your name, sweetheart?'

'Siriana,' she breathed.

'Siriana, that's the sexiest space-suit I've ever seen.'

'What is *sexy*?' She asked, and abruptly understood what she liked so much about Star Merchants – the way their mouths curved upwards and completely transformed the geography of their features.

'Get away from that human!'

Her father's furious command tidal-waved through her and drowned all her own thoughts even though no one else heard him. She leapt off the chair as his cloaked form appeared at the other end of the bar.

'Hey, where are you going?' Simon caught her arm, but instantly released it. 'You're *hot*,' he said beneath his breath.

The human's touch sent such intense currents of sensation through her body that even with the powerful tide of her father's displeasure flooding her awareness she found it nearly impossible to move away from him. His hair was fine and luminous as Web threads touched by the suns, and in the dark space of the bar his eyes were like her world's two moons, small silver orbs emanating a mysteriously powerful gravity. Her veils rose and fell in growing swells towards him like twilight-stained waters.

'Too hot for me,' he added quietly, staring down into her violet eyes, his mouth hard as the horizon.

Her father – a turban of atmosphere wrapped around the lower half of his face – was almost upon her, his white cloak billowing around him.

He never reached her. He was abruptly surrounded as if by his own shattered reflection as two groups of men from her world entered the bar from opposite sides and rushed towards him, their intent clearly approved by the human security officers who followed them in.

She was about to run to her father's side when a force such as she had never known flung her in the opposite direction.

She spun into the shadows at the far end of the bar and grabbed on to the first object she encountered to keep herself from falling. Vaguely, she realized it was the man Simon who had shoved her away, but shock and fear only enabled her to take shallow breaths and she couldn't dive beneath the choppy surface of events to grasp what was happening. Cowering on her knees in a pitch-black corner, she saw Simon's head rise over her.

'Don't make a sound,' he whispered, and left her there.

She was completely alone for the first time in her life; her father's emotional current, disapproving or otherwise, was no longer flowing into her. His angry thoughts had stopped breaking on the shore of her awareness in the same instant the human pushed her away.

'You're under arrest,' the cold, implacable voice sounded very loud, 'for the manufacture and sale of an illegal substance. By the law of...'

She stopped listening as she waited desperately for her father to send her at least a trickle of reassurance, one small, secret word she could hope on, but his silence was a painful desert protecting her; one of his non-human captors would immediately sense the thread of their communication. She knew this, yet it took all the restraint she possessed not to broadcast her anguish and concern. Drops of it slipped through her tightly clenched will, but they only evaporated in the blank, burning sand of his anger.

It was a terrible relief when she heard the authorities leading him away. Webs of empathy could only stretch so far. Once solid walls of alien alloys rose between them no connection would be possible.

'You've jumped into light-speed one too many times, Simon.' The man who had called her a "little mermaid" spoke in a tone that disturbed her pulse's harmonious frequency. 'What are you going to do with her now?'

'I couldn't just let them arrest her, she's only a kid, and you know what those holy bastards are like. Everything's a damned web to them. A baby's as guilty as its parents. Whole families are wiped out if just one member does anything wrong.' He crouched down beside her. 'It's all right, little one.'

'Oh, now she's just a kid. A minute ago you were ready to–'

'Shut-up.'

'Okay, she's beautiful, but she's hotter than hell, in every sense. You can't *do* anything with her, man.'

'I guess he just wanted to help her, Nick.' The other human in the bar spoke up.

'It's more like he wants to keep her.'

'What *am* I going to do with you?' Simon asked her quietly.

'I'm not getting mixed up in this,' Nick said, and she heard the heavy sound of his boots retreating.

'I'll help,' the other man offered.

Simon was silent for a moment, and his distinct human scent became overpowering. 'Fetch me a laundry bag,' he said.

'A laundry bag?'

'You heard me. Now. Hurry!'

'Okay, but I don't know anything about this!'

Simon was suddenly emanating such arrogant confidence that she half swooned beneath it. She had never been in such close contact with this distinctly human scent and she found it staggeringly delicious.

'It'll be all right,' he promised. 'We'll figure something out.'

'I thank you, Star Man,' she replied formally.

'Don't thank me yet. How long will those veils… you know.'

'Two more sunsets.'

'Four days,' he translated to himself.

'If I remain,' she searched for the right word, '*calm.*'

Simon rose when he heard his friend return, and she followed him up.

'Thanks, Jim.' He grabbed the black sack. 'I owe you one.'

'Forget it. I don't know anything about this.' He hurried away.

'Okay, baby, into the bag. Quick.'

Siriana had no reservations about assuming a temporary cocoon. She took the sack from him, slipped into it feet first, and with one last look up at the moons of his eyes, she disappeared into its black cloud.

It proved a fascinating journey. She had no trouble breathing of course, wrapped as she was in her violet atmosphere, and curled up against his back she found the rhythm of his strides down the corridors of the Space Port strangely soothing. It seemed to her that she had always known this would happen. Taking slow, almost contented breaths, Siriana understood this was her destiny. The seeds planted by her father's first visit to the Port would finally begin to bloom when she rose from the sack's soil-like warmth. She was so engrossed in the mysterious certainty expressed by the images flowing through her that she only half heard Simon occasionally speaking and laughing.

It was almost too soon when he set her down with a gentleness that surprised her. She only reached half way up his chest, but her feelings during the journey had been so heavy she had half expected him to drop her.

The pale rays of his fingers ripped open the darkness, and she followed them out.

She was in his room. She couldn't tell this by looking around her, it was simply the only place she could be, and her curiosity was boundless. Her gaze floated from one unfamiliar object to another.

'I must be crazy,' he said.

She planted herself in front of him. 'You are good. My people are wrong when they say humans care only for the Webs.'

'Oh, no they're not. Nick was right. It was a selfish impulse.'

'You helped me,' she articulated clearly, because for some reason he seemed confused about this.

'Yes, I did, but why?'

His intent regard paralyzed all of her except her veils, which still wafted towards him. 'I do not know. Why, Simon?'

'Jesus.' Turning away, he ran his fingers through his hair and paced from one end of the cramped space to another. 'I'm in deep shit now,' he mumbled, 'deep shit.'

'What is *shit*?'

He made a sound like the hard, empty shell of the current she had come to know as human laughter. 'I've lost my mind,' he concluded calmly, stopping before her again.

'Then I will help you find it, Star Man.'

'Okay, let's think. If I get you out of here, where will you go? Do you have any other relatives? But they'll all be... oh, hell.' He dropped onto the edge of a soft surface and his head sank like a sun at the end of a long day into the furrows of his hands.

Watching him, Siriana's delicate breasts heaved beneath a tidal wave of realizations. He was not going to help her free her father because it was impossible. She could do nothing for her sire. He would be thrown into a Web and she would never see him again, and unless this human was able to think of something, the same fate awaited her.

She understood now this was not what she wanted to happen even though it was considered an ecstatic experience to be embraced by one of the sacred Spinners. It was said you did not feel any pain as you were consumed. First the Spinner's sweet poison numbed and stiffened your limbs, and then you just watched the black jaws feasting on your body. Yet humans considered themselves superior to the sacred Spinners and used the Webs to feed their own hunger...

'Please, Star Man, help me!' she cried, and Simon looked up with a stunned expression as she flung herself into his arms.

She heard him groan, and felt pain where he gripped her to push her away, but then there was a sound like a long sigh, a violet mist enveloped them, and their arms coming around each other became the horizons of an ideal climate.

'Baby...' he whispered.

Even when she felt him reaching down to lift her veils, she couldn't find it in herself to pull away from him. 'No,' she protested weakly, confused she didn't really mean it even though what he was doing could prove fatal to her.

'It's all right,' he said gently. 'I won't hurt you...'

Scarcely able to breathe, she believed him.

* * *

Her veils so much resembled the diaphanous material of harem fantasies, Simon was taken aback when they flowed through his hands like warm water stimulating all the nerve-ends in his fingertips like a carbonated liquid, only he knew it was really a pure energy he was feeling. If he lifted her veils all the way off her she would die within minutes, and so it seemed perfectly natural that he should join her beneath them. He laughed quietly feeling like a kid again agreeing to play Arabian Nights with his pretty new neighbor, except the intimacy of this 'tent' was not in the least bit claustrophobic; it was like being surrounded by an infinitely soft twilight where her unknown mouth opening trustingly beneath his felt like the miracle of reaching the horizon and all its mysterious promise. Now he was the one who couldn't breathe as his tongue dove between her lips, and for a few profoundly delicious moments his awareness of everything drowned in her kiss... his tongue was his whole body and she was the sea arching in deep warm waves around him, her smooth little teeth a rocky harbor... he pulled himself up gasping for air, and quickly slipped out from beneath her veils. She moaned, reaching for him, and her violet eyes above the seductive harem girl's outfit shone like amethysts blindly pleading with him. A stab of guilt sharpened by desire made him shove her back across the bed less gently than he intended, but she languidly accepted his violence; it was just another human trait she was eager to accept because she believed in him, and the knowledge that he could do anything he wanted to her was going dangerously to his head.

'Oh, Siriana,' he whispered, and impatiently shoved her veils up out of his way again. He unzipped his pants, and intently observed her eyes watching as he freed his erection. Her vivid black pupils expanded and contracted in response to her first glimpse of his penis, and the unexplored mystery of her turned him on so much his hard-on grew almost painful. Her legs were as slender as a girl's but more exquisitely shaped than any woman's, and his desire for her intensified almost unbearably when he realized there wasn't any hair between her thighs at all; all he could see was smooth skin as white as ocean coral tinted a delicate rose by the setting sun. Joining her on his narrow mattress, he lay on his side next to her as he caressed her veils further up her body, revealing her achingly delicate torso. The knowledge that he could go were no man had gone before was threatening his usual control, but gritting his teeth he steeled himself and tentatively slipped a hand between her legs. She was unbelievably tight, tighter than any earthly virgin could possibly be… not that he had ever been with a virgin so he couldn't really be sure…

'My God,' he breathed, 'I can't find… where is…?' He was stunned. This exquisite creature lying utterly submissive beneath him didn't have a pussy! He was afraid he had hurt her with his incredulous groping when she reached down and grasped his hand, bringing it up to rest over her navel. 'I'm sorry, Siriana, I didn't mean to…' He raised his hand. Only how rampant his cock was enabled him to understand what he was seeing. He wasn't looking at a cauterized wound that had once housed the umbilical cord of a growing fetus. He was gazing down into a puckered hole in her belly. At first he thought he was only imagining the faint sheen of violet-tinted warmth emanating from this sphincter-like crater in the smooth valley of her flesh, but his own skin told him the glowing need emanating from her was real. He had fucked more than one woman up the ass before – his cock had forced its way into more than one little hole – but this was different, he had no idea where it was going or what it would feel like. An earth woman's anus was stimulatingly tight, but he knew where he was and he also knew the pain he caused her wasn't truly going to hurt her…

Siriana's back arched as she abruptly yanked her veils up around her throat, exposing her breasts, and it was her desperate willingness to be used combined with the sight of her aureoles that undid his resolve to be careful. Her conical little tits appeared to have leach-like starfish clinging to their tips, and even as he watched they turned purple as if dining on her blood. She didn't have any nipples, but he didn't care because he was able to get her entire breast into his hungry mouth. Her skin was firm and yielding, resistant and vulnerable, like any young woman's flesh, yet for some reason its appetizing qualities were intensified a hundred fold in all his senses and nerve-ends as he devoured the tender mounds of her bosom, licking and nipping and sucking them ravenously.

'Oh, Star Man... Star Man!'

Without thinking he rolled on top of her and launched his erection into her belly. His reason warned him he wasn't sure he could penetrate her this way but for once his desire felt mysteriously smarter than his brain. The way she reached above her to clutch his pillow might have been an expression of pain as he pushed his way inside her, but he didn't think so... he didn't feel so... the moist warmth engulfing his hard-on as he slowly penetrated her encouraged its stabbing entry as her back arched, urging him to force his cock in deeper. He couldn't be careful anymore; he plunged his erection all the way inside her, groaning from the intense pleasure he experienced when his groin hit the cushion of her belly. Her innermost flesh was deliciously clinging and yet also yielding, warm and slick... and bottomless... there seemed no end to how far up into her chest he could drive his selfishly swelling dick. He groaned from the effort he made to control himself, but there was no resisting the lust that possessed him. Supporting his weight on both arms he pulled his erection out of her belly, but only to relish stabbing her with it again fast and hard. He plunged into her over and over, he couldn't help it; he fucked her violently, watching her breasts quivering in response to his thrusts; to his ruthless gutting as his cock reaped a hot, rich feast of sensations. He stopped caring whether or not he could hurt her. The sense that he could ram himself all the way up into her throat if he didn't hold himself back was threatening to drive him mad, her absolute silent submission a vicious aphrodisiac he was

thankfully too far gone to analyze. Whatever control he still possessed slipped away completely on her enigmatic little smile as he
stabbed her... he ejaculated fiercely, and for a few blissful moments
he feared he would be lost in her forever as her pupils swallowed the
twilight of her irises like night falling, and he saw his sperm glimmering in their black depths like a distant galaxy being born.

* * *

'Are you proud of yourself?' Nick's hard eyes stared down at
the creature dying on the cot.

Sitting beside her, Simon was holding her small hand as the struggle to take a breath consumed all her energy.

'I hope you at least used protection. The last thing the earth needs
is another fucking virus.'

Simon glared up at him. 'In case you haven't noticed, *she's* the one
dying.'

'Naturally she is,' Nick retorted coldly. 'Did you think you could
just keep her in your room like a fish in a tank? She's a sentient life
form, for Christ's sake, not your pet.'

'I want to take her home with me,' Simon stated with quiet passion.
'We could harvest as much of their atmosphere as she'll ever need
without their ever–'

'If I was you,' Nick interrupted harshly, 'I'd worry about how you're
going to dispose of her body. She'll be dead within the hour, so stop
dreaming. I'll help–'

'Get out.' Simon returned his full attention to the bed.

'Fine, but if you're not careful you'll end up in a Web yourself
and your parents will always remember that their son died like a fly.'
He left.

Simon wondered what his judgmental friend would say if he knew Siriana could give head for hours... he had wrapped his cock in her veils and shoved them both into her mouth and down her throat, where they had stayed until he almost passed out from the pleasure washing around him in endless currents growing deeper and more powerful until his consciousness nearly drifted away on them... but she had only one veil remaining now, and it was worn so thin it might just have been a faint sheen of sweat.

To Simon's guilty eyes, she looked like a beautiful gift trying to break out of the pink cellophane she had been wrapped in just for him. He was determined to save her and keep her.

Her palm was hot as molten gold – the element casually spun by her world's sacred Spinners – yet she had become much more precious to him than the valuable filament.

Rising, he removed a small purple vial from a special niche built into the wall, and returned to the bed with it.

She had stopped struggling for breath; she was utterly still, her eyes closed.

He slipped an arm beneath her and pulled her up into a sitting position. Her head hung back limply, her mouth gaping open. It was an easy matter for him to pour the shimmering liquid down her throat.

Encouraged by the fact that she didn't gag or cough as he had feared she would, he lay her back down gently, and she suddenly took an ecstatic breath.

Nothing had ever tasted as sweet to Siriana as that breath. There was something strange, something very different about it, but she didn't care. It was life, full and delicious and... intoxicating, dazzling! So much information was carried on it she couldn't even begin to process it all. It was all so overwhelmingly fascinating she had to let some of it out. The urge was like a terrible itch and the sound that bubbled out of her was the only way to scratch it...

'I think it's going to be all right now, sweetheart.'

She opened her eyes. Simon's hair nearly blinded her, and his eyes drew her whole body up towards him, not just her veils. She wasn't wearing any veils... she gasped in terror.

'Don't worry, baby, I know what can sustain you now, at least until we can get you some real atmosphere.' He handed her a small violet flask.

She took it from him in wonder, and began experiencing that oddly delightful sensation again.

'Siriana,' he stared down at her very seriously, 'are you laughing?'

'Yes, laughing... thank you.' She slipped her arms around his neck. 'Thank you, human, for giving me back my father in this laughter.'

'Things won't be easy,' he warned, and crushed her against him.

Light After Breath

A Parallel Universe – Date Unknown

I n a rush to get to his ship, he collided with her in the Station's main corridor. The Roman numeral clocks decreed it was three o'clock on a civilized afternoon even though space was timelessly dangerous around them. She was wearing a tight black mini dress over which her full blood-red lips seemed to leap out at him, his gaze tumbling to a pleasant rest on the glowing green oval stone against her chest.

'Excuse me,' he murmured, and her smiling mouth was softly forgiving. He made himself keep walking. Her brown eyes shaded in dark-green had abruptly made him remember the centuries-old jungle movies he had loved as a kid. He smiled to himself feeling as though he had stepped in quicksand but managed to escape, and the encounter lifted his bored mood.

Alex served as an Immigration Pilot. His job consisted of ferrying new arrivals from earth to the Station's three neighboring planets. As he neared the off limits docking areas, the crowds thinned out until only a few other registered personnel in black uniforms dotted the pure corridors like mysterious dominoes. That afternoon he was the only one around. He was late, but it didn't matter; his passengers would just have to wait, and he enjoyed feeling like the last, most vital piece in a cosmic game... he was alone on the three-dimensional board of a luminous energy eternally playing the lord of darkness bending threateningly over it. Alex knew the fate of hundreds of souls – the wager these two supreme forces made when making their moves at the speed of light – rested on his toy-sized yet mysteriously strong shoulders, and he relished the act of raising a defiant fist in order to set the blue-diamond on his ring into the security niche on the console.

Like an onion's layers white doors peeled open before him down a curving passageway as the proximity of the energy ships began sting-ing his eyes. He slipped on black glasses still thinking about the sooth-ing liquid color of the green stone against the woman's chest. Damn it, why hadn't he asked her name? There were always young female passengers aboard his vessel, and as always he enjoyed their gasps when he entered the long capsule's brilliant atmosphere which he knew made his blonde hair shine like a sun over the black space of his uniform. Their jewelry flashed spectrums at him as they raised their hands to whisper to each other; innocently launching prisms that con-verged demandingly in his eyes. He frowned, and the colors vanished as all the young women on his ship folded their hands demurely in their laps. But his relaxed bravery continued to widen their eyes as they stared up at him from beneath the shadows of protective lenses. Looking at them, he was reminded of small ponds in a thick, dark for-est no one had explored and that he could dip into and wade in for a while before walking casually away. He smiled down at a girl in the front row whose eyes were algae dappled with sunlight, and bent over to adjust the strap across her breasts. She sucked in the luminous foggy atmosphere as she caught her breath, and sent a ripple of small waves down the ship as she sighed.

* * *

Morgan was dreaming... observing vast gaseous clouds rolling in the white of her sleeping eyes creating suns, an impossible power blinking them out of pure darkness touching and feeling itself with the fingertips of planets. She gazed at the world nearest the Station and in the distance saw a golden snake hissing towards it. She imagined the pilot sitting calmly in its burning head and the space around her felt as warm as his chest when she ran into him. She noticed a second planet, so far away it might have been a coin fallen out of his pocket, and she wanted to give it back to him even though she imagined he had enough of them not to miss it. How long would he live if he stopped aging on each trip...?

I would much rather obey his strong arms in that black uniform than these thin meaningless ones, Morgan thought sullenly as she found herself staring at her digital clock, its cold male voice telling her to wake destroying the universe of her dream.

There was never much to do in the commercial shipping department where she worked because most of what the Station produced it kept for itself, barring the innumerable scientific experiments only certified personnel were allowed to handle. The harmless gift objects she dealt with had made the job entertaining at first since she was entitled to free samples. Her favorite items were the intricate webs in crystal cubes spun by spiders in zero gravity especially bred to produce silver and gold thread. She had kept two of these to use as book ends, an amethyst butterfly (her birth stone) trapped in one, a sapphire fly in the other. As soon as she saved enough money they would look stunning in a room with a window, preferably one looking out only on stars as the sight of a planet would merely annoy her with depressing possibilities.

Morgan cherished little hope for mankind's three new worlds, fresh though they still were. Every morning as she got dressed for work her mind slipped into the same depressing thoughts, which she promptly zipped to a stop with the cynical mantra, *It doesn't matter.* There were an infinite number of worlds out there to be used and abused, an unimaginable harem of wonders. It annoyed her that the world where she had happened to be born was dying, but it was nothing to ruin her life over. Nevertheless, moving to another planet so soon would have felt like leaving the bedside of her dying mother, although she had always felt rather detached from her parents, perhaps because they had conceived her in a test tube; the growing amount of toxic chemicals in earth's atmosphere made it more and more difficult for people to have children the natural way. It comforted Morgan to live in a place that was everywhere a hard white faceted with lights like a crystal, its environment strictly controlled, always pure. The shape of the Station (which she had first seen six months ago as her ship was docking) reminded her of a picture in her elementary school hologram book of an ancient Hindu statue with six arms twirling slowly around so she could view him from all angles. He was alone in the hologram's inky depths, smiling as if in his mouth he held a magic morsel he could savor forever, a secret that kept Morgan suspended out in space because she was somehow determined to taste it herself.

* * *

It was midnight according to the Station's sentinel clocks. The residential corridor was deserted, a bright cocoon behind whose walls she sensed peoples' uniquely colorful dreams stretching like butterfly wings into the dark universe. Morgan stood waiting for the local transport to her room wishing she hadn't drunk so much wine. She stared intently at the dark crack between the doors, seeing it as the manifest line of time… and how much of it remained in her life that no one truly interesting would ever illuminate…

The transport arrived and the doors sighed open.

Secretly elated, she stepped inside next to the blonde pilot, reluctant now to press the button that would take her to her level.

'Hello,' he said, smiling.

'Hello…'

'I wanted to ask you your name the other day, but I was late.'

'Morgan.'

'Alex.' The doors parted for him and her heart swelled painfully with the air that in a moment he would no longer occupy. 'Can I see you tomorrow night, Morgan?' he asked abruptly.

'Please,' she replied at once, infinitely relieved he had taken control of her. 'I'm on level thirteen, number nine.'

* * *

The following day dragged by in a meaningless march of seconds like caterpillar legs crawling all over her heart. Only the black-and-white computers around her soothed her somewhat with their perpetual subtle purring. That was in the morning. Later in the day the old-fashioned clock she kept glancing at began to weigh her excitement down like an endless chain of minutes linked to a prisoner's ball. When she was finally free to leave, Morgan felt weak from a lashing of cynical thoughts about her date even as her imagination rose passionately to his defense.

After she showered and began dressing, the colors and textures of her clothing and jewelry revived her positive spirit. She selected a very short, sea-green dress gently revealing the soft waves of her figure with matching bikini panties; translucent stay-up silver stockings that made her legs feel light as foam; and ankle-high black boots. On her arms she slipped bracelets the colors of Saturn's rings, and on her ear lobes she gently hooked silver fish that rippled as she moved.

The buzzer sounded sooner than she had expected. She picked up the remote control, but then tossed it impulsively on her bed and ran to open the door intimately with her hands.

He stood on the threshold in his black uniform, the zipper over his chest down a few inches to indicate he was off duty, a bottle of wine cradled in his left arm. Alex smiled as he rocked it gently. 'A very special vintage I've been saving. It was a gift from a grateful passenger.'

'I'm honored,' she replied, smiling.

The evening began with the inevitable conversation about their home planet. 'Heard anything new?' he asked indifferently, obviously more interested in opening the wine.

'Not really, although they say the sky is nearly always purple now from all the pollutants.'

'Yes, and I hear it's killing the bees except for the queen. I guess she likes purple.' He winked. Their world's atmosphere was still healthy and whole in his blue eyes.

'Be serious.' She didn't meant to speak sharply, but in those moments she was single mindedly mining for his worth, desperately hoping his sensitivity would equal his intense good looks. She already knew he was intelligent; a lightship pilot couldn't be stupid.

'I am being serious.' The plastic cork slipped smoothly into his hand. 'A purple heaven is deadly to bees. I find this an intriguing scientific fact.' He laughed and she felt as if it was some of her blood he was pouring into the crystal glass; he had the power to shatter her illusions, yet she trusted his intensity as instinctively as she knew he wouldn't spill a drop. 'Let's toast,' he commanded.

'Toast to what?' She felt as if she was falling waiting for his answer to catch her.

'To us, of course.' He sat on the edge of the bed beside her. 'I can tell you're trying to sound me out, Morgan. "Is he just cute," you're thinking, "or is there something under his brilliant hair?"'

'It's not just a brain I'm looking for.'

'Right, there's the quality of both heads to consider.'

'Don't be crude.' She looked shyly away at one of her crystal-encased spider webs, excited because she knew she was caught.

'I think I'm being rather subtle, Morgan.'

His voice was too soft for her thoughts to walk on; they stumbled, and she couldn't manage to line them up into a clever sentence with which to fence him. She stood up. 'Would you like to hear some music, Alex?'

'No.' He caught her arm, and she willingly sat back down beside him. 'I'd rather listen to you're voice, Morgan, it's beautiful, and I'm sorry, you have every right to wonder if I'm just an ordinary clone, I was conceived in a test tube, after all.'

'So was I.'

They were silent for a moment.

'Well then, come.' He sounded determined. 'Let's drink to the fact that we have at least one thing in common.' He raised his glass.

Light After Breath

To her horror, Morgan saw herself snatch it out of his hand and fling it along with hers across the small room. The crystal glasses hit the plastic wall with dull thuds, and promptly bled all over the floor, making it look a deathly white. She was utterly appalled by what she had done, yet the sight pleased her in a strangely morbid way. 'To us.' She smiled at him wickedly.

'Morgan!' He whispered as if in shock, and pushed her down across the bed. He stood up, and she let him lift her dress to slip her panties down her legs. He repeated her name reassuringly, but she didn't really hear him; she was too desperate to submerge her awareness of everything in a sensual whirlpool where he would become everything while she sucked his cock as if there was no more important act in the universe. She sat up to this purpose, clutching his uniform, but he shoved her back down gently.

'I'm going to come in you, Morgan,' he warned. 'I want to come deep inside you!'

The zipper of his uniform came down like lightning and the blackness of space seemed to part over her full of his pale skin's contrastingly luminous warmth. Her body in the sea-green dress undulated like a wave longing to sink his erection in her wet depths, but all she succeeded in doing was wetting the cool tip of his head with the warm lips of her sex, sending ripples of delight through her. Yet for her making love had never been so much about bodily parts or physical sensations as about desire, intangible but absolute, illusive yet overwhelming. With Alex's big cock penetrating her, and then patiently but relentlessly stroking her, Morgan's thoughts and senses, her feelings and fantasies, her sense of touch and her sense of the infinite, all came together as one heady, delicious brew in her blood. It had been a long time since a man opened her pussy up around his thrusts, yet the sensation of her innermost flesh caressing his hard-on was secondary to the more deeply stimulating penetration of his eyes. His unflinching regard stoked her excitement with the arousing knowledge that it was a lightship captain driving himself into the tight vessel of flesh mysteriously docked between her legs, the increasing speed and force of his pulsing hips transporting her into another dimension of perception where she felt much wiser than she was when she wasn't being energetically fucked and filled up by a beautiful man's hard cock.

He didn't need to pin her arms up over her head for her to hold them there submissively as his own strong arms kept his body arched over hers, his balls beating against her rousing a ghost of pain at the base of her slit where his dick was almost too thick for her labial lips to comfortably embrace. His strength and self-control had her moaning with literally profound admiration and gratitude, his bare chest and sleek black suit turning her on like two different forms of nakedness, like hot light and a bottomless darkness coming together inside her. Maybe it was because they were lying on a bed in a room floating out in space that her physical senses were merging with her deeper feelings in a uniquely stimulating way... on one level a man she had only just met was silently banging her, and on another the languid peace suffusing both her mind and her body was mysterious proof that she had at last found her soul-mate, a cosmic reality much more vital to her than an orgasm. In the end he was fucking her so hard there was no way her clitoris could assert itself and achieve a few seconds of blinding pleasure, until he abruptly lowered his head and thrust his tongue into her mouth, then all the nerve ends buried beneath ecstasy's stubborn little seed branched out into the beginnings of a climax. She almost believed it was possible she could come without touching herself, and if she believed it she could make it happen because with this man anything was possible, she knew this in her soul. The certainty was at once so relaxing and so inspiring that when he looked down into her eyes again and stopped moving inside her, she arched her back, crushing her clit against him, and her orgasm was made even more potent by the fact that she didn't needed it to feel fulfilled.

All night words were unnecessary between them; what they were feeling was more meaningful and could be expressed only with their flesh.

* * *

Morgan was walking down an empty corridor when she saw a pilot standing directly in front of a star-filled window. She paused. It was if he had appeared out of nowhere. She looked to make sure, but there was no door anywhere near where he suddenly stood. Amazement and anxiety twined mysterious twin shoots up her spine as she shivered, suddenly so aware of her body's vulnerable warmth that she felt paradoxically powerful; hot with her identity. His back was to the stars, his eyes were closed, and his stance was so relaxed she actually wondered if he had fallen asleep on his feet like a horse. She reasoned that she hadn't seen him when she first turned the corner because his hair and uniform were as black as the universe behind him, and his pale face could have been a far away moon whose undulating surface she was only imagining into strikingly attractive features... she kept on walking, and the sound of her boots seemed to wake him. His hair was a shoulder-length mane unconfined by Station regulations.

'Do you always sleep standing up like a horse?' She raised an ironic sword in passing to hide the fact that he made her feel intensely nervous.

'I've been waiting for you, Morgan.'

She stopped because she could not believe his eyes were violet, her favorite color. 'Are you a friend of Alex?' she asked. 'Is his ship delayed?'

'Yes.'

Vaguely, she wondered how he had known to find her in this corridor, but disappointment clouded her ability to think, as did a sudden lightning flash of fear. 'Is he alright? Nothing happened to his ship, did it?'

He grabbed her left arm just below the shoulder and began leading her in the opposite direction she had been walking, the ache in her flesh where he clutched it only a reflection of the hopeless pain in her heart getting all her attention. 'Oh, my God, please tell me nothing's happened to Alex!' She imagined the worst – that his ship had crashed or vanished through some rift in time during light speed – and his friend's profound silence only fed her growing dread.

'Don't be so distressed, Morgan, there are billions of other men.'

As if a serpent's tail had coldly lashed her brain, she felt dizzy with terror and desperate to get away from him. 'Let go of me!'

'Don't be afraid, my lady.' His quiet, seductive voice lulled her against her will. 'Your lord still lives, but he must fight me for you.'

When he smiled down at her she tried to feel relieved. He was teasing her, tormenting her like a boy enjoys pulling a cat's tail, and she was ashamed she had played his game and become hysterical so easily. Yet who the hell did he think he was dragging her around with him like this? She told herself she was only allowing him to lead her somewhere because he knew where Alex was; she didn't dare acknowledge his physical power over her.

'Where are we going?' she asked him, and the submissive softness of her voice truly scared her. They reached a transport and she fervently hoped there would be other people inside it, but the Station suddenly seemed deserted.

Somehow she knew they had reached his level when they stepped into a dimly lit corridor covered with a plush black carpet – the richest residential area of the Station where she one day hoped to live because in lieu of walls each room was surrounded by floor-to-ceiling windows that literally transformed the apartment into your own personal space. The anxiety she was still feeling for Alex made her strangely weak, as if she had been stabbed and was still bleeding fears; too absorbed in staunching their flow to find the strength to defend herself from another danger. Suddenly, she found herself alone in a stranger's room, with a man whose his name she didn't even know, but it didn't seem to matter as she was overwhelmed by the vision of stars burning in an infinite space all around her. It was as if the warmth of countless galaxies was embracing her and lifting her up in the form of a man's arms, an experience impossible for her to resist. He spread her across a deep white fur covering the bed and she lay there oddly paralyzed by its perfect comfort... and then by shock that for some reason she wasn't resisting as he lifted her dress off over her head, and then slipped her sapphire-blue panties down her long legs.

She had never seen her flesh strictly by starlight. There seemed to be a hundred suns for every cell in her body, white and red, and the faint blue of blood beneath her skin not yet exposed to oxygen. Her nipples hardened beneath all the pulsing lights licking them, and glancing down the length of her naked body, she could almost believe it was the pure and perfect flesh of her soul she was seeing and not just corruptible skin stretched over muscles, sinews and bone... her skeleton was made of a hot white light, indestructible and eternal...

She cried out when the beautiful pilot began crawling towards her from the foot of the bed, sleek and slender in his black suit as a panther or a jackal… Anubis, the ancient Egyptian god of the dead… yet not even the possibility that Death had come for her in an irresistibly attractive form made her feel like resisting what was happening. Instead she was ashamed to realize that the eternally virginal force of desire was at high tide inside her, pounding through her heart and drowning all guilty thoughts of Alex so there was nothing left except her flesh, sensually undulating beneath another man's amazingly warm caress. An absolute stranger's hand was traveling slowly down the length of her body from her throat to her sex, his touch a prolonged electric shock arching her back and making her gasp as she thought it would kill her how desperately she longed for him to reach her pussy. At last he cradled her cunt in his hand, his hard thumb and rigid fingers a fierce jaw clamping hungrily around her juicing tenderness.

'Oh, my God!' she breathed. 'Who are you? What are you doing?'

He unzipped his suit with his free hand, and the unreal dimensions of his erection stunned her. Then she lost sight of his star-lit hard-on as he shoved her over onto her stomach. It was all happening too fast, and yet at the same time she seemed to have a small eternity to contemplate the humiliating fact that she still wasn't fighting him; that she wasn't resisting him because some irresistible part of her didn't want to. Body and soul she felt caught in the gravity of a black hole as he docked the head of his cock in her impossibly tight sphincter. She couldn't really be allowing this to happen; she couldn't possibly survive the pain of being fucked up the ass by such a big dick, lubricated or not, compounded by the emotional agony of betraying her love for Alex.

'Oh, God, no, no!' she begged helplessly. If he had diluted his haunting command over her with words, she would have bucked beneath him, she would have tried to get away from him, but he didn't speak; he didn't break the dark spell of his impossibly big cock surging into her bowels with a rending thrust that nearly caused her to blackout beneath a glorious rush of agony. The excruciating sensation of his hot shaft expanding her innermost horizons was so shocking it burned though her shame and fear. Clutching the cool fur, Morgan crossed an event horizon where morality as she knew it could not survive as she found herself unable to distinguish the difference between violence and virtue, humiliation and fulfillment, pain and pleasure... and the longer the brutal experience dragged on, the more perversely sublime it became as though it was her very soul he was possessing and claiming. When he pulled out of her abruptly her anal ring was burning hotter than the stars as she collapsed against the soothing fur, longing only to rest forever... until he shoved her over onto her back again, and black as the universe his eyes told her this was what she had always wanted and would always want because it would never end...

The arrow of a lightship taking off from the Station suddenly flooded the room with golden light.

'Alex!' she cried.

The stranger groaned, folding in on himself as if in pain.

With an enormous effort of will, she forced herself off the bed, and the blue-and-white door knob looked like the earth in her hand as she dared to look back.

There was no one in the room with her.

Desperately, she tried turning the knob, but it was locked in place, trapping her in the fear that her time had indeed run out. 'Alex, help me!' she prayed beneath her breath. 'I love you! I love you! Help me!' She pushed against the door with all her strength. 'I love you!' The black barrier burst open and she plunged into the corridor. She crawled across the carpet for a few feet, until she trusted her balance enough to stand up and run.

* * *

Morgan gazed out at the blue towers of the city. During the day they were almost invisible against the sky, but now their tall young forms were alive with bright, self-centered lights. Night fell much more quickly than on earth. Standing in front of the floor-to-ceiling window, her vulnerable imagination perceived the encroaching darkness as the shadow of a huge mythical bird soaring down on the city from above, the setting sun burning a compassionate intelligence in one god-like eye even as the rising moon was cold and blind with hunger in the other. She sipped her drink, enthralled, as the coal-black universe swooped down and the day instantly burned out. Darkness descended in a single wave, wetting the buildings into their full shine, and like foam the stars all appeared at once.

She turned the lights to their dimmest setting, transforming the light-gray carpet into a lunar surface, and activated the tiny springs beneath it, enjoying the playful illusion of a world with low gravity. These days Morgan appreciated anything that distracted her, and she searched the hotel room for other curious special effects, but there were none she didn't already know about so she went and stood in front of the window again. The pyramid lamps were faintly reflected in the pane as if they had just been erected on the horizon. *One for me, one for Alex, and one for…* The pyramids trembled when she struck the glass with her fist, but they survived this slight earthquake. Hope was like this reflection, indestructible and yet just as unreal. She thought about the ancient kings of earth who had been buried beneath shapes that pointed up to a divine source transcending the cutting sharpness of fear, and she felt a little better. She wouldn't allow herself to miss the star-warmed embrace of life on the Station because it felt the same as desiring the stranger with the violet eyes of her birthstone...

A shaft of light harmlessly speared her when Alex entered the room, closing the door behind him and leaning back against it as his eyes adjusted to the dim light. He studied her figure silhouetted against the luminous blue buildings as she turned to face him. After a moment he was able to make out the thin mist of her dress and a crescent moon floating above it – the silver necklace he had given her. Golden asps given birth by the lights of the city slivered up and down her black vinyl boots as she approached him. There was something chillingly remote about her. He had felt it as a slight, unusual frost in her distracted silence a few days ago, and now her mood struck him like a blizzard of unspoken thoughts and feelings as subtle and complex as snow flakes. He felt they could be dissolved if she would only let her fears fall into the warmth of his understanding, but her beauty had become an almost physical ache in his chest as her refusal to communicate with him mysteriously froze the air between them. It made his physical desire for her almost brutally sharp; he was desperate to break her cool reserve and feel her melt lovingly around him again. It had been his idea to get away from the Station for a while. They had arrived on the planet three hours ago, but he had post-flight duties to attend to before he could join her in their room.

Morgan's nerves screamed like a cat's claws struggling not to fall into an inner abyss as she approached him, but he didn't move and meet her half way. If he didn't make an effort to win her back to him, all was lost. 'Alex…'

'Is there something you want to tell me, Morgan?'

'Yes…'

'I know you haven't been yourself lately.'

'Please hold me…'

He reached her in a heartbeat.

She clung to him for a moment before looking trustingly up into his eyes from which his being radiated so generously and supportively. She knew the spreading weed of fear would eventually kill their growing love if she didn't kill it first, and she marveled again at how his loving regard brought her beauty to life for her in a way no mirror ever could. She had always felt her looks were a reflection of her innermost self, yet all the men she had been with before had only superficially appreciated her. It was Alex who had broken the mirror's corruptible husk so that her beauty recognized it magical nature as the form of his eternal pleasure.

'What's wrong, Morgan?' he whispered. 'Please tell me.'

'Something happened the other day, Alex, and I just don't know how you're going to take it…'

He stiffened the way he did every time he thrust into the space between past and future and felt reality slip terrifyingly out of their grasp as urgent pulses of light swallowed everything except the black limbs of his suit. As her arms slipped from around his neck a cold, murderous darkness filled his mind, and staring at her white dress against the blue city, he held his breath as if what she was about to say might destroy the atmosphere.

'There's a man on the station who isn't a man,' she began quietly.

He thought handling a lightship was nearly impossible, but he realized now it was nothing compared to understanding and mastering a woman. He transformed a painful urge to slap her into a sarcastic, 'You don't say?'

'I was walking down a corridor when he suddenly appeared out of nowhere, you have to believe me, Alex. He was wearing a pilot's uniform, and he implied he was a friend of yours when I asked him if your ship was delayed. He knew my name, and when he saw how afraid I was that something had happened to you, he laughed and said, "Your lord still lives, but he must fight me for you." I was so worried about you, and I wanted to find out when you'd be back, so I... I went with him... but I didn't really have a choice; he was gripping my arm so hard I couldn't get away. He took me to his room...'

'I see...'

'No, you don't, Alex, please believe me, I couldn't resist him, it was like being in a terrible dream until I cried your name when a lightship shot out of the station and it seemed to hurt him. I ran to the door but it was locked, and when I looked behind me he was gone and there was no one in the room with me. Yet I'm even more frightened now than I was then because it's coming between us. I couldn't tell you before... I was so afraid you wouldn't understand. You won't believe me, but I know this happened because I love you so much, if that makes any sense at all. He told me not to be distressed, that there were billions of other men out there. He knows how much I love you and that's why he wants me. Whoever, *whatever*, he is, I can sense he's determined to win me from you.' She gazed at him helplessly and sank to her knees before him, slipping her arms around his thighs to press her soft cheek against his latent force.

'So...' He caressed her hair, staring intently out at the stars, 'I'm truly challenged at last.'

guilty pleasures

* * *

Morgan's happiness felt like perfect health. It was hard to remember the pain of loneliness and how the days had dragged by before the stimulation of Alex's company. He rented a ground ship and they set off to explore the wild planet. She enjoyed filling the intimate little vessel with supplies, the challenge of striking a perfect balance between gourmet pleasures and physical necessities delighting her. The storage units could only hold so much, yet she wanted them to have all they desired on their journey. As the head of their personal little economy, she made sure nothing went to waste, recycling their plates and napkins for the next meal, burying organic garbage in the soil every morning before they took off, and stacking their bottles of wine in the back of the ship every night to be recycled when they returned to the city.

'If we keep drinking like this we should buy some land and plant our own vineyard,' he teased.

'Maybe.' The playful suggestion annoyed her, and then depressed her because she didn't understand why she reacted with such an intolerant sense of exhaustion to it. Part of her longed to be restfully embraced by deep space again... distant stars infinite dream-worlds not quite graspable by her mind, which could be as pleasurably lazy as a baby's fist in a pure, temporary cradle... The planet's sunlight struck her as harsh – as an intense responsibility to her vision and an unavoidable pressure on her flesh whenever she left the cool confines of the ship.

Morgan's favorite time was after dark when they ate what she had prepared in the galley outside beside a fire Alex kindled and continued feeding throughout the cool night. Stars crowded as if curiously above the tall, earth-like trees surrounding them. Little suns quivered restlessly through the atmosphere like children silently laughing as they spied on the two lovers. Larger suns flashed hot, encouraging looks as Alex rolled her over the alien ground in his familiar arms, and all the stars pulsed in rhythm with his hips rising and falling between her open thighs. He had claimed all her orifices for himself – her mouth, her pussy and her ass – but there was always a tenderness to even his most violent penetrations that turned a perverse part of her off. She couldn't help wondering if she had been spoiled, perhaps even damaged for life, by her experience with the stranger who appeared out of nowhere and fucked her like she had never been fucked before; and he had clearly not even begun with her before she somehow managed to resist a suicidal desire to surrender every fiber of her being to him. Alex's considerate love-making gave her pleasure; her clitoris loved surfing his cresting tongue and dissolving into a crashing climax. She enjoyed it when he sucked on her nipples and lodged his cock deep in her cunt without moving so she could touch herself and make herself come. He let her bring herself to orgasm once, twice, even three times before he began thrusting and taking his own pleasure from her slick and clenching depths. She liked it most when he urged her down onto her hands and knees and fucked her pussy from behind, clutching her hips and riding her hard. She loved everything about him except the fact that desire always felt like a safely contained force in the loving gravity of his arms, a force that would never overwhelm and devastate her as her soul longed to be. In the stranger's starlit room she had discovered that there was a haunting strength in absolute submission. She had asserted a metaphysical power by yielding to his totally unrestrained lust, and experienced a pleasure deeper than any she had ever known while offering him the blessing of ecstasy without seeking it for herself…

'You know,' Alex spoke softly as they lay in each other's arms inside the purring ship, 'I feel like a man whose first wife died and whose second one looks so much like her he can't tell the difference between them, as if they're actually the same soul… it's still strange how much this planet looks like earth.'

'I know, sometimes I even think it's an illusion we're wishfully projecting around us.'

'That makes us pretty powerful, Morgan.'

'Yes, but apart from a few strange flowers here and there, and some odd trees, everything looks and feels the same, and I think it's because we want it to; because it suits us this way.'

'For now,' he agreed neutrally. 'I fancy I might be a little more daring and avant-garde with my next world.'

'You couldn't very well wear a suit with eight arms or with buttons where your face is, could you?'

'No.' He laughed.

'Doesn't it seem as if natural laws are sort of like an outfit we put on, that the naked energy we're ultimately made of wears to enjoy looking at Itself?'

'You mean earth-type forms are only the current fashion our timeless spirit is into? Doesn't that make time and space an open magazine on God's lap?'

'On *our* lap,' she corrected him. 'Our spirit's.'

'I'm one leg and you're the other?' he teased.

'I'm being serious, Alex.'

'So am I, and I definitely like this page; you're as beautiful as I could possibly imagine you… for now.'

'Good night, then.'

'I love you, Morgan. I love you more than anything. I'd be lost without you.'

'So would I.'

* * *

She awoke unusually irritable and Alex suggested they spend the day where they were, bathing in the stream instead of being cooped up in the ship. She shrugged, trying to shake off the weight of the planet around her, morosely feeling its lush beauty offered her no divine security in return for her intense appreciation. She stared longingly up at the blue sky impossibly searching for a glimpse of the Station. She was unreasonably sullen as she watched him fix breakfast from where she sat cross-legged on the ground, pouting because she didn't feel well. The world and everything in it was so bright it hurt her eyes... Alex's hair, the scrambled eggs, the sun leaping off the wet leaves dancing mockingly around her as branches jeered at her for being such a fool as to imagine her little heart had anything to do with the creation of worlds... the grass stuck possessively to her bare thighs as she stood up, but there was nowhere to run from her own imminent decay.

'Morgan, are you okay?'

Her soul was a butterfly perched for a briefly precarious moment on the limbs of her body, anxious to fly away from the fear of being caught in the net of a disease and the dread of being paralyzed by grief, forever trapped in mourning black if something should happen to Alex. She was desperate to return to the Station right away, its corridors white and smooth as her own bones buried in darkness alive with luminous seeds from which worlds bloomed and died without her knowing any pain... because she was lying where creation and destruction were the exciting rhythm of her own unending pleasure…

'Morgan?'

The world splashed all at once into her sight, light diving into her pupils' black pools and making her aware of her body again supported by Alex's arms.

'Are you okay?' he asked again.

'Yes… I just felt a little dizzy.' Why did she lie?

'Was it Him, Morgan?'

'Yes…' She saw darkness embracing every world that had ever come into being, possessing it even as its golden lord watched powerless, a full moon His cold engagement ring around her slender finger of gravity… 'Tell me you'll always love me!' she begged, fervently caressing his blond hair.

'I'll always love you, Morgan, you know that, *always*.'

'Your feeling for me won't… it won't burn out?'

'Never, it'll only grow so strong it has to break the boundaries of this world into a better one, I swear it.'

'Please don't let Him take me away from you forever, Alex!'

'We belong to each other, Morgan, he can't come between us except through ourselves if we're afraid, so don't be afraid. I'm here and I'm part of you, you're not alone anymore, you never really were because I was always looking for you, my love… my *life*!'

* * *

The sounds are different, Morgan thought, pushing away Alex's heavy arm and leg. He didn't wake up, which made her angry, because how could he protect her when he was asleep? She sat up in bed and gazed down at him. *He's only a man*… Tenderly, she covered the smooth expanse of his back with the sheet and got out of bed. She felt restless listening to the symphony of sounds playing outside. Until that night she hadn't discerned the gasping tone behind all the other nocturnal noises and it was making her feel as if the planet was a woman sensually enjoying the energy of all the life moving on top of her and inside her as living creatures ceaselessly caressed her. Glancing back at Alex, she pressed open the vessel door, excited by her fear of what she was doing.

The night was cold against her naked skin. A frigid breeze felt her out, and then abandoned her indifferently, leaving her deliciously shivering. Reason told her to at least put on a jacket, but her body was already descending the plastic steps onto the damp ground. She sensed the ardent touch of all the stars overhead gazing down at her, the circular glade in which their ship was parked an arena across which she was irresistibly drawn. Her mind processed countless fears large and small – catching cold, being killed by some unknown wild animal, Alex's angry displeasure with her foolish behavior – yet she kept walking.

She felt Him waiting for her, and she was afraid that if she didn't give Him what he wanted the next time Alex went out in his lightship the darkness would swallow him forever. She had to appease Him with a sacrifice, but all she could offer was her dreadful fear as she ritually stabbed it with her straight, unflinching approach towards the deep menace of the forest. *Perhaps I can make him love me...* Perhaps He would share some of his power with her and she could use it to protect Alex, to keep him safe with her forever...

The trees grew so close together it was as if they sought to embrace her, catching her long, soft hair with roughly curious fingers, eagerly scratching her tender breasts as she stumbled, tossed from one indifferent embrace to another until she somehow began enjoying the profound thrill of her terror. It became horribly delicious to trip on roots and fall into hard, strong arms passionately prodding her when she tried to get away. A short limb thrust out from the impenetrable darkness directly between her thighs and made her cry out with mingled pain and pleasure. She clung to the rough bark for protection when she suddenly saw Him standing before her, his eyes the precious reflection of her life.

'Morgan.'

'You can have me if you swear never to hurt Alex!'

'My dear, no man is immortal, only I can hold you forever. Come to me.'

Far away she heard Alex calling her name. 'Oh, God...'

'Don't be afraid, Morgan, your unique beauty touches me. I will give you all you desire.'

She tried to move but discovered that the tree's branches had ensnared her. 'It won't let me go!' she cried.

'It's hungry for you, Morgan. It wants your sweet legs to wrap around its roots, your arms to help it reach for the sky, and your heart to nest as a bird in its branches.'

'Please, help me!'

He stepped around behind her.

She closed her eyes wondering if it would hurt and how long it would last. She gasped, 'Alex!' as a two-edged agony and joy thrust into the base of her spine, transforming it into a serpent coiling wildly in and out of blinding misery and intense pleasure. She rose swiftly, leaving her legs heavily rooted below her as His dark arms lifted her up without the slightest effort, but then she chanced to look back and saw that it was really Alex holding her body. The sight jarringly anchored her, pulling her down again. The last thing she remembers is seeing Alex rising over her and a beautiful ray of light emanating from his hand into the darkness...

*   *   *

The Station corridor was deserted. Morgan avoided it whenever possible because it was the one in which the man who wasn't a man had appeared out of nowhere. He was like the scar on her back, she couldn't see him yet he was always there; she still felt him just behind her...

She quickened her pace. Alex's ship was due any minute. Once she was in his arms again she would be safe. She was passing the window in front of which the stranger had stood when the sound of her scream astonished her as it reverberated from wall to wall like a trapped bird, her heart fluttering with terror when she saw His face just outside the glass smiling in at her. Then suddenly Alex appeared in his black uniform at the other end of the corridor. She knew it was him even though he was so small and far away she couldn't see his face. He was running towards her, shouting her name, but then the distant sound of his voice was lost in a deafening explosion behind her. She refused to believe it even as she heard the fatal exhalation of oxygen being sucked out into space and felt an infinitely strong grip on all her limbs. Red emergency lights flashed her heart a useless hysterical sympathy, screaming for her as her lungs cowered helplessly, 'Alex!' caught forever in her throat. It was no use fighting the pull of the vacuum. She turned and willingly flung herself into its relentless desire, her body tossed as lightly as a sweet between the shattered window's jagged teeth. She only hoped Alex would make it into an airlock and live, without her...

She was icy with jewels flowing in sharply frozen streams over her naked body, cascading between her breasts and legs and down her back so she could barely move from their cold, chaining weight. She was in a dark space of vast proportions. She could see other women in the distance as frostily motionless as herself. And then He appeared before her, his eyes reflecting the amethyst burning against her womb.

'Mine at last,' he said, never smiling.

'What happened to Alex?'

'Close your eyes and see…'

Her lover's golden hair gloriously filled her mind's eye, but then she noticed there was blood streaming everywhere from it, the wound in his head burning red as he grew cold forever. He was lying on the Station floor in his black uniform, only a brief charcoal sketch already being erased as someone spread a white sheet over him. 'Alex!' she sobbed. 'Oh, Alex, no!'

'Listen to me, Morgan…'

'No! Oh, my God, I love him. I love him more than anything! You can't take us away from each other, it's not possible!'

'I said open your eyes, Morgan!'

'Alex?'

'What the hell were you dreaming?'

'Oh, Jesus!'

'It's all right, baby, nightmares are the only power he has over you. Getting rid of him is as easy as waking up. He's gone. We've killed him.'

'Thank, God! Thank God, Alex!'

'Thank *us*.'

'Thank *you*. I'm the fool who left you to try and seduce some power from him.'

'Because naturally, being a woman, you didn't listen to me. It was

315

your fears that almost killed you.' He held her close, lightly caressing the burn scar on her back. 'Does it hurt?'

'No, it was my love for you that hurt because I couldn't really believe in its power, but now I know its really true, Alex...'

They were silent. He would never forget the sight of her caressing the tree as she sank slowly to her knees, the energy blade quivering hungrily as it slipped deeper inside her, vibrating with intense satisfaction as it slowly sucked the life from her. The red-hot hilt burned his hand when he pulled it out of her body. No longer half suspended on the weapon's rising volts of force, she collapsed in the tree's arms. He swiftly cut them from around her, but she was cold and still. Then he saw the specter of their fears standing a few yards away, waiting for her. Spreading her gently across the grass, he rose over her, and with all the force of his grief and rage, he flung the blade still shining with her life straight at its heart. The next moment the sun rose instantly as it always did on that world, rays of light flowing between the skeletal branches so they suddenly breathed with leaves awakening from their nocturnal sleep, and he saw her breasts rise and fall. Her brown eyes opened, infinitely deeper, and as vital to him, as the earth beneath his feet...

'Alex, do you think that one day you'll be able to hurt me?'

'I should ask you what the hell you mean by that, but somehow I think I know, and the answer is yes, because I love you.'

Maria Isabel Pita began her career with three BDSM Erotic Romances – *Thorsday Night*, *Eternal Bondage* and *To Her Master Born*, re-printed as an exclusive hard-cover edition by the Doubleday Venus Book Club, where they were all featured selections. She is the author of two Paranormal Erotic Romances *Dreams of Anubis* and *Rituals of Surrender*, and of two Contemporary Erotic Romances *Recipe For Romance* and *Cat's Collar*. Maria has also written two best-selling non-fiction books, *The Story of M – A Memoir* and *Beauty & Submission*, both vividly detailed accounts of her training as a slave to her Master and soul mate. You can visit her at www.mariaisabelpita.com

as *A Weekend Visit, The Modern Eveline, Misfortunes of Mary, My Secret Life, The Man With A Maid, The Life of Fanny Hill, The Mournings of a Courtesan, The Romance of Lust, Pauline, Forbidden Fruit* and *Venus School-Mistress.*
0-9755331-0-X   **$15.95**

Guilty Pleasures
Maria Isabel Pita

Guilty Pleasures explores the passionate willingness of women throughout the ages to offer themselves up to the forces of love. Historical facts are seamlessly woven into intensely graphic sexual encounters.

Beneath the cover of *Guilty Pleasures* you will find intensely erotic love stories with a profound feel for the different centuries and cultures where they take place. An ancient Egyptian princes… a courtesan rising to fame in Athen's Golden Age…a Transylvanian Count's wicked bride… and many more are all one eternal woman in *Guilty Pleasures.*
0-9755331-5-0   **$16.95**

September, 2005

The Collector's Edition of The Lost Erotic Novels
Dr. Major LaCartilie, Editor

The history of erotic literature is long and distinguished. It holds valuable lessons and insights for the general reader, the sociologist, the student of sexual behavior, and the literary specialist interested in knowing how people of different cultures and different times acted and how these actions relate to the present. They are presented to the reader exactly as they first appeared in print by writers who were, in every sense, representative of their time: *The Instruments of the Passion & Misfortunes of Mary*–Anonymous; *White Stains* - Anaïs Nin & Friends; *Innocence* - Harriet Daimler
0-9755331-0-X   **$16.95**

November, 2005

The Ties That Bind – Vanessa Duriés

The incredible confessions of a thrillingly unconventional woman. From the first page, this chronicle of dominance and submission will keep you gasping with its vivid depictions of sensual abandon. At the hand of Masters Georges, Patrick, Pierre and others, this submissive seductress experiences pleasures she never knew existed. Re-print of the French bestseller.

0-9766510-1-7   **$14.95**

Cat's Collar - Three Paranormal Erotic Romances by Maria Isabel Pita

Dreams of Anubis – A legal secretary from Boston visiting Egypt explores much more than just tombs and temples in the stimulating arms of a powerfully erotic priest of Anubis who enters her dreams, and then her life one night in the dark heart of Cairo's timeless bazaar.

Rituals of Surrender – Maia Wilson finds herself the heart of an erotic web spun by three sexy, enigmatic men – modern Druids intent on using her for a dark and ancient rite…

Cat's Collar – Interior designer Mira Rosemond finds herself in one attractive successful man's bedroom after the other, but then one beautiful morning a stranger dressed in black leather takes a short cut through her garden and changes the course of her life forever.

0-9766510-0-9   **$16.95**

Send check or money order to:

Magic Carpet Books
PO Box 473
New Milford, CT 06776

Postage free in the United States add $2.50 for
packages outside the United States

MagicCarpetBooks@aol.com